A SAINT, MORE OR LESS

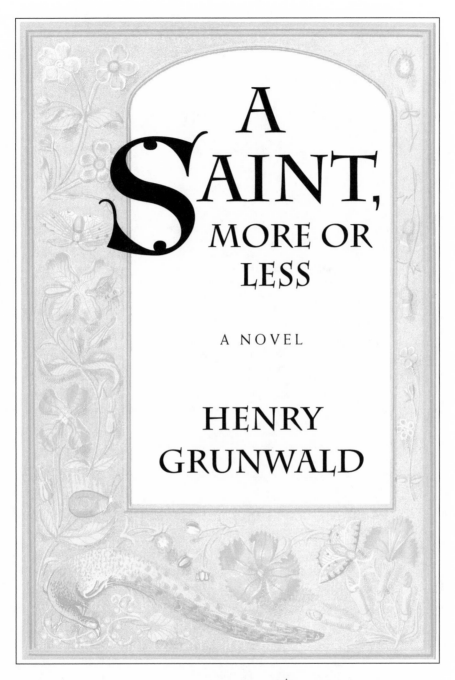

A Saint,
MORE OR
LESS

A NOVEL

HENRY
GRUNWALD

RANDOM HOUSE 🏠 NEW YORK

Library of Congress Cataloging-in-Publication Data

Grunwald, Henry A. (Henry Anatole)
A saint, more or less : a novel / Henry Grunwald.
p.   cm.
ISBN 1-4000-6149-0 (alk. paper)
1. Marie de l'Incarnation, Blessed, 1566–1618—Fiction. 2. France—History—Henry IV,
1589–1610—Fiction. 3. Women healers—Fiction. I. Title.
PS3607.R76S25 2004
813'.54—dc21   2003054809

Printed in the United States of America on acid-free paper

Random House website address: www.atrandom.com

246897531

FIRST EDITION

Book design by Carole Lowenstein

For my grandchildren
Elizabeth, Jonathan, Benjamin and Caroline
And their parents

ACKNOWLEDGMENTS

Faith is at the center of this book, and faith is what Sarah Lewis brought to this project. She believed in the story and she believed in the characters; in fact, I suspect that she felt a mystical connection with one of them. This is the third book on which we have worked together, and, as before, Sarah not only indefatigably took down my words but offered huge quantities of ideas and inspiration. She was, in effect, my first editor and critic, and my gratitude to her is immeasurable.

Solange Soloman, my researcher in France, was indispensable. Her command of French history and culture is impressive and she has the talent of knowing where to look and what to look for. She provided a mass of detail on the political, social and religious aspects of the period as well as on the lives of the historical figures in the story. Also, with great ingenuity and imagination, she helped me with the fictional parts of the book, and she always strove to keep my inventions plausible. Together she and I explored the Paris neighborhoods in which much of the story takes place and made the trip to the Carmelite convent at Pontoise. I am extremely fortunate to have found her.

Valuable research was also contributed by Susanne Washburn, as well as by Shane Butler, Paul Chaney, Robert Frumpkin, Elizabeth Hatcher and Stephen Shapiro.

Communication with these researchers, and with the outside world generally, was ably managed by my assistant, Dorothy Paulsen, who also helped in countless other ways.

I am especially grateful to my friend and agent, Lynn Nesbit, and to my editor, Kate Medina, who gave me unstinting support.

I am indebted to my son, Peter, and my daughter Lisa for important and very valuable suggestions. My daughter Mandy was also always part of the family cheering section.

The loudest cheers came from my wife, Louise, who admired the book from the beginning, including even the sections I discarded, and whose love and enthusiasm sustained me in moments of doubt.

"Lord, I believe; help thou my unbelief."

Mark 9:24

"A miracle, my friend, is an event which creates faith. That is the purpose and nature of miracles. . . . Frauds deceive. An event which creates faith does not deceive: therefore it is not a fraud, but a miracle."

George Bernard Shaw, Saint Joan

A SAINT, MORE OR LESS

A CONFESSION

"Why do you pursue me, Nicole? Why do you haunt me?"

For years I spoke those words in my mind to a woman who had been dead for more than three centuries. She had seized my imagination and would not let go.

I first encountered her long ago in a book I picked up from a remainder table. It was called *Miracles.* The title jumped out at me because, despite a certain sturdy skepticism, I have always been fascinated by the supernatural and apparently inexplicable. The book was a sort of catalog of miracle workers and visionaries. Nicole Tavernier appeared in one brief section. She lived during the terrible religious wars that ravaged France and much of Europe in the sixteenth and seventeenth centuries. Seemingly out of nowhere, Nicole emerged in Paris one day preaching repentance and trailing tales of wonders she had performed. She crossed paths with a very pious woman named Barbe Acarie. Their lives became intertwined in a drama and a mystery.

The book stayed on my shelf for many years, but its orange cover kept catching my eye at odd moments, as if reminding me of a task neglected. With the passage of time, the reminders did not fade; they grew stronger. Nicole Tavernier took shape in my mind, feature by feature, act by act. I must confess that she seemed to speak to me and I to her.

"What do you want from me?" I would say.

"I want you to tell my story," she would reply. "I want you to show that I was treated unjustly. Tell how it really was."

I would counter that I did not know how it really was, and, with reproachful eyes, she would urge me to find out. "I will help you," she would say. "I will show you the way."

Occupied with other work, I tried to put aside these promptings, but they grew more insistent. They came without warning in the midst of busy days, sometimes during restless nights.

I knew that if I tried to tell her story I would have to take the reader into a strange world in which saints and angels were as real as kings and peasants, if not more so, a world in which God spoke to people and the Devil lurked around every corner. I would have to evoke an era drenched in faith and blood in which Christians killed one another by the tens of thousands in the name of God. But then I asked myself if that world was really so very far from ours. Regardless of our individual faith or lack of it, are we not still inspired—or tormented—by religion? Do we not still look for miracles, saints and devils, if, perhaps, by other names? Do people not still slaughter one another in the names of their deities?

At long last I gave in. I went in search of the real story of Nicole Tavernier, which inevitably was also the story of Barbe Acarie. I read histories and biographies, journals and other documents of the period. My explorations led me to libraries and archives, churches and monasteries. I discovered that a great deal was known about Barbe but very little about Nicole. After I had pinned down all the available facts, there were still large gaps. I decided to fill in the gaps by using my imagination. I had to make some choices: Nicole might have gone here or there, done this or that. To my surprise I found that the choices were easy, inevitable. I seemed to be quite sure about her every step. It was as if she really were guiding me along the way.

This, then, is her book as well as mine.

CHAPTER 1

"Not another procession! This is the third in a month."

"I love processions! I wish they had one every day."

"This one is special. Why else would everybody have to close their shops? Lord knows how much business we will lose."

"But what is it about?"

"It is about penance. The archbishop ordered it. But I will tell you who is really behind it. That girl from Reims."

"The one who has been healing the sick and doing all kinds of miracles?"

"That's the one."

"Look, there is the archbishop walking behind the statue of the Virgin."

"He does not seem very steady on his feet."

"And there are all those other priests and monks. I have never seen so many in one place."

"But where is she? The girl?"

"I see her now. There, after all those choir boys singing their hymns. There she is, walking by herself, all in white."

"She looks like a bride."

"Pray for us, blessed Nicole. Give us your blessing."

"She is not looking at us. She is just looking up at the sky."

"What did you say the girl's name was again? Nicole?"

"Yes. Nicole Tavernier. The girl from Reims."

A mysterious girl whom no one knew had been given a solemn procession in her honor with all of Paris at her feet. How had she come to this moment? She had appeared in the city only a few weeks before, in the spring of 1594.

Father Pacifique de Souzy had just finished hearing confessions at the Capuchin church on the rue Saint-Honoré when the sacristan approached him. He looked puzzled.

"Father," he said. "There is a young woman who insists on seeing you. She says she has come with a very special mission."

"What sort of mission?" asked the priest.

"I don't know, Father. I am not sure what to make of her. She is very earnest and sure of herself and she has a kind of"—he groped for the right word—"a kind of authority."

Before the priest could ask any further questions, a small, slim girl appeared from behind the sacristan. She wore a threadbare traveling cloak with a large wooden cross hanging around her neck. Her shoes were scuffed, her hair disordered. Her face was flushed. Her eyes were fixed on the priest. She stared for a few moments at his tonsured head, his narrow face with the small pointed beard.

"Yes," she said. "It is you, Father. You look exactly as you did in my vision."

"Your vision?"

"Two weeks ago, during evening prayer, my mind stood still. I saw your image. And a voice told me that you would become my spiritual director. Here I am. I ask your help, Father."

De Souzy was baffled.

"Help you how, and to do what?" he asked.

"Help me to save the true faith and to bring all sinners to repentance."

De Souzy knew well that the religious upheavals of the time

produced a great many self-appointed saviors. He felt skeptical about this young girl, and yet there was something about her that drew him.

"I am extremely busy and I cannot give you any special attention. But of course, like everyone else, you are welcome to confess here whenever you feel the need."

As Father de Souzy turned away, the girl said firmly, "You are wrong to refuse me, Father. God has given me rare powers and I believe you will yet recognize them."

To de Souzy the words sounded almost like a threat, but he put the incident out of his mind. He was surprised the next day to see the girl again, standing on the church steps surrounded by a small crowd. She was speaking to them passionately.

"You have suffered great misery," she was saying. "You have seen your wives and children cry with hunger and writhe in pain, you have seen death everywhere. War is destroying the country. Why is this happening? It is God's punishment for your sins and iniquities. You must confess and repent, you must surrender your hearts and souls to the Lord. You must win over the heretics and prepare the path toward peace."

De Souzy was irritated. Not that he disagreed with what she said. Pacifique de Souzy had been a firebrand in his youth, but lately his attitude had begun to match his given name. His own sermons, while full of the necessary condemnation of the Protestant heretics, always appealed for reconciliation and peace. To hear a woman preach, however, and in front of his church, was offensive. To his astonishment he noticed that the people surrounding her were rapt by her words. They looked at her with a radiance that seemed to mirror her own. Some even knelt.

De Souzy went on about his usual church business, but the next day he was amazed to see the girl in the same place preaching to an even larger crowd. Her words were much as they had been the day before, but de Souzy now became aware that she was supplementing her message with biblical quotations.

When at length she finished, he approached her and asked her to follow him into the church. She did so matter-of-factly, as if she had expected the invitation.

"What is your name," he asked, "and where do you come from?"

"My name is Nicole Tavernier and I come from Reims."

"How old are you?"

"I am nineteen."

He recognized in her drawling speech, with its softly elongated words, the accent typical of that city.

"I have been traveling from town to town bringing His message to all who were willing to hear me."

"And what gives you the right to do that?"

"I know in my heart that God wants me to do this. A voice tells me that it is so; the same voice that sent me to you, Father."

De Souzy shook his head. "I noticed that you recite passages from scripture when you talk to people. Do you know what the words mean?"

"I do."

De Souzy decided to test her. "I will read you a passage and you will try to tell me what it signifies."

De Souzy opened a Bible on his desk and leafed through it for a few moments. Then he read from the Song of Songs.

" 'Let him kiss me with the kisses of his mouth: for your love is better than wine.' What does that mean to you?"

"It means God's love for His Church. It also means that our love of Jesus is better than any earthly love."

It was a good enough answer, but de Souzy asked, "Did someone, a priest, say those things and did you then commit them to memory?"

"I have heard sermons from many priests, but my interpretations came to me from the Holy Spirit."

De Souzy was still doubtful.

"What does scripture say about the Trinity?" he asked.

"It says many things."

"All right. What does Saint John say?"

"John says that there are three who in a common one are one in stateliness and therefore in power and will."

There was no hesitation as Nicole answered. "This means," she continued, but Father de Souzy held up his hand. He decided to try something trickier.

"What did Jesus say when He was taken to the temple? How old was He? How long did He stay?"

Nicole smiled.

"He didn't say anything the first time; He was forty days old. That was the custom, to take children to the temple forty days after their birth. When He was twelve," and she emphasized the number, "He was found in the temple after three days. When Mary and Joseph told Him they were worried"—she paused as she easily and correctly quoted scripture—" 'Son, why hast thou thus dealt with us? Behold thy father and I have sought thee sorrowing,' Jesus said"—Nicole continued with a slight nod to the priest to signal that the rest of his answer was coming—" 'How is it that ye sought me? Wist ye not that I must be about my Father's business?' " She was looking at Father de Souzy and yet looking inward as well.

De Souzy was no scholar, but he realized that this young, uneducated girl had given very learned answers. He suddenly felt out of his depth and decided to temporize.

"I will consider your request," he said.

"Thank you, Father, but I hope that you will not take too long to consider. There is much to be done."

De Souzy was taken aback by such arrogance, but above all he was puzzled. He felt that he needed more information about this odd creature and some sound advice about how to treat her.

For that he turned to the Jesuits. Although they were widely distrusted, even their enemies agreed that they were the best-informed people in Paris. He sought out Father Pierre Coton, who had a reputation for shrewdness and good sense. Coton was a tall, lean man with a shock of brown hair that was prematurely turning gray, lending him a paternal air. He gave anyone he spoke to the feeling of being at the center of his attention, and he was unfailingly gentle.

After hearing Father de Souzy's request for information about one Nicole Tavernier, Coton contracted his brow as if to retrieve an invisible dossier from his memory. Twice he repeated the name and then said, "Nothing comes to my mind but I will try to find out what I can."

When de Souzy returned a few days later, Coton was ready with his report.

Glancing at a sheet of paper in front of him, he said, "Nicole Tavernier is a young woman from Reims. Nothing is known about her family. She has been roaming from town to town affecting the role of a wandering preacher. She has attended sick people and there have been rumors of miraculous healings. She seems devoted to helping the poor and she gives them food when she can. One story has it that some mysterious messenger gave her a loaf of bread that multiplied in her hands so that she was able to distribute bread continually. She lodges at the hospital of Sainte-Catherine."

The nuns at this establishment were in charge of shrouding and burying corpses found in the street or in the river. The place also gave shelter for a short time to women looking for work.

"She wants me to help her and to be her spiritual director. What should I do?"

"God knows we have seen many visionaries and healers and wonder workers," said Coton. "Some of them are pretenders and hysterics, and we must always be on guard against such persons. On the other hand they must not be lightly dismissed. Some may be genuine. And they may help fortify the faith, which is why the Holy League is always eager to take them up."

"Ah yes, the League," said de Souzy, sounding apprehensive.

The Holy League was a powerful combination of Catholic nobles and wealthy bourgeois who had banded together to fight the Huguenots, as the Protestants were called in France. They raised armies, subsidized preachers to denounce the heretics and bitterly attacked fellow Catholics who seemed insufficiently enthusiastic on behalf of the true faith.

It was now nearly eighty years since the German monk Martin Luther had posted his theses on the church door of Wittenberg, theses that attacked the corruption of the Roman Catholic Church, its greedy hierarchy, its practice of selling indulgences that supposedly shortened the time sinners would have to spend in purgatory. In the intervening decades Protestantism, as it came to be known, spread everywhere in various forms. Bitter wars between Catholics and Protestants followed, interrupted by peace treaties and short periods of uneasy calm, only to resume again. Christendom had once been united, more or less, under the vast dome of the Catholic Church. But that dome was now broken and every part of Europe claimed its own fragment of it. Catholic Spain, under the lugubrious Philip II, was in conflict with Protestant England, under the allegedly virginal Elizabeth. Most German princes had followed Martin Luther into the Protestant camp; Switzerland had become the Protestant fortress of John Calvin. France was still largely Catholic, but the Church was increasingly alarmed by the steady growth of the Protestant forces. Coton was pained by the continuous bloodshed among Christians. He was a moderate who had Protestant friends and did not share the Holy League's zealotry, but it was his principle to be on good terms with all factions.

"The League must be reckoned with," he told Father de Souzy. "They are bound to hear about this girl. They may try to use her to stir up fervor among the faithful who may be tiring of this endless war. My advice to you is to move first and arrange for this Nicole Tavernier to meet some of the leaders of the League and especially their pious ladies. It would be interesting to see what they make of her."

Thinking aloud, Coton pronounced several names but dismissed each, until he finally said: "The Acaries. Yes, I believe they are the right family for this."

Pierre Acarie was one of the leaders of the Holy League—distinguished, rich and active. Moreover, his wife, Barbe, was celebrated everywhere for her good works, her piety and her shrewdness.

"I even know some priests who have gone to Barbe Acarie for advice," said Coton.

De Souzy nodded. "I know her, yes. She has sometimes attended my church."

"Good," said Coton. "I suggest that you arrange for the Acaries to meet the girl. And keep in mind that Madame Acarie's opinion will count as much as her husband's, if not more."

De Souzy wanted to know if Father Coton would be present if and when the meeting took place. "I would rather stay in the background for now," replied Coton.

That afternoon Coton went to the Golden Racket, an establishment on the Left Bank, where he regularly played tennis, a game highly popular among gentlemen of the time. He faced his usual opponent, Dr. René Monnet, having tied his cassock around his waist so as not to be hampered in his movements. The priest beat the physician handily. After the match they talked over a cooling drink. They had met at the Golden Racket some years before and had become friends. They had several things in common, including a Jesuit education and an abrupt change in their careers. Father Coton had started out as a lawyer but had become increasingly disgusted with what struck him as the inhumane pettifoggery of the law. He realized that he had been drawn to the Church all along and he entered a Jesuit seminary.

It had been the opposite with René Monnet. His devout parents had wanted him to be a priest and he persuaded himself that he had a calling. He too had entered a Jesuit seminary, at a much younger age than Coton, and he proved to be an excellent student. But he discovered that he was not cut out for the religious life. René Monnet developed too warm a feeling toward the gardener's voluptuous daughter and an unusually strict prefect abruptly ended his clerical career. He decided to take up the study of medicine, turning from the care of souls to the care of the body. The dividing line between the two, he thought, might not be all that clear. He always remembered something written by the great François Rabelais, who was a physician as well as a priest and believed that body and soul, virtues and vices, appetites and dreams, are all mingled together in God's human creatures. As Rabelais's character Pantagruel said: "Everything we are and that we have is made up of three things: the soul, the body and our property."

Monnet became a well-respected physician in Paris but was always ready to discuss religion.

"I have great difficulty with this business of celibacy," he told Father Coton when he described why he had left the seminary. "Priests commit themselves to chastity because the Church demands it and that, one could argue, is a form of duress. Moral philosophers tell us that no oath taken under duress is binding."

"I am afraid that is what people call a Jesuitical argument," said Coton. But he was tolerant of Monnet's foibles and his skepticism. He liked him and trusted him. Now he said, "I believe you are friendly with the Acaries."

"Yes, I have been their doctor for several years and I can say that I am also their friend."

"I arranged for them to meet a young woman who has begun to make a stir in Paris." He summarized briefly what little he knew about Nicole Tavernier.

"Father de Souzy will bring her. I myself do not yet want to be identified with her, but as a friend of the house you could easily be present at this meeting. If you agree, perhaps you could let me know later what the girl is like and what sort of impression she made on the Acaries. Or on you, for that matter."

René Monnet was a wiry man in his middle years with reddish, bristly hair. His left eyelid drooped slightly, which gave him a deceptively sleepy appearance. It was always a little surprising when he flashed out with a sharp look, as he did now.

"Why are you interested in her?"

"My instinct tells me that eventually a great many people may be interested in her."

Dr. Monnet promised that he would try to attend the meeting and to let Coton know how it went. He pulled out a timepiece, an extraordinary watch made of silver and shaped like a death's-head.

"Do you have time for another game?" Monnet asked.

"I do. But put away that awful watch of yours. In these times we hardly need a reminder of death."

CHAPTER 2

The Acaries lived on the rue des Juifs, not far from the Hôtel de Ville, a street that had once been part of a Jewish quarter but had long since been taken over by wealthy Parisians who had put up sedate and elegant residences. The Acarie mansion consisted of an imposing main house, two smaller houses, stables and gardens.

Father de Souzy and Nicole Tavernier arrived at the appointed time and were shown into a large reception room. Against a backdrop of walls hung with elaborate tapestries and elegant walnut furniture, a group was waiting as if for a performance. There was Pierre Acarie, his wife, Barbe, and Barbe's companion, Andrée Levoix, as well as Dr. René Monnet.

Father de Souzy was clearly nervous, but Nicole strode into the room without hesitation.

"Monsieur Acarie, may I present Nicole Tavernier, the young woman I have told you about," said Father de Souzy.

Pierre, a tall man in his thirties with an air of being accustomed to deference, nodded formally. Before de Souzy could introduce Nicole to the others, she was in front of Barbe, and made a deep bow. "Madame," she said. "I ask your blessing."

"I have no power to bless you," said Barbe, her tone reserved. "It is God's blessing we all need."

Barbe at twenty-eight seemed matronly, and she was very much aware of her position as mistress of a large household. She took in Nicole's rather disheveled appearance, her poor clothes, her drawling accent. Nearly a decade younger than Barbe, Nicole seemed almost childlike but with far more than a child's presence.

"Madame," said Nicole, "all Paris knows that God has particularly blessed *you*. Your piety and good works are praised everywhere. I ask no better than to follow in your path."

When her husband had suggested this meeting, Barbe had only reluctantly agreed to receive this stranger, who sounded like something of a vagrant and had the audacity to preach in the streets. Now Barbe began an interrogation.

"We understand that you come from Reims," she said.

"That is right," said Nicole.

"Will you tell us something about your family?"

"I have no family," said Nicole.

It was a puzzling answer but Barbe let it pass for the moment. She next asked what had brought Nicole to Paris and the girl repeated the story of the vision in which she saw Father de Souzy.

"Do you have such visions often?"

"Often enough."

"What do they tell you?"

"Sometimes they have guided me toward my next destination— a town especially sinful, a family especially in want."

"And how do you live?" asked Barbe.

"God provides for me. People take me into their homes and share meals with me. I do not need much food. Occasionally someone will give me a gold piece or two and I accept it, not for myself, but so that I can go on spreading God's word."

As Barbe and Nicole faced each other, the room around them appeared to recede and the two figures stood out as if on a stage.

At length Barbe spoke again. "You said that you wished to follow in my path. You seem to have your own path. I merely perform works of mercy for the poor and the sick."

Pierre Acarie broke in. His stiff and dignified manner had softened and he said to Nicole with a smile, "I am sure that my wife will be grateful for your help."

Barbe glanced at her husband for a moment and said with a slight shrug, "Very well. I will be going to the Hôtel Dieu tomorrow morning as usual to assist the sisters. You may accompany me if you wish."

Nicole replied with a note of triumph. "Thank you, Madame, it will give me great joy to do that. I will consider it the first step of my mission in Paris."

Father de Souzy beamed like a teacher whose favorite pupil had just successfully passed a test. "I too thank you, Madame. This young girl came here in search of spiritual direction and I believe you will be a better guide than I could be."

Dr. Monnet and Andrée Levoix had been silent observers. Andrée was Barbe's contemporary—they had known each other since childhood—but she looked younger. Her plain face was carefully neutral, the face of someone who has learned to mask her thoughts, but when she felt that she could speak out she did so sharply. She obviously trusted the doctor and said quietly as they left the room, "Did you notice the part about this being the first step of her mission in Paris? *The first step.* My guess is that she has a lot more in mind than changing bandages at the Hôtel Dieu."

On the next morning Barbe and Nicole arrived at the Hôtel Dieu together. It was widely feared as a terrible place—overcrowded, corpses being carried out daily, a gruesome stench emanating from its walls into the surrounding streets. Barbe remembered her own frightened impression when, years before, she had insisted on going there to help the sisters. The first time she had to change a blood-soaked bandage and clean a wound while the patient screamed in pain, she thought she would never get used to it. But she eventually conquered her revulsion and became a familiar figure in the hospital.

Despite its forbidding aspect it was a well-organized institution. The sick were segregated in different rooms—the most serious cases in the infirmary, intermediate cases in another ward called the Saint-Denis room, convalescents in the Saint-Thomas room and mothers in the Birthing room.

The powerful hospital smells did not faze Nicole, but the size of the place and the number of patients astonished her. "So many sick," she kept saying. "So many sick."

She had been in hospitals before but none as large as this huge warehouse of disease with its three hundred beds, many of them occupied by four or five patients. Throughout the day she followed Barbe on her rounds, handing her fresh bandages, helping her to sponge patients and holding them down when they writhed in pain while Barbe ministered to them. She carefully listened to the comforting words Barbe spoke to the very ill who were nearing death.

That night Pierre asked Barbe how the girl had done.

"I have to admit she did well," replied Barbe. "She is skilled with her hands, she is patient and she does not tire easily."

Nicole's second day at the hospital passed much as the first, but the third day was different. As soon as the two women arrived in the ward Nicole left Barbe's side. "I think I now know what to do," she said, "thanks to you, Madame."

With that she started her own progress from bed to bed, bandaging, washing, soothing. The sisters who watched her curiously realized that she was as competent as Barbe and equally adept at comforting patients.

"Do not be afraid," she would say. "God will heal your wounds," or "mend your bones," or "cool your fever. Trust in His power and His love."

Barbe observed her as curiously as the sisters did. It occurred to her that Nicole was finding it much easier to do this work than Barbe herself had during her own beginnings at the hospital. She felt a flicker of resentment but suppressed it, telling herself that this was unworthy.

The next day brought a startling incident. It involved a patient who for days had been shaken by violent convulsions that the physicians could not diagnose. On this day he seemed in extremis. Nicole, approaching his bed, looked at him intensely for a few moments and then knelt by his side in silent prayer. The man's wife stood by tearfully. Suddenly Nicole rose and placed her hands on the man's shoulders. "The Lord will bring you peace," she said. "Peace and rest. Trust in Him to bring you peace and rest."

Soon afterward the patient's convulsions became markedly milder and within an hour had ceased altogether.

"A miracle!" the wife pronounced. "This girl has performed a blessed miracle."

The word quickly moved about the hospital and out into the city. The story spread from mouth to mouth, jumping across streets and squares, in and out of taverns and shops.

Barbe had been in another ward at the time of the incident and heard about it from the excited sisters. Later in the day she asked Dr. Monnet whether he had any medical explanation for this recovery.

"I have no explanation," he said, "but that does not mean it was a miracle. I have seen many spontaneous recoveries and our physicians' art, alas, cannot explain everything."

Barbe nodded and said, "We are taught, after all, that miracles are not performed by the living."

But Nicole's reputation as a wonder worker grew. The patients in the Hôtel Dieu and their families asked for her, and more healings were reported. She was even invited into private houses to tend to the dying. She would usually declare, almost in passing, that she could not perform the functions of a priest, but she nevertheless heard confessions. She had a way of mentioning sins that had been omitted in these confessions.

"You have not told me about the money you stole from the collection plate in church some time ago," she might say. Or, "You have had impure thoughts about your maid." And so Nicole became widely considered not only a healer but a reader of minds and souls.

Nicole's slight, dark figure was soon familiar all over Paris, and wherever she went people crowded around her. Some merely wanted to see her or listen to her preaching or touch her robe. Others wanted to claim her miraculous powers and put them to work.

"My father is desperately ill, please come to his bedside," they would say; or, "A demon has possessed my son, who raves and rants. I beg you to come to our house and cast out this evil spirit."

Nicole obeyed many of these requests and, unlike Barbe, freely granted her blessing to anyone who asked for it.

The leaders of the Holy League were delighted with her, and sympathetic priests often mentioned her in the pulpits. "This saintly maid, this Godly virgin," they said, "was a living rebuke to the heretics who denied saints and miracles."

One day she confronted de Souzy. "Father," she said, "I must meet the archbishop."

The priest was taken aback and asked her why.

"I have a special request that I wish to discuss only with his eminence," she replied.

"The archbishop carries many burdens and has little time to spare," said de Souzy. "Why not tell me what it is you want?"

"What I want only the archbishop can grant," Nicole said.

De Souzy was afraid to approach the powerful archbishop, but was also afraid *not* to approach him. Nicole, after all, had by then acquired many followers in Paris, including his own Capuchin order.

Treading carefully, de Souzy submitted a request that an audience be granted to Nicole Tavernier on grounds of the spiritual role she had begun to play. The audience was duly granted.

Accompanied by Father de Souzy and Pierre Acarie, Nicole walked into the vaulted chamber where Archbishop Pierre de Gondi was seated on a gilded throne. She knelt, kissed the large ring on the archbishop's extended hand and rose again quickly.

"Your Eminence," she said, "I have been able to take God's message to people here and there, at street corners and in their houses. But that is not enough. People have not sufficiently atoned for their sins, the sins that have brought down on us the punishments of war and heresy. I ask Your Eminence to order a procession of penitence so that Paris will repent."

Gondi was astonished.

"A procession!" he exclaimed. "We have heard much about your good works and inspiring words and we do not doubt your devotion, but I do not believe that such a ceremony is either necessary or fitting."

Nicole went on as if she had not heard him. "In addition," she said, "during the procession all places of business in Paris must be closed and the entire court of Parliament must be present."

The archbishop's face reddened, approximating the color of his robe. He repeated his refusal.

Nicole's brow contracted in anger; her whole body stiffened and she shouted, "I am not asking this for me but for God. Bishop you may be, but He has sent me here and He will punish you severely if you ignore His command. You will be dead in three months' time unless you grant me what I ask in God's name."

Father de Souzy and Pierre Acarie were shocked, and the archbishop rose abruptly, anger flexing the cords of his neck. "Leave us," he shouted. But Nicole had already turned and was hurrying out of the room.

"Why do you bring such a creature to me?" cried the prelate.

Father de Souzy tried hard to recover his composure. "I beg Your Eminence to make allowances for this young girl's zeal," he said. "She should not have spoken as she did, of course, but she is animated by genuine faith and burning conviction. I do believe that she is divinely inspired and so do most of my brethren in the Capuchin order."

"And why do you believe this?" demanded Gondi. "What is your evidence?"

"Eminence, I have examined her. She is a simple girl without much schooling and yet she is well spoken, and well versed in scripture. She has given me interpretations to rival the insights of many a learned cleric. Such knowledge surely must be the result of special grace."

"Besides," said Pierre Acarie, who had been silent so far, "I have seen her preach in public places, and she has an extraordinary effect on people. They see something holy in her."

"Be that as it may," said Gondi, still angry, "it is outrageous for her to presume to threaten me, the archbishop."

De Souzy tried again. "My Lord, I am reminded of Saint Catherine of Siena. As Your Eminence undoubtedly remembers, this young nun lived a life of extreme humility and self-mortification, yet acted and spoke with great audacity. She lectured scholars, hectored princes and even the Holy Father. To Pope Gregory XI, she once wrote, and I think I quote accurately, 'Up, Father! No more irresponsibility! You ought to be using the power and strength that is yours. If you don't intend to use it, it would be better, and more to God's honor and the good of your soul, to resign.' "

The archbishop said sarcastically, "I see you have thoroughly studied Saint Catherine's life. But are you suggesting that this Nicole is a future saint?"

"I make no judgment as to that, although many believe she is. I merely cite Saint Catherine to show that deep and consuming faith can lead to what sounds like insolence."

Pierre Acarie spoke again. "I do not know whether or not Nicole Tavernier is divinely inspired. But I do say, in the confines of this room, that this does not matter at the moment. What matters is that many people *believe* that she is. I feel that we can use Nicole Tavernier to bolster our cause. In fact I think we need her. The zeal of even the most faithful is weakening and everywhere there are calls for compromise with the heretics."

Pierre ignored the fact that Gondi himself might be willing to compromise for the sake of peace and that Nicole was preaching repentance and reconciliation. He felt that, regardless of her specific message, Nicole was seen as a shining witness to the Church's miraculous powers and would thus enhance the League.

Gondi rose again. "Let me reflect on this."

The archbishop, who had served as France's ambassador to the Vatican under three popes, was a politician at heart. He well understood the significance of processions in Paris. They were popular almost as a kind of entertainment; occasionally, the participants were only lightly clothed and a certain amount of quite unspiritual activity resulted.

While some of these marches were spontaneous, many were organized by the Holy League, which favored them as a form of propaganda. Gondi did not want to antagonize the League because, like Coton, he knew that it was still powerful.

Perhaps yet another factor helped influence him. No one had ever considered the wily old man to be especially superstitious, but he may have taken Nicole's prophecy of his death seriously. After a day of reflection, the archbishop approved a solemn procession in honor of Nicole Tavernier. Once he had made his choice, he decided to back the event with his full prestige and lead the march himself.

The procession had formed in front of Notre Dame Cathedral. At the head of the parade two strong Capuchins in gray habits carried a statue of the Virgin, pink of face, dressed in white and blue. After the archbishop, leaning heavily on his crozier, and assorted clerics came monks of various orders, some covered from head to toe, their eyes peering out from behind narrow slits. Then a group of nuns, their white wimples swaying as they walked, some carrying huge crucifixes, others leading little children, presumably orphans. Soldiers holding swords in one hand and pictures of the Virgin in the other. Physicians displaying medicines and herbs, accompanied by people with stumps for legs or arms. The city fathers, wrapped in ermine and dignity, chains of office glittering around their necks. Ordinary citizens, some dressed in burlap as a sign of penitence, others in their Sunday best.

The procession slowly moved from the narrow square in front of the cathedral, past the cloister of Notre Dame and past a house known as the Red Donkey; at one of its windows, a group of foreign ambassadors watched the scene. The route was lined with eager crowds, some merely curious, some pious. The marchers filed through the rue Neuve, past the Hôtel Dieu. They went on through narrow streets and alleys and then past the tall, graceful spire of Sainte-Chapelle, which had been built to contain the precious relics—supposedly the crown of thorns and fragments of the true cross—brought back from the crusades by Saint Louis. At the sight of the spire, some of the marchers crossed themselves, some wept, some exclaimed, "Christ is with us!"

Barbe Acarie had been astonished and indignant that Archbishop de Gondi had approved this event. She did not believe that Nicole deserved such an honor. But in the end, drawn by curiosity, Barbe decided to witness the spectacle. With Andrée, she watched the procession from the steps of a building not far from her house. When Nicole approached and saw her, she left her place in the march and rushed toward Barbe. She seized her hand and said, "Madame, please join this procession. It would please all Paris."

Barbe withdrew her hand and shook her head. "Thank you," she said. "But this is your day."

Then the parade turned around and headed back toward Notre Dame. At the entrance of the cathedral, the archbishop stood waiting for the girl who had been at the center of the procession— Nicole Tavernier in her white dress, barefoot, her dark eyes glowing as if with a fever. He led her inside the church, where she presently could be seen kneeling and praying before the altar, amid the familiar smell of incense, candles and ancient stone—the deep breath of centuries.

The morning after the procession, de Souzy called on the Acaries. This time he was accompanied by Father Coton, who no longer felt the need to keep his distance. Dr. René Monnet had reported to him that Nicole had been well received by the Acaries, and besides, there had been the procession led by the archbishop himself.

"We have witnessed an extraordinary event yesterday, an outpouring of adoration for this girl," said de Souzy.

Father Coton added, "She cannot go on staying at Sainte-Catherine's indefinitely."

"In that case," said Pierre, "she should come to live with us."

"It is precisely what we hoped for, Monsieur Acarie," said de Souzy.

After the two priests left, Pierre turned to his wife.

"I assume you have no objections." It was more a statement than a question.

Barbe was puzzled by this peculiar girl, and suspicious. Although she would not admit this to anybody, not even herself, she was irritated by the way Nicole had almost usurped her place at the Hôtel Dieu and been so easily acclaimed as a miracle worker. And yet—it was confusing—she was also drawn to the girl and had been touched by Nicole's attempt to include her in the procession.

"If you wish it, I will welcome her," she said to her husband.

A servant was sent to fetch Nicole. Barbe and Andrée led her to a large, sunny bedroom close to Andrée's own.

"You should be comfortable here," said Barbe.

Nicole looked about her at the wide bed, the chest and a small oak armoire. "More comfortable than I have ever been before."

That evening, as Barbe was about to say the rosary in her chamber, Nicole appeared at the door. "Madame," she said, "will you allow me to pray with you? It would give me such comfort on this first night in your house."

After a moment's hesitation Barbe agreed. The two women knelt and began to pray. When they reached the first Our Father, Barbe suddenly fell silent. Looking up, Nicole realized something had happened she did not understand. Barbe was stock still, rigidly holding the crucifix at the end of the rosary in front of her. She was barely breathing.

"Madame?" Nicole said in a low voice. Barbe did not seem to hear. Nicole said, "Madame, are you ill?" Again Barbe did not stir. Nicole rose and went to fetch Andrée.

"There is something the matter with Madame," she said. "We were saying the rosary and she suddenly stopped. She does not move and when I tried to talk to her she did not seem to hear me."

Andrée showed no sign of surprise or alarm. "This happens to her occasionally. It is nothing to be concerned about."

At that point Pierre Acarie appeared and overheard Andrée's words. "Is it another of her weaknesses?" he asked. And Andrée nodded.

"I think we had better send for Dr. Monnet."

"Sir, do you really think that is necessary? I am sure she will soon be herself again."

"These things have been happening too often lately," said Pierre. "I would prefer to have the doctor examine her."

When Dr. Monnet arrived nearly an hour later, Barbe was still rigid in her trance. As Pierre, Andrée and Nicole watched, the doctor approached her and touched her gently. He spoke her name several times. Slowly she began to stir. Her eyes, which had been lifelessly staring at the crucifix, moved and focused on the doctor.

"It happened again," she said. "Did it last very long?"

"That does not matter," said Monnet. "But I see that you are very flushed and very warm to the touch. Perhaps you should be bled."

"That usually just makes me tired," she said.

"Do not contradict the doctor," said Pierre.

But Monnet actually agreed with Barbe, having never found that bleeding helped her much. Instead he prescribed a tonic— rhubarb wine—and left her to rest.

Later, after Monnet had gone, Nicole quietly returned to Barbe's room. Barbe was stretched out on her bed, half asleep. Nicole looked down at the pale face and said, "Madame, even though the doctor was here, I now know that you are not ill. I believe that you were in a special state, close to God."

Barbe opened her eyes wide in astonishment. "What makes you think that?"

"I simply know it. I sometimes have the same experience. I believe it is a sign of special grace."

The same experience? Barbe resented the comparison. After all, she thought, she did not claim to have visions or to possess special powers or to be clairvoyant. But she sighed and said only, "I must rest now."

CHAPTER 3

Dr. René Monnet had first met Barbe Acarie thirteen years before, when she was fifteen. One day in December of 1581, he was summoned to the house of the Avrillot family, one of the richest and most distinguished in the city.

He was received by a handsome woman with strikingly green eyes whose manner matched her severe black dress.

"I have called you to examine my daughter. There is something wrong with one of her feet," said Madame Avrillot.

Monnet was led to another wing of the house and ushered into a chamber. A young woman lay on a bed, her pale, delicate face setting off her eyes, which were of the same green as her mother's. One of her bare legs extended from below a coverlet and was elevated on a cushion. Next to her sat a girl of about the same age, her hand resting on the other girl's shoulder.

He examined the foot and quickly recognized chilblains, an extraordinary condition in so wealthy and warm a house—crackling fireplaces were everywhere. Barbe's foot looked badly swollen and discolored.

"This has been ignored too long," he said. "One of the toes is badly infected. I am afraid it will have to be removed."

"Do what you must do," said Madame Avrillot.

Most physicians would have left such an operation to one of the many barber-surgeons who were looked down on as mere craftsmen by university-trained doctors. To Monnet, that division of labor made no sense and, like a handful of colleagues, he had trained himself in surgery.

After he had performed the painful operation and Barbe was sleeping uneasily, he again faced the mother.

"Chilblains!" he said belligerently. "How could this have happened?"

Madame Avrillot looked at him coldly, said, "Good-bye, doctor" and left the room.

By then the young woman who had been sitting with Barbe and who stayed with her throughout the surgery had joined them. Monnet had not been introduced to her and now she said, "I am Andrée Levoix. I am Barbe's companion." Presently she explained what Barbe's mother would not.

Marie Avrillot had lost several babies shortly after they were born. When she was again with child, she dedicated the expected infant to Our Lady and vowed to dress it, until the age of seven, all in white. This set Barbe apart from other children, but she did not mind. On the contrary, it gave her a sense of devotion. At eleven she was sent to the convent school at the Franciscan Abbey of Longchamp, where she met Andrée, another of the "little boarders," as they were called. She took with enthusiasm to the cloistered life, its deliberate commitment and strong discipline. She diligently learned her lessons, chanted the Divine Office flawlessly and accepted the Church's teaching without hesitation.

"Some of the other girls asked questions," Andrée recalled. "But Barbe never had any doubts.

"One night before we went to sleep," Andrée recalled, "Barbe said that she wanted to tell me something very important. 'I want to stay right here forever,' she said. 'I want to become a nun.' I told no one else about this, but Barbe was not as good at hiding her feelings as I was. The nuns soon guessed what was in Barbe's mind and they told Madame Avrillot, who was appalled. She felt that the dedication of her daughter to the Virgin had perhaps gone too far. She certainly wanted Barbe to be a good, devout, Catholic young lady, but she also wanted her to make a brilliant marriage. Barbe was abruptly withdrawn from the convent."

Barbe cried before she left the serene and ordered atmosphere of Longchamp with its regular round of devotions and chants and the camaraderie of the "little boarders."

"I don't want to leave any of you," she sobbed to Andrée. "Especially I don't want to leave you."

As it turned out, she did not have to. Andrée's father, who owned what had been a large and profitable estate in Normandy, was given to hazardous land speculations. He was by then nearly bankrupt. The mother superior suggested to Madame Avrillot that she might take Andrée into her household as a companion to Barbe, and she agreed, thinking that Andrée would be useful.

"I was happy to stay with Barbe, although I was soon troubled by my position here. To Barbe I was simply a friend. To Madame Avrillot I was Barbe's maid."

Now began what Andrée described as the time of silks and satins. Madame Avrillot had a dressmaker come to the house almost weekly with ever more dazzling clothes for Barbe. Barbe hated them. To her they symbolized vanity and worldliness, qualities she felt she must avoid, for she still hoped one day to enter the religious life. But as a dutiful daughter she allowed Andrée to dress her night after night in the silks and satins and brocades. That lasted for a few months. Then Barbe rebelled. The plague had broken out in Paris—more and more houses displayed the wooden cross that signified the presence of a plague victim. Barbe announced to her mother that she wanted to go to work as a nursing sister at the Hôtel Dieu. Madame Avrillot felt that the dreaded hospital was no place for her daughter. Furthermore, she suspected that Barbe's desire to work there was a step toward becoming a nun after all. She forbade it absolutely.

"If you want to live like a nun, my child," she said, "you can do so right here in this house. I will be pleased to help you."

At a stroke all the pretty dresses were locked away, her soft bedding was replaced by a hard pallet, her meals were meager. In the harsh winter of 1581, Barbe was forced to dress in front of an open door. She accepted it all silently, without complaint.

"I often tried to make things a little more comfortable for Barbe," recalled Andrée. "But Madame Avrillot would not even let me take her near a fireplace to warm herself."

That was the explanation for the chilblains.

One evening eight months later, a liveried footman arrived at Dr. Monnet's rooms in great agitation and handed him a note that bore the name of a well-known and wealthy financier. The note asked the doctor to come to his residence as quickly as possible to treat someone who, it was feared, had suffered a stroke. Monnet mounted his mule with its saddlebags full of medical instruments while the footman trotted alongside.

After arriving at the house, Monnet found a corpulent middle-aged man in an antechamber where he had been hastily bedded down on several cushions on the floor. A quick examination showed that he had not suffered a stroke but was incapacitated by excessive drink and food. The doctor was able to assure the host, who was hovering nervously at the door, that his guest was in no danger. He gratefully invited the doctor to join the party. In a large ballroom perhaps fifty couples were lingering indecisively, and at the host's signal the musicians resumed the gavotte. Meeting several of the guests, Monnet suddenly found himself facing an extremely pretty girl. There was something vaguely familiar about her face, about her green eyes. She was introduced to him as Madame Barbe Acarie. He realized with amazement that since he had last seen her, Barbe Avrillot had married. She had been transformed from the pale and wretched girl into a radiant creature. Before the evening was over he would learn that she was already known in the more fashionable circles of Paris as "the beautiful Acarie."

A strapping young man, obviously her husband, stood at her side. "The doctor and I have met before," she said. "Dr. Monnet once attended me at my mother's house."

Despite his youth, Pierre Acarie was self-assured and somewhat condescending. "Dr. Monnet," he said tentatively, as if trying to remember where he had heard the name before. "Ah, yes. I hope you will do us the honor of calling on us some afternoon." He added with a smile, "Even if nobody is ill."

Before leaving, Monnet sought out Barbe and said, "I am extremely pleased to see you so well and happy."

"God has been very good to me," she replied.

Knowing what he knew of Barbe's miserable condition only a short time ago, it seemed that God had performed something of a miracle.

Yes, God had been good to her, thought Barbe as her maid was preparing her for bed that night. But He was also confusing. Surely it had been God who had prompted her to want to be a nun, to become His bride. But it also must have been God who told her that she must not go on defying her mother. Wasn't it also God who had brought her a handsome and attentive young man who wanted to marry her? This strong feeling she had for him and the sudden thoughts of being a wife and mother—did not all this also come from God?

When Andrée came into her bedchamber to say good night, Barbe repeated these musings.

"What God wants us to do is not always clear," said Andrée. "And surely He is entitled to change His mind."

A few days later René Monnet decided to act on Pierre Acarie's invitation and to call on the Acaries. They were away visiting one of Pierre's estates in Champagne. In their place Andrée Levoix did the honors.

"As you can see," she said, smiling over hot, spiced wine, "I am still with Barbe." From the way the servants treated her it was clear that her position in the new household was more elevated than it had been under the severe regime of Barbe's mother. As soon as seemed decent, Monnet began to ask questions about the extraordinary transformation that had taken place in Barbe.

"I sometimes think," Andrée said, "that there are two Barbes. There is the pious and otherworldly creature. But then there is the intensely practical Barbe, intelligent, with an orderly mind, who can face up to reality. There simply came a point when this second Barbe understood that she could not win out over her mother and decided to make the best of the inevitable. And when the inevitable turned out to be an attractive suitor, the decision was not all that difficult."

Andrée was silent for a few moments but stopped Monnet when he was about to ask another question. "Do not believe, Doctor, that the first Barbe is gone forever. The first Barbe will reappear someday. When the two are joined together"—she laughed in anticipation—"I think we will have a very formidable woman with us."

For a long time Barbe thought about what Andrée had said about God changing His mind. She mentioned this to her confessor, who was indignant.

"God is unchangeable and eternal," he said. "We cannot presume to know God's mind. We can only hope and pray that our actions will please Him."

"And how do we know when they do?"

"God will always give us a sign, a sign that is the expression of His grace."

Barbe gladly accepted this explanation. She went about her usual devotions—the Mass, the rosary—which were a part of her daily routine, her regular and reassuring communication with God. She thought of Him as an omnipotent king who had delegated the rule over her household to her. She performed that duty with growing competence. René Monnet, who was often at the Acarie mansion as a physician and increasingly as a friend, observed her confident way with the servants and eventually her children.

She bore the first three in quick succession and three more would follow later. Barbe was an attentive and cheerful mother, clearly relieved at being free of her own mother's tyranny, but she showed traces of the older woman's strong will. There was a constant stream of guests, with many parties and musical entertainments. Barbe—the second Barbe—enjoyed them all. In an odd way Pierre Acarie seemed like a guest too. He was affectionate but condescending toward his wife, spent a suitable amount of time with the children and was always a good host. But he rarely gave an order to the household staff or took any direct hand in guiding the Acarie establishment, a role he left increasingly to Barbe. Yet he was sharply critical when anything displeased him, whether an undercooked bird or an insufficiently stoked fireplace.

One evening in Pierre's library Monnet observed him crossing the room to take a book from a shelf. He thought that he dragged his left foot slightly. "Did you injure yourself, Monsieur?" he asked.

Pierre stopped short and replied almost angrily, "You doctors are always looking for defects. There is nothing wrong with my foot."

A moment later he added, "Well, I did have a minor accident when I was a boy. It still troubles me occasionally."

He obviously hated to admit any imperfection in himself.

And he clearly expected perfection in Barbe. She had taken to reading the romances translated from the Spanish that were popular in Paris. When Pierre found out about this, he forbade such frivolity and handed her a list of spiritual volumes suggested to him by a priest. It included such titles as *Collection for the Faithful Soul,* containing *The Spiritual Mirror, The Ring, The Crown* and *The Spiritual Treasure Chest; On Knowledge of God and Ourselves* and *The Instruction of the Christian Woman.*

Barbe dutifully read these books and if some part of them seemed boring or incomprehensible, she either did not admit it to herself or blamed herself for insufficient understanding. Then one day she read a passage quoted from Saint Augustine: "He is indeed a miser to whom God is not enough."

For reasons she did not grasp, the words made a deep impression on her. She was so struck by them that she had to put the book down. She felt dizzy. Questions filled her mind: Was she being a miser? Was she withholding too much from God and giving too much of herself to the world? No, she decided, surely she was not guilty of that, surely she always did her duty and thus God's will. But then things began to happen to her that once again made her wonder just how to discern God's will.

One day she went to Mass as usual at her parish church of Saint-Gervais but did not return at the expected time. Alarmed, Pierre sent Andrée and several servants to the houses of friends she might have visited. She was nowhere to be found. Finally Andrée went to the church and saw Barbe sitting stiffly in her pew. When Andrée shook her, Barbe seemed to awaken and said, "Is Mass over?"

She hurried home, reproaching herself for having neglected her household duties that day. She could not understand what had come over her. During the next few months such trances occurred again and again.

Pierre Acarie was at first sympathetic and then increasingly irritated by these "weaknesses," as they were referred to in the household.

"I wonder whether you are suffering from some ailment," he told Barbe. "We should ask Dr. Monnet to examine you."

Barbe was shocked by the suggestion of illness but agreed to submit to an examination. Monnet could find no physical cause for her condition. But Barbe's trances became more intense and she was embarrassed. She tried to prevent them by distracting herself. Once in the middle of a conversation she rose and began to play a tune on the spinet to avoid slipping into one of her suspended states. Another time Monnet saw her gripping a pair of scissors so hard that her hand started to bleed.

"What are you doing?" he cried, reaching out to take the scissors from her.

"I felt a 'weakness' coming over me and I thought I might stop it by hurting myself."

To his repeated questions she said, "I simply do not know how these things happen to me or why. I start to pray or I think about

God and I am overcome by a wave of intense feeling. Sometimes the feeling is so strong that I must close my eyes and I think I cannot bear it any longer."

Ever since childhood she had seen the face of Jesus on a thousand crucifixes, but in these trances the physical image of Christ faded away and what she felt more than saw was a glowing presence that overwhelmed and enveloped her. It was a presence that seemed to radiate goodness and bliss. And yet, as she tried to describe it, Monnet realized that she was afraid.

"I do not know, Doctor, whether all this is sent to me by God or"—with a shudder—"by the Devil. Why would God want to try me so?"

He replied that he did not feel qualified to answer that question. He urged her to seek spiritual advice, prescribed one of his tonics that he hoped would soothe her, and left. As always, he was struck by the doubts and torments, the spiritual tribulations, that seemed so often to beset believers.

CHAPTER 4

Dr. René Monnet had never felt such tribulation himself. In hindsight he realized that even in his seminary days, when he had tried to convince himself that he had a calling, he had a problem accepting all the teachings of the Church. He gradually found he could not believe that the body of Christ was literally present in the bread or His blood in the wine. The Protestants, of course, did not believe that either, but Monnet did not become a Protestant; he became a skeptic. He was sometimes tempted to blame science and reason—the astronomers who were trying to show that the world was not at the center of the universe and the philosophers who were asserting that man was at the center of the world. But his doubts came quite apart from such knowledge. Perhaps, he thought, that showed a lack of imagination because, after all, the world was full of equally miraculous and inexplicable phenomena, including life itself. He conceded that the universe does not make sense without God, or something like Him, but he could not accept the idea of a personal God who supervises and commands every human action, including the worst crimes and brutalities. As with God, so with the Devil. He believed that there are forces of evil, but he could not quite see them embodied in the horned and cloven-hoofed fiend who incessantly plagues man and beast with infinite guile.

He could not say this to anyone at the risk of being denounced as an atheist and blasphemer, and even in his long conversations with his tolerant friend Father Coton he dared to discuss such matters only in theory. He often wondered how many other people felt the same way behind their masks of pious propriety. Yet for all his skepticism he was fascinated by the phenomenon of faith and observed it with the curiosity—perhaps envious curiosity—of a man observing lovers even though he himself cannot love.

He had great compassion for Barbe when he saw how mortally afraid she was of the Devil and how real he was to her. But he could not help Barbe because he still had no explanation for her trances. Pierre had asked him whether his wife might be suffering from epilepsy, but the doctor had found no trace of this. He knew that many of his colleagues might have given a diagnosis of melancholy, but he had no idea what that term really meant, and he doubted that anyone else did either. Her confessor tried to reassure her but he failed.

Then she met a remarkable man, a Capuchin known as Benet of Canfield. Many priests frequented the Acarie mansion and Canfield was especially welcomed by Pierre, for he always had news about conditions in England, where Catholics were savagely persecuted. Canfield was an Englishman who had been born a Protestant but converted to the Church of Rome in his youth. He had fled to France and settled there. He was a tall, lanky man who never quite seemed to know what to do with his arms and legs, but his very awkwardness made him sympathetic.

To Barbe's surprise, he listened to her concerns without astonishment, as if they involved something quite natural and familiar. Then he told her his own story.

"When I was a novice in the monastery, I had precisely the same experiences that you have described. I would fall into prolonged trances that greatly alarmed the friars. During one of my raptures, doctors were called in. I was pricked with large pins in my thighs and shins without being roused. Eventually I came out of it on my own. In time the friars were wise enough to leave me alone, and my trances grew shorter and happened more rarely. They became part of my life and they still are."

He took Barbe's hand.

"Like you, I used to fear that they were inspired by the Devil, but I realized that if they had been, I would not have been so concerned. The same is true of you. I now know that these trances are from God, and I take them as a special sign of grace."

"A sign of grace," Barbe repeated. Had she not been told before that God gives such signs as a mark of His approval? She seized on Canfield's words with relief and joy. She believed in what Canfield had said, not only because he seemed wise and kind, not only because he had gone through similar experiences, but because she wanted to believe him. "Yes," she thought. "God is sending me these things to test me, and these tests are a special grace."

Before long she hardly remembered that her trances had ever frightened her; instead, she took satisfaction from them.

At Pierre's insistence, Dr. Monnet still looked in on Barbe from time to time. On one occasion, Pierre took him aside and said he wanted a word with him. He led the doctor into the garden and, as it was a chilly day, a servant handed him a hat—a black toque with a shell-and-pearl brooch. Pierre had something of a passion for hats, of which he had an extraordinary collection: fur and silk and velvet, bespangled and plumed. As they strolled along the neat, pebbled paths Pierre was limping noticeably.

"I told you an untruth some time ago, Doctor," he began, "or at least a half truth, when I said that my limp was the result of an accident. Well, it was not exactly an accident. Once, when I was a young boy, probably eight or nine years old, my father took me along, as he often did, on a visit to our estate at Ivry. Our house stood on top of a hill with a great view of vineyards below (the wine was both good and profitable), and on a clear day one could see Paris and Notre Dame in the distance. I was particularly fond of the local church, Saint-Pierre and Saint-Paul, with its picture of the Virgin and child—the baby Jesus was holding a bunch of grapes. One day we were attending Mass there with a group of my father's friends and retainers. Suddenly, from across the square came the sound of people singing. A crowd of Huguenots, as they were wont to do, had gathered and intoned a hymn to disrupt the Mass. My father sent one of his men to ask the Huguenots to stop their singing until the Mass was over, but they refused. Instead, they stormed into the church, singing all the while. Our men tried to push them out. Swords were drawn. My tutor, who was with us, tried to protect me, but I stumbled and was suddenly struck by a blade. The wound never properly healed. People on both sides were killed, including my tutor. I had loved him very much."

Pierre's voice sounded a note of bitterness that Monnet had never heard from him before, and he realized that there was more to the charming, spoiled and rather foppish gentleman than he had perceived. A few inquiries made it clear that Pierre Acarie was one of the leaders of the Holy League. Like his father-in-law, he was contributing large sums to the cause and had mortgaged some of his country estates.

The Acarie house was so well-ordered and calm that it was sometimes difficult to remember the terrible struggle going on in the outside world. The war between Catholics and Protestants had been a fact of life as Barbe grew up, always there, like the weather or the occasional outbursts of the plague. She had been taught to hate the Protestants, which was not difficult when she heard how they broke the statues of saints, abolished the Mass and trampled on the Host. But for a long time the war did not directly touch her. That was about to change.

The force behind that change was King Henry of Navarre. Barbe was only a child when she first overheard grown-ups mention what seemed to be a dreaded name. He was a heretic, they said, a scoundrel, a menace to the True Church. As leader of the Protestant forces, he was winning battle after battle against the Holy League.

When she returned from the convent at fourteen, Barbe began asking questions about this Henry, but her family was not inclined to talk about such serious matters with a young girl. Even after her marriage two years later, Barbe's husband refused to discuss war, politics and his own involvement with the Holy League, feeling that his young bride's function in life was devotion to the household, the children—and himself. Ultimately it was Dr. René Monnet who gave her a thorough picture of the man who eventually became king of France.

Navarre was an ancient realm between Spain and France, linked to the French crown through an intricate web of marriages and treaties. The monarchs of France belonged to the house of Valois. The rulers of Navarre were part of a great rival family, the Bourbons. The Valois line was to end with the successive deaths of three inept, if not deranged, Valois kings. The last, Henry III, was dispatched by an assassin in 1589. This series of fatal events would have taxed the imagination of most dramatists. (Shakespeare, then busy writing plays to the applause of Queen Elizabeth's court in England, could have done justice to the story.) With courage, cunning and luck, Henry of Navarre had survived a maelstrom of plots, counterplots and attempted murders. With the death of Henry III, his brother-in-law, King Henry of Navarre was now king of France as well—at least in theory. The notion of a Protestant on the throne of France, "the eldest daughter of the Church," outraged most French Catholics. Determined to prevent his ascension, the Holy League prepared to take the field against him, backed by King Philip of Spain. Although Spain had only just recovered from the disastrous defeat of its great armada at the hands of the English, Philip sent troops to fight alongside the League armies. Henry in turn was joined by English troops sent by Elizabeth, and also had help from some German princes.

In March 1590, at Ivry, Henry faced the Catholic forces. At daybreak, armored and on horseback, the king prayed aloud that God grant him victory if he was worthy but, if not, he was ready to die in the hope that his blood would be the last to be shed in this war. He affixed a white plume to his helmet and charged his men to rally to it. Although heavily outnumbered by the League's forces, Henry won an overwhelming victory. He was now ready to move on to Paris and soon laid siege to the city.

He had often referred to Paris as "my mistress," but the Holy Leaguers, who professed to be shocked by his many amours, still swore that he would not conquer this one. They formed the sixteen wards into a revolutionary government, thereafter known merely as "the Sixteen."

Cut off from the surrounding countryside, Paris quickly ran out of food. As the usual meat began to disappear from butcher shops that now displayed old pieces of mules and cats, people chased dogs and rats. Eggs, butter and the occasional remaining fowl cost as much as precious jewels. Dr. Monnet, like all the other physicians in Paris, was kept constantly busy by the diseases of hunger. On his rounds in the hospital, Monnet became accustomed to the usual symptoms—swollen bellies, dysentery, bleeding gums. One day, outside a church, he observed a man chewing furtively. As Monnet came closer he realized that the man was gnawing on a candle, trying to extract the grease from it. Such a diet, he discovered, was becoming widespread. Worse, someone made the incredible suggestion that the bones of corpses should be dug up and ground into meal with which to make bread. As Monnet or any competent physician could have foretold, this "bread of the dead," made from the decaying remains of human bodies, killed many people.

At length hunger became so fierce that some people started to hunt children as well as dogs and cats. A few priests proclaimed that it was better to kill your own children than give in to Henry the heretic. Sermon after sermon announced that those who died of hunger would thereby gain paradise.

Amid such misery, Barbe grew stronger and more resolute. She worked tirelessly, nursing the sick and comforting the dying. She cooked soup and distributed it to the hungry. No longer called "the beautiful Acarie," she was now known as "the good Acarie."

Barbe was infuriated when she learned that many in Paris were hoarding food. During a visit to her mother's house she noticed that the mattresses in the bedchambers gave off a strange crackling sound. They had been filled with grain.

"Mama," she said, "you are helping to starve the poor by hoarding."

"I am only taking care of my family," replied her mother, "which is something that you neglect very easily in your pious trances. Your father and your husband are important to the Holy League."

Barbe was unmoved.

"We will hardly starve by sharing our grain with others," she said.

"Don't presume to instruct me in charity!"

"I am not instructing you, Mother. I am simply warning you that if you really mean to keep this grain you had better hide it where I cannot find it, because otherwise I will surely give it away."

Andrée was astounded by the change in her friend. Only a few years ago, Barbe had yielded to her mother by making a desirable marriage instead of going into the convent. Was the first Barbe returning? When Andrée questioned her, Barbe was surprised.

"I don't believe that I have changed at all," she said. But after thinking about it she admitted, "Perhaps you are right. I could not be the same after watching the misery and suffering of these poor people. And when I realized that my 'weaknesses' were not weaknesses at all but divine grace, I knew there was only one path to follow and it was not my mother's."

As the siege wore on, more and more people managed to slip out of the city, past the enemy lines and into the countryside, in search of food. Among them late one night was Dr. René Monnet, but food was not his mission. He made his way to a modest farmhouse and knocked.

"Yes?" came a voice from inside.

"Navarre," said Monnet and the door opened.

He was greeted by a stout man of military bearing. "I was afraid you might not come tonight," the man said.

"I am sorry, but I had a great many sick to attend," replied Monnet.

"Take a glass of wine," said the man, pouring. "And then let me have your report."

Monnet took a few sips and said, "My report is simple. The city is miserable but it is holding out. More and more people are getting away, which makes things easier for the rest. Why are your men allowing so many to leave?"

"The king is too softhearted. He is sorry for the sufferings of the Parisians. And he does not want to storm the city with all the terrible bloodshed and carnage that it would bring."

"There may not be much time left. We keep hearing rumors of a Spanish army on its way to lift the siege."

"We hear the same rumors. I believe the king may think it wiser to wait and try for Paris another day. Now, do you have any other news?"

Monnet recited some details about conditions in Paris. Then the two men shook hands and Dr. Monnet returned to the city.

The rumors had been correct: a well-equipped Spanish army advanced toward Paris to lift the siege. Henry, still hoping eventually to take Paris without violence, retreated. The Spaniards entered the city and virtually occupied it for several years. Henry now realized that he had reached a fateful deadlock. Paris—and most of France—would never accept a Protestant king. He began to consider conversion to Rome. His Protestant advisers furiously argued against it, feeling that it would amount to a betrayal of the Reformed faith his followers had fought so hard for. He also realized that many Catholics might never accept his conversion as genuine. But he finally concluded that if there was ever to be peace in France—and he passionately wanted peace—there was no other way. In May 1593 he took what he called the perilous leap. He sent word to the pope that he wished to take instruction in the Catholic faith.

There followed dreary weeks during which relays of church-men drilled him in dogma. He did not give them an easy time. He balked at the notion of purgatory but eventually he accepted the concept because, as he put it sarcastically, purgatory was after all a big source of income for the Church, through the sale of indul-gences. Moving through the liturgy, he did not want to hear the prayer for the dead. "I am not dead yet," he said. "And I don't want to be."

His instructors finally decided to leave well enough alone, and the day came when he walked through the flower-strewn streets of Saint-Denis, past houses hung with flags and tapestries, toward the abbey. He was preceded by drummers and followed by trumpeters. Normally he did not much care about what he wore, but on this occasion he felt that some show was required. He was dressed all in white with a black cloak over his shoulder.

The Church had organized quite a show of its own. At the mas-sive door of the abbey he was met by monks of Saint-Denis bear-ing cross and holy water and by the archbishop of Bourges, who asked his name.

"I am the king," he replied.

"What do you seek here?"

"I seek to be received into the bosom of the Apostolic and Roman Catholic Church."

He knelt, read the recantation of his Protestant faith and the pro-fession of the Catholic faith, received absolution and was led into the church. Sunlight from the tall windows lightened the gloom. He confessed to the archbishop and heard Mass. Saint-Denis was the traditional burial place of French monarchs, and their coffins were everywhere in the church. And so Saint Louis and François I, along with all the others, were silent witnesses to the conversion of Henry of Navarre.

As he made his way out of the crowded church, a high-pitched voice was heard in a triumphant shout: "God bless you, Sire. This is the beginning of the redemption of France."

In the tumult he could just glimpse the pale face of a young woman, features contorted by passion and dominated by shining, dark eyes. A moment later the girl had been swallowed by the crowd, but her face and her shout stayed in his mind. He considered the incident a good omen. He would soon be ready to try for Paris again.

CHAPTER 5

"Have you ever seen such a crowd? They are going wild."

"They won't even let him move."

"See, the guards are trying to push the crowd back, but he is calling them off."

"Look at him smile—he wants the people to come close."

"They are going to frighten his horse."

"Oh no, that horse is an old campaigner."

"Well, so is Henry. He looks older than I thought."

"So would you if you were in his place. He has been through more battles than I bet he can remember."

"And through more mistresses too."

"He has always talked about forgiving and forgetting. Still, I wonder what he is going to do with those Leaguers and the Spaniards. I would not want to be in their boots."

"Long live the king! Long live the king!"

Henry had held to his determination not to take Paris by force. He did not want his reign in his future capital to begin in a welter of blood. Money had been the solution. The governor of the city was a greedy man named Brissac. He drove a hard bargain. He finally settled for a hefty pension, the governorship of two cities and a marshall's baton in exchange for opening the city to Henry. In the small hours of March 22, 1594, Brissac unlocked the Porte Neuve to the west and the Porte Saint-Denis to the north. The king and four thousand troops entered the city silently. Paralyzed by surprise, neither the adherents of the League nor the Spanish occupying troops resisted. There was virtually no bloodshed, no fighting. As Parisians stirred from their sleep, the news spread from street to street, neighborhood to neighborhood: Henry was among them. Slowly, preceded by five hundred soldiers, the king, on horseback, made his way through the streets of Paris toward Notre Dame.

From all over the city, from the busy commercial center of the Right Bank, from the abbeys and centers of learning on the Left Bank, from every quarter, square and street, people surged to see their new monarch. A huge crowd jammed into the square in front of the cathedral, blocking the nearby bridge and overflowing into surrounding areas. In keeping with the holiday mood, hawkers sold food—meat and vegetable pies, oatcakes, nuts. Men, women and children strained to get a glimpse of the king: ruddy, cheerful face; full head of dark hair; slightly lumpy, aquiline nose. Guards tried to hold back the crowd but Henry stopped them.

"Let the people come close," he said. "They are hungry for the sight of a king."

"Long live the king!" The shouts mingling with the booming of church bells made Henry intensely happy. Nothing like it, he thought, except perhaps love with a beautiful woman. A man in the crowd with a red, laughing face was shouting something else. Henry could not make it out at first but then he recognized the words.

"Paris is worth a Mass," the man was shouting. "Paris is worth a Mass."

Henry was not sure that he had actually said it that way after his conversion to Catholicism the year before, but he must have said something close to it, and the remark had become famous. If they remembered nothing else about him in the future, they would remember that.

So he had Paris at last, thought Henry. But it had not been easy, even after his conversion.

He kept getting reports, especially from that excellent fellow Monnet, that the Holy League continued to struggle. One procession in Paris included an effigy with a straw crown and a cow's tail followed by young people who shouted: "See the devil of the heretic king!" The effigy was supposed to represent Henry. The die-hard preachers proclaimed that his conversion was fraudulent. One priest fulminated that even if the pope accepted the conversion (which Henry was sure would eventually happen), it would not be valid, and a particularly intolerant Jesuit said that even if an angel of God should come down from the sky and say "Accept him," his words should be doubted. But as Henry now looked around him at the cheering crowd, he knew that for the vast majority of Parisians he was Catholic enough.

He also knew that there were still enemies to deal with. He would take care of the Leaguers later. For the present he needed to cope with the Spanish forces in the city. He did not want to take revenge on them, only to get rid of them. He sent a message to their commander saying that he would make a gift to them of their lives and property on condition that they leave the city at once. Having suspected a far worse fate, the Spaniards were much impressed by Henry's generosity and in short order marched out of Paris through the gate of Saint-Denis. Observing them from a window, the king doffed his hat and called out, "Adieu, gentlemen, adieu. Go in peace but do not come back again."

During the tumultuous scene in front of Notre Dame, a young girl had been wedged in the crowd, almost crushed by shoving, gesticulating people. It was Nicole Tavernier. Having made her way to Paris, she had arrived weeks before the king, a few short weeks

during which she had accomplished her extraordinary triumph—
the procession, the adulation of the people, the reception by the
Acaries. Now, her eyes dancing with excitement, she followed
Henry's every movement. In her mind the picture blended with an
earlier, similar scene of a year ago.

At the time of Henry's conversion, there had been the crowd in
front of the cathedral at Saint-Denis, a smaller crowd than in Paris
but just as enthusiastic, with the Te Deum still ringing in the air
and the bells pounding overhead. And there she had been, trying to get a look at the king from amid the mass of people, and, on
a sudden impulse, crying out at the top of her voice that Henry
would be the savior of France. She was tempted now to shout it
again but she was suddenly aware of a man staring at her from a
few feet away. He looked familiar.

It had taken René Monnet a few moments to recognize Nicole
Tavernier, although he had seen her several times since she had
gone to live with the Acarie family. He came over to her and said,
"Do you remember me? I am Dr. René Monnet."

"Of course," she said. "My mind was elsewhere."

By now the king had disappeared into Notre Dame Cathedral
and both Nicole and Monnet turned to go. He offered to walk her
back home, as he intended to call on the Acaries. They made their
way through the slowly dispersing crowd and he said, "The people seem very happy with their new king."

"They should be. He will finally bring peace. He will save
France."

Monnet certainly agreed, but he said, "Monsieur Acarie would
not like to hear that."

"I will not say it to him. I am saying it to you because I believe
you feel the same way about the king as I do."

Monnet gave her a searching glance from underneath his droop-
ing eyelid. Here was a girl who had become a heroine in Paris with
the help of the League, and yet she was praising a man whom the
League hated. Was she naïve, he wondered, or was she clever—
clever enough to say the right things to the right people?

René was sharply aware of his own duplicity. He was a re-spected physician in Paris who was also an informer for the king. He was regarded by Pierre Acarie as a friend while he secretly served the king whom Pierre loathed.

As they continued on their way back from Notre Dame to the Acarie house on the rue des Juifs, Monnet took out his watch. Be-fore he could put it back in his pocket, Nicole reached for it. He let her take it from his hand. She looked at the small, silver death's-head for a long moment and cradled it in her palm. "The king gave you this," she said.

"What makes you think so?"

"I felt his presence."

Monnet was startled. The watch, indeed, had been a gift from Henry, offered in gratitude for Monnet's work. "This is a rare piece made in Germany," the king had written in an accompany-ing note. "You may find it somewhat macabre but I hope it will ward off what it represents."

Monnet was astounded by what Nicole had said—after all, there was nothing to connect him to the king—and he began to under-stand why people believed in her. Her face seemed to glow, her voice was vibrant with conviction.

When they reached the Acarie mansion Monnet suddenly changed his mind about calling on the family. He clearly imagined Pierre's state of mind. "If Henry ever takes Paris, he will have all our heads," Pierre had often said.

Pierre was bound to be furious as well as anxious, and Monnet decided this was not a good time for a social call. He said good-bye to Nicole, and before she went into the house she looked at him with a smile.

"You must not worry, Doctor," she said. "I will not mention the watch. That is our secret."

CHAPTER 6

Reflecting on his duplicitous role, René Monnet could not feel guilty about it. He clearly remembered the event that ultimately had led him to Henry more than twenty years before. It was in the days when one of the hapless Valois kings, the weakling Charles IX, ruled France and his formidable mother, Catherine de' Medici, ruled him. She had maneuvered her son into ordering the assassination of Gaspard de Coligny, a brilliant and popular commander of the Protestant forces.

A band of hired assassins broke into Coligny's lodgings, ran him through and tossed the body out of the window to the street. The corpse was dismembered, the head sent to the royal palace, the hands and genitals severed and offered for sale. Amid rumors of a Protestant conspiracy against the throne, the assassination unleashed a rampage against all Protestants. Soldiers spread through Paris shouting, "Kill! Kill! The king commands it!"

Corpses soon littered the streets and children played among them. Embryos were torn from the bodies of their dead mothers and smashed. It was August 24, 1572: Saint Bartholomew's Day.

Monnet had not yet finished his medical studies, but he ventured into the streets to see if he could help the wounded and dying. He was so appalled by the carnage that he recklessly ignored whether he was ministering to Protestants or to Catholics (who, to distinguish themselves from the heretics, wore white crosses and armbands). That night Paris was eerily silent. The next day brought a fatal misunderstanding. A hawthorn started to bloom out of season in the Cemetery of the Innocents. This was considered a miracle. Church bells rang out to proclaim the event, but the mob mistook it for a signal to continue the hunting of heretics. The Protestants fought back but they could not prevail against the much more numerous Catholics. When it was finally over, thousands had died. King Charles received congratulations from the Parliament of Paris; in Rome, Pope Gregory XIII celebrated a thanksgiving Mass and had a coin struck to commemorate the Church's great victory.

Looking back on these terrible scenes, Monnet often wondered what a stranger—from far away—from Turkey, from China, from another world—would make of them. Monnet knew that the conflict was not only religious. There were issues of power and property: nobles and the crown envious of the riches amassed by the Church, French resentment at having to take orders from those Italians at the Vatican, rivalries between great aristocratic families. Monnet asked himself whether religion was using politics as a weapon or politics using religion as a pretext. And yet the overwhelming fact remained: the combatants on both sides were Christians who believed in the same deity and worshiped the same Jesus. If called on to explain this, thought Monnet, he would find it extremely difficult. Perhaps he might say: "Think of us as a tribe. Men are especially bitter when they believe that their God is being betrayed by their own. There is apt to be greater anger against them than against people who are outside the tribe, or faith, entirely."

But Monnet was not sure that this answer would be adequate to illuminate what separated Catholics from Protestants and how their differences justified thousands upon thousands of people slaughtering one another.

He kept wondering what drives people into lethal religious frenzy. Was it at bottom the fear of mortality and the desire to overcome it? Could it be that we inflict death on one another to escape death? If that paradox was true, would the killing ever end? Or was France doomed to a permanent Saint Bartholomew's Day?

Gradually Monnet became convinced that there was one man who could free France from this endless cycle of death. In the years following the massacre, Henry of Navarre emerged as the leader of the Protestants. He was the kind of man who inspires legends. As a boy he had a rugged upbringing, received neither toys nor flattery, climbed rocks in his bare feet and ate peasant fare. He had a keen intelligence, absorbing Latin and Greek with ease, and a daring nature, choosing as his motto when he was a mere child: "To conquer or to die." Stories about him circulated almost as a form of entertainment. He developed into a brilliant general but hated killing and habitually forgave those who tried to kill him. Once he seized the pistols of a would-be assassin, but instead of shooting him, fired the pistols into the air, leaving the man to try again later. During one battle he climbed to a church steeple to survey the action and a cannonball flew between his legs; he lowered himself to the ground by a rope before the tower collapsed.

Aside from the stories of his martial prowess he was famed for his prowess as a lover. As a young man Henry had been maneuvered into a political marriage with Margaret of Valois, in a vain attempt to unite the Valois and Bourbon families. The couple actively disliked each other and lived apart. Henry kept a dazzling series of mistresses, often several at the same time, whom he juggled with great finesse. In pursuit of women he would take extraordinary chances, once crossing enemy lines disguised as a peasant to woo a beauty (who, as it turned out, was not impressed).

Monnet relished the tales of Henry's gallantry, both on the battlefield and in the bedchamber, but what he admired most of all were the reports of Henry's hatred of bigotry, his determination that the fratricidal wars must end. As he would say on one occasion: "Perhaps the difference between the two religions is not so great. Perhaps it is caused mostly by the animosity of the men who preach them."

By 1580 Monnet had established himself as a physician in Paris. But as he kept hearing about Henry's exploits, the notion formed in Monnet's mind that he wanted to join this man. Apart from his admiration of what Henry was trying to accomplish, Monnet had to admit to himself that he had another motive. The practice of medicine in Paris—prescribing for corpulent citizens and their vaporous ladies—was getting to feel rather tame. He was thoroughly familiar with the array of medications from the vegetable, animal and mineral kingdoms, including ground pearls, mummy powder, passion flower and snakeskin, but he was disappointed by their limited healing powers. He was amused by antimony, a purgative in wide demand, because it passed through the body and could be used again and again, which appealed to frugal bourgeois.

He had no wife or family to hold him in Paris. He loved women and there had been many since the gardener's daughter in the seminary, but he prized his independence and had never met anyone for whom he was willing to give it up. The idea of settling down with one partner in an endlessly repetitive cycle of domestic routine did not appeal to him.

One day Monnet quietly rode out of Paris. At the time Henry was preparing for action in the southwest. At Coutras, not far from Bordeaux, on October 20, 1587, Henry faced a Catholic army twice the size of his own. The Catholic troops were arrayed in shining armor with brilliant banners overhead, while Henry's soldiers were encased in rusty metal and stained leather. When an aide remarked on the contrast Henry said, "So be it. The enemy will make better targets."

As always, Henry was far out in front of his forces, white plume waving from his helmet.

Monnet arrived the day following the king's overwhelming victory, and, after being searched by guards for concealed weapons and having established bona fides as a physician, he was admitted to the king's tent. He found Henry behind a cluttered campaign desk piled high with maps and reports. He was a stocky man in a torn, rumpled vest, with a face that was both exhausted and exhilarated. His long, thin nose seemed to disappear into his moustache, which, like his beard, had begun to show flecks of gray. Monnet explained that he was a doctor, that he believed in Henry's cause and that he wanted to offer his services. Henry smiled broadly.

"Well, we could certainly use you," he said. "Our own medicos leave much to be desired. Take a look at this."

He came out from behind his desk and pointed to his thigh, which was wrapped in a bulky, bloodstained bandage. Underneath the bandage Monnet found a deep ugly cut, which had been clumsily sewn up.

"I think I can do better," said Monnet. In a matter of minutes he had reopened the wound, cleaned it and patched it up expertly.

Henry called for brandy and began to question Monnet about what was going on in Paris, the mood of the people, rumors from the court, the doings of the League. After nearly an hour of this Henry said, "An idea has just occurred to me, Doctor. You certainly would be very valuable to me as a physician—and I thank you for the way you have just handled this wound of mine. But I think you could be even more valuable in another way. The most important ammunition in war is information. You could serve me best by going back to Paris, resuming your practice and reporting to me what you see and hear. As a physician you are obviously in and out of all sorts of houses in the city. Whatever you can glean about my enemies—the money they raise, the troops they recruit, the plans they hatch—would be most useful."

Monnet had not thought of himself as a potential spy, but the idea appealed to him. It suggested a double life, and that certainly would not be boring. If he felt any scruples, he suppressed them quickly. In these terrible times he had long since decided that all means were permitted if the end was peace. He accepted Henry's suggestion and was pleased by his almost brotherly clap on his shoulder. Thereafter he regularly reported whatever news he could gather to one or another of the king's intermediaries.

• • •

When Monnet returned to the rue des Juifs a few days after the king's entry into Paris, the usual serenity was gone. The faces of the servants, always an indicator of the mood of a house, were glum and apprehensive. The household was in disarray, piles of books and papers stacked on tables, packing boxes everywhere. Pierre was striding up and down and talking loudly, in angry bursts.

"Ah, Doctor," he said when he noticed Monnet's arrival. "What do you prescribe in this situation? I am afraid your medicines will not help."

He held out a document on which Monnet recognized the royal seal. He knew what it was: the order for Pierre Acarie to leave Paris.

Pierre had been certain that Henry would deal harshly with all who had supported the League. He had loudly declared himself ready for martyrdom. But Henry had no intention of creating martyrs. The king had sent heralds around the city proclaiming that there was to be no retribution against his enemies and had leaflets printed with the same message. Still, he did not feel it safe to have the leaders of the League near him in Paris. Pierre, who had thought himself ready for a heroic death, was outraged by the prospect of mere exile.

"This is the house where I have lived all these years, where our children were born," he said to Barbe. "What is to become of me now? And what is to become of you?"

Turning to Monnet, he said, "I trust, Doctor, that you will take care of my wife when she succumbs to one of her weaknesses."

Monnet said that of course he would, but it occurred to him that at the moment, it was Pierre more than Barbe who needed taking care of.

Pierre was in a flurry of indecision about what to take and what to leave behind—clothes, books, documents. He also was undecided about where to go—he was allowed to choose his own place of exile. In the end he settled on the Charterhouse of the Carthusian Order at Bourgfontaine, a reasonably safe thirty leagues from Paris.

Andrée, who quietly supervised the packing with Barbe, whispered to her, "Monsieur is not taking this very well."

Barbe made no reply but she secretly agreed with Andrée. She had been watching her husband in amazement. Naturally she was dismayed that he would have to go into exile, but she also knew that far worse things could have happened to him if Henry had been vengeful. She wondered whether her husband was being as strong as she would have expected him to be. His complaints and lamentations—did they suggest a lack of courage? She guiltily suppressed such subversive thoughts and did her best to reassure him.

When the time came for his departure Nicole suddenly appeared. "I will pray for you, sir," she said gravely. "I will pray that our Lord will keep you safe."

"I am grateful," said Pierre, "but you must pray for my wife as well. Stay with her and help her."

One evening two weeks after Pierre had gone, there was a commotion outside. Barbe, Andrée and Nicole were at supper when, brushing a servant aside, a man wearing the black toque of a minor official strode into the room. From a leather pouch attached to his belt he drew a document.

"Madame," he said, "I have here a court order requiring me to seize your property and this house for nonpayment of certain obligations undertaken by your husband."

As the bailiff spoke, other men came in and started lifting pieces of furniture. Barbe looked on silently, stunned, and Andrée rose to put a protective arm about Barbe's shoulders.

Nicole also jumped to her feet, confronted the bailiff and shouted, "You cannot do this! God will punish you!"

The kind of threat that had impressed the archbishop was lost on this petty functionary. He shrugged his shoulders and started to remove the dishes from the supper table, including the plate from which Barbe had been eating.

If King Henry was forgiving, Pierre's creditors were not. Seeing the Sixteen collapse and Pierre in exile, they suddenly demanded repayment of the debts he had incurred and the pledges he had made on behalf of the League. Barbe, who had been told little by Pierre about his financial affairs, now found, to her horror, that the Acarie fortune was virtually gone.

The attorney looked about the house with dismay. Almost all the furniture had been removed, and on the wall he saw the ghostly outlines where paintings had hung. The curtainless windows seemed bare and harsh. Antoine Lenoir, long Pierre Acarie's lawyer, faced Barbe with an air that was more reproachful than sympathetic. He had often warned Monsieur Acarie, he said, that pledging so much property for the League was imprudent; but, alas, Monsieur had not listened. What to do now to avoid complete disaster? Of course money was needed. For one thing Monsieur Acarie had held the important position of counsel to the treasury of the Parliament of Paris. That position could be sold, although it would not fetch as much as it would have earlier. If he was not mistaken, continued Lenoir, one or two country estates were still unencumbered, and, although they had been devastated by the wars, careful nurturing might eventually make them profitable again. Perhaps Madame Acarie could borrow some funds. Otherwise Madame would have to throw herself on the mercy of the creditors. Barbe shook her head at those words. Lenoir ignored the gesture. There might of course be certain legal tactics, he said, to avoid or at least delay the forced sale of this house and other properties. Normally he would be glad to be of help, but he would have to insist on the usual fees and he was afraid that under the circumstances Madame Acarie could not take on such a burden.

To Andrée, who was at Barbe's side during this meeting, the conversation sounded familiar. She had been only a child when her father had run into financial difficulties, but for years after she left the convent and came to live with Barbe she had been aware of the old man's desperate and futile struggles to retrieve his properties. She was therefore accustomed to the idea that a comfortable life could suddenly fall apart, but she wondered how Barbe would take to this stunning reversal of fortune.

When the lawyer had finished, Barbe rose and said evenly, "I understand, Maître Lenoir. Thank you for your explanations. I will not trouble you further."

After Lenoir had left, Barbe said, "What an unpleasant and ungrateful man. But I do not need him. I will do what must be done on my own. First of all, I must find a place for us to live."

That proved to be easier than she had expected. Her cousin, Louise Bérulle, a well-to-do widow, lived in a large house not far from the rue des Juifs and she gladly offered it to Barbe as a temporary refuge. Barbe and Andrée prepared to move, aided by tearful servants for whom there would be no room in her cousin's house, even if she could still afford to pay them.

"What about Nicole?" asked Andrée. "Do you mean to take her along? I wonder whether your cousin would want to have yet another boarder. Besides, Nicole might be quite content to leave you after everything that has happened. She could easily find a place with some other family or in a religious establishment."

But when Barbe suggested this, Nicole pleaded, "Please, Madame, do not send me away. Monsieur Acarie asked me to stay with you and that is what I want. I will be glad to do anything to make myself useful."

Barbe was astonished. Like Andrée, she had suspected that Nicole had attached herself to the Acaries because they were important in Paris. Barbe said, "You see what is happening to our family. Our wealth is gone, our reputation counts for nothing. My husband is in disgrace. Do you really want to tie yourself to me?"

"With all my heart."

Barbe could not help being affected by Nicole's profession of loyalty. She felt this especially because there was no help and little sympathy to be had from friends or relatives other than her cousin. Her mother was now dead and her own father, like most Leaguers, was in the same situation as Pierre. In the end she agreed to take Nicole along.

The respected and prosperous lady suddenly was a supplicant.

Barbe began with extraordinary tenacity to try to restore the Acarie fortune and to retrieve the mansion on the rue des Juifs. She
wrote petitions, abjectly pleaded with creditors, waited for hours
in the antechambers of magistrates. Pierre wrote regularly, offering some advice, but mostly complaining about the solitude of his
exile. Barbe went to see him several times, but, returning from one
visit, she suffered a bad fall from her horse. One of her legs was seriously injured and she could not make the trip again.

Andrée was away much of the time, as her father had died and
her mother needed her help. In Andrée's absence, Nicole seemed
to be always at Barbe's side. She sat up with her till late at night
while Barbe wrote her petitions, accompanied her on her endless
rounds calling on officials who as often as not refused to see her.
Barbe and Nicole became a familiar sight, kneeling side by side in
church or walking to the hospital together, where both still tended
to the sick. Often, in the evenings, they would talk. Whenever
Barbe asked her about her family or her childhood, Nicole would
say, "Forgive me, Madame, but it was an unhappy time for me. I
would rather not talk about it."

Nicole would then change the subject and ask her about some
spiritual matter. And Barbe always welcomed such questions. Observing their growing closeness, Dr. Monnet wondered whether
Nicole was gradually replacing Andrée in Barbe Acarie's life. He
did not want to put it that way to Barbe, but he did ask her how
she really felt about Nicole.

"I am not sure," said Barbe.

She admitted that her emotions were in conflict. She had been
suspicious of Nicole from the first. She distrusted her claims of
special powers and was put off by the arrogance with which she
described her "divine mission." But in that very arrogance Barbe
also sensed a strength and fervor that appealed to her. Besides, she
was affected by Nicole's obvious devotion to her, a devotion that
had turned Nicole into a disciple and almost a daughter.

On his regular visits, René Monnet was invariably amazed by
the energy and determination with which Barbe tried to salvage
what she could of the wreckage of the Acarie fortune. At the same

time he often found her deep in conversation with her cousin's son, Pierre Bérulle. He was an extremely earnest and intense young man who had just been ordained. Sometimes other clerics were present, paying close attention to Barbe's words on such matters as the rules governing religious establishments or the proper use of certain prayers. How, Monnet asked himself, had Barbe Acarie, without any scholarly training, acquired such authority? Monnet recalled the occasion when Pierre Acarie had directed his wife to read a whole collection of religious volumes. But Monnet guessed that Barbe did not speak merely about what she had read, but what shrewd observation and instinct had suggested to her about the spiritual life. As for her trances, they kept recurring. He found this remarkable in a woman now so active in worldly affairs, and told her so.

She smiled indulgently. "You seem to think, Doctor, that there is a connection between my inner and my outer life, as between two vessels linked to one another. You assume that if one is fuller, the other must be emptier. I believe you are thinking of some physical law. But this does not apply to the soul. I know that my trances are a sign of God's favor, and He will give me all the strength I need to do my work in the world."

One day during a stay in Soissons, where she had gone to visit an ailing family friend, she went to church where a priest, substituting for the regular pastor, was celebrating Mass. Something about him—she could not say exactly what—drew her attention. After the service, she approached him on the church steps and asked him some questions about his training and his previous parish. The man's answers were halting and confused. At that moment she experienced a kind of flash in her brain, resembling the onset of dizziness or the first pulse of anger. With this came absolute certainty. Abruptly, she said, "I do not believe that you are a priest at all. You are playing a role."

A small crowd had gathered and he loudly protested his innocence, but within hours he fled Soissons, leaving behind a note confessing that he had never been ordained.

News of the incident spread, and with that began a new kind of fame for Barbe Acarie. In addition to charity and wisdom, she was now renowned for her ability to read the secrets of a soul.

Nicole's own fame in Paris lingered, but many people were disappointed that she was much less active in preaching and healing. Soon after Barbe's feat at Soissons, Father de Souzy spoke to Nicole.

"As your spiritual director I must ask you whether you have given up your mission. I realize that the Holy League is no longer here to support you, but the faithful still long for your words and wonders."

"My mission lately has been to help Madame Acarie," said Nicole. "But I know that other work still remains to be done. I will do what I am called to do."

One morning during the fourth year of Pierre's exile, in 1598, the tread and clatter of guards was heard outside Louise Bérulle's house. The king walked in without ceremony, more carefully dressed than usual in a bottle green doublet and the soft leather boots he favored—which most gentlemen in Paris were copying. He was followed by several attendants and Father Coton. The household hastily assembled—Madame Bérulle, her son Pierre, Barbe, Nicole and Andrée, who had returned from visiting her mother. The servants were in the background.

Barbe lifted herself from her armchair, struggling to her feet with the help of a cane. Since the time she was thrown from her horse, she had suffered two more falls. She attempted a curtsy but Henry quickly waved her back into the chair.

"I have heard about your unfortunate accidents, Madame," he said, "and I wanted to come myself to ask about your well-being."

In truth, Henry was here for political reasons. In April 1598, at Nantes, he had issued an edict allowing freedom of worship to Protestants in most of his kingdom but not in Paris. Catholic worship was restored in places where Protestants had abolished it. An amnesty was declared for all acts of violence committed in the course of war.

"The memory of everything which occurred on one side or the other . . . will remain extinguished," the document proclaimed. "We forbid all our subjects . . . to renew the memory thereof, attack, resent, injure or provoke each other with reproaches for what is past . . . but to contain themselves and live peaceably together as brothers, friends and fellow citizens. . . ."

It was like Henry to believe that he could suppress memory by royal fiat, could impose brotherhood by decree. But the pope and most of the French clergy were outraged. By wooing prominent Catholics like Barbe Acarie, the king hoped to bolster his cause.

"I am well enough, Your Majesty, and all the better for your visit," replied Barbe. "But I would be even better if I could be finally reunited with my husband."

"I know. You have sent me any number of petitions—and I must say, Madame, that you are a very persuasive advocate. And now—" The king paused, with a flare for the dramatic and relishing the moment of suspense.

"And now?" Barbe asked.

"And now I have decided to end his exile. Moreover, I believe he should return to his own house. I will find a way of restoring it to you."

Although his treasury was dangerously depleted, he believed that such gestures of reconciliation were worth the expense. As he said to the Parliament on one occasion, "I restored houses to some who had been exiled, their faith to others who had lost it."

Barbe burst out with words of gratitude but he cut her off.

"Madame," he said as he prepared to leave, "my throne is not the most comfortable of seats and my crown is sometimes very heavy. I only ask for your prayers."

As he walked toward the door everyone bowed. Before she too made her obeisance, Nicole took a step forward. The king paused in front of her, a puzzled look on his face. Father Coton quietly said a few words to him. "Ah yes," said the king. "I am told that you have worked many wonders. Well, I am trying to work a few myself—I am trying to bring peace to France. I hope you too will pray for me."

But he kept looking at her. "I seem to remember seeing you before. Where could it have been?"

"Sire, I think perhaps it was at Saint-Denis after the Mass when you joined the True Church."

The king clapped his hands. "Precisely. You were the girl who broke from the crowd and shouted that I was the savior of France. I believe you are a good prophet. Thank you."

With that he strode out.

Barbe watched the exchange in amazement. Hearing about the encounter at Saint-Denis and observing the king's warm response to Nicole, Barbe felt unsettled, as if something she should have known had been kept from her.

"I thought I had come to know her," she said later to Andrée. "But she keeps surprising me."

Andrée said, "I do not think we know her at all."

CHAPTER 7

The chapel was small but—René Monnet could find no other word for it—elegant. The altar cloth was embroidered in shining gold thread, the crucifix skillfully carved and subtly painted. Not many houses in Paris had a private chapel where Mass could be said, but the archbishop had permitted this as a special favor to Barbe Acarie in view of her spiritual reputation and her injured leg.

On this day Pierre Coton had come to say Mass for the Acarie household, now resettled in the mansion on the rue des Juifs, less than a year after Pierre's return from exile. René Monnet, by now a virtual member of the family, surveyed the group. There was Barbe, comfortable and serene, although he knew that she found it difficult to kneel. There was Pierre, markedly older-looking than before he went away, with a prematurely white beard. Andrée's plain, angular face looked as impassive as ever and Nicole was still girlish, still slightly disheveled and following the Mass with fierce intensity.

When it was over Barbe moved toward the door and looked into the adjoining room, where several men sat waiting.

"Who is it today?" she asked Andrée.

"There is Father Duval with a colleague from the Sorbonne. I

believe they want to tell you about a treatise on Saint Teresa of
Ávila and how she differed in her devotions from Saint Francis of
Assisi. There is Pierre Bérulle, who is looking for advice about a
young Benedictine nun. She wants to leave her order and he is trying to convince her to stay."

Barbe nodded.

"Finally," continued Andrée, "there is a young seminarian named
Vincent de Paul who is very concerned about our wretched medical care for the poor."

"If we are going to talk about medical care, perhaps Dr. Monnet will join us."

Barbe was about to walk into the other room when she turned
to her husband. "Will you join us too?" she said.

"I don't think your visitors really want me. They are here to talk
to you."

Pierre was still not accustomed to his new situation. Although
the king had finally allowed him and other Leaguers to return
home, there was no way of returning to the old life.

Pierre's consuming work for the League was gone. There was
nothing to replace it. He was much given to reminiscing about the
old, exciting days of combat and intrigue, and he found that
Nicole was always ready to listen to his stories. Barbe was too busy
for this. She had not only grown accustomed to running all family
affairs, but she had also become a revered figure in Paris. The
house on the rue des Juifs seemed to be overrun by priests, semi-
narians, monks. A kind of spiritual salon had formed around
Barbe. At first Pierre tried to join in but his reception was chilly.
Where once she had been excluded from his League business, he
now found himself excluded from her religious business.

From the door Pierre surveyed the waiting group, nodded
briefly and turned to leave. He paused a moment for a word with
Monnet.

"Believe me, Doctor, it is not easy to be married to a saint."

Barbe took a chair among her visitors, who clustered around
her as if receiving an audience. She presided over the meeting with
authority. She discussed the two saints with Duval and his col-

league and promised to read their paper carefully. She listened to Pierre Bérulle and agreed to interview the nun he was concerned about but remarked that it sounded like a difficult case. She drew out Vincent de Paul, who told a rambling story of how he had once been captured by Barbary pirates. With a flicker of impatience, she asked what this had to do with his present concerns, and he explained that his sufferings had given him a burning sense of compassion for all unfortunate people, especially the sick. He offered his ideas about improving conditions in the hospitals, with Barbe asking pointed questions and inviting Monnet to comment. Several times, she remarked that she was not nearly as wise as the learned gentlemen in attendance, but she nevertheless spoke with the utmost self-confidence. Throughout the discussion Nicole Tavernier sat behind Barbe, following every word.

The meeting was about to break up when Father Coton spoke. He said that he had some unfortunate news. A venerated relic had been stolen from the Church of Saint Geneviève the day before. It was part of the saint's arm bone and was contained in a precious gold reliquary. Searches all over the city failed to find the missing treasure. Any help in retrieving the holy object would be blessed. Amid murmurs of concern and outrage, Nicole rose.

"I will gladly do whatever I can to find what is missing," she said.

Barbe looked at her with some asperity. "I am sure that we are all ready to do just that."

"Nevertheless, I would like to go to the church, if you have no objections. Perhaps God will show me where to look."

Once again Barbe was offended by Nicole's presumption. Why, she thought, would God especially favor and guide Nicole Tavernier in the search?

But before she or anyone else could object, Nicole was gone. She made her way to the church, where disconsolate parishioners were keeping a vigil. She knelt before the altar, prayed and meditated for a long time. Finally she announced, "Go to the Cemetery of the Innocents, where you will find the relic buried in the ground beneath the oak tree near the entrance."

The curate of the church, surrounded by a squadron of other

priests and monks, hastened to the place Nicole had designated. After some minutes of digging, the gleaming reliquary was found. Shouts of joy and thanksgiving went up. Apparently the thieves had buried the object here intending to retrieve it later and sell it, presumably in some foreign country.

Nicole's fame was now greater than ever. Soon after the incident a servant announced a visitor at the Acarie mansion.

"Henriette de Balsac d'Entragues," said Barbe, repeating the name questioningly. It sounded like an important name but she could not place it. The caller had taken off the mask that many Parisian ladies wore outdoors, not so much to hide their identity as to protect their complexion. Her face was darkly beautiful under a mass of brunette curls. After thanking Barbe for receiving her, she looked about the room as if expecting to see someone else. "I have come to seek advice, Madame," she said.

"I will be very glad to offer you whatever advice I can. Is it about some spiritual matter?"

"No. It involves a question about the future, about the nature and the time of a possible future event."

Barbe's attitude stiffened. "I'm afraid I cannot help you. I may occasionally have certain insights into the character and motives of people. But I do not foretell the future."

Henriette was embarrassed. "In truth, I was not looking for advice from you, Madame. I was hoping to see the woman who stays in your house and to whom you have given your patronage. I mean Nicole Tavernier."

Barbe was silent for a few moments, staring at her visitor. Then she said coldly, "I will have someone fetch Nicole. Good day."

Within a few moments Nicole appeared. Again Henriette said, "I have questions about the future."

Nicole looked at her sharply. "Is it about bearing a child?"

Henriette was startled. "So people are right when they say that you are clairvoyant."

Henriette d'Entragues was the king's latest mistress. He was so enamored of her that he had paid her father a considerable sum to have Henriette in his bed and even recklessly promised to marry her once his earlier marriage to Margaret of Valois was annulled. Henry's sole condition was that Henriette become pregnant within six months and bear him a son. Now she was anxious to know if this might happen.

Nicole took Henriette's hands into her own and closed her eyes. After some minutes she announced that Henriette would conceive in three months.

Gossip spread that the king's mistress had consulted Nicole Tavernier, which brought many more requests for her prophecies. Grain merchants wanted to know about the outlook for next year's harvest. Powerful lords wanted her advice about the outcome of political intrigues.

The servants at the rue des Juifs learned to ask visitors immediately whether they were there to see Madame Acarie or Nicole Tavernier. Barbe was increasingly irritated by the flow of strangers in her house, who seemed to crowd her own visitors. But whenever she was on the point of confronting Nicole about this, some kind gesture or deferential word by Nicole would stop her.

Barbe carried on her sessions with her spiritual salon. As she had promised, she went to see the young nun Pierre Bérulle was concerned with. She found Charlotte Lasserre confused and distraught, saying tearfully at one moment that she did not want to break her vows, angrily the next that she felt imprisoned by life in the convent.

"My advice to you is to give up on this young woman," she told Pierre Bérulle. "I do not believe that she ever had a true vocation to begin with."

"Respectfully I disagree with you, Madame," said Bérulle. "I will continue to try to save her for the religious life."

But within a week Charlotte Lasserre left not only the convent but the Church, married a Protestant minister and went to live with him in Geneva. Pierre Bérulle was deeply embarrassed and did penance for the soul of the apostate. The incident only strengthened his deference toward Barbe. Nine years her junior, he treated her as he might one of his professors at the Sorbonne. He began to visit her almost daily and she found that she enjoyed talking theology with him. Gradually his self-confidence increased, and they often argued. Amicably, they agreed that if either one of them went too far in these arguments, they would warn each other to stop.

Meanwhile, the scandalous episode of Charlotte Lasserre further confirmed Barbe's sagacity, and she was frequently called on as a diagnostician of souls. In the case of two other women who had become prominent for their visions and prophecies, Barbe bluntly told their priest, "I think they are inspired by self-love."

The pair quickly lost their following.

Then there was the instance of the nun who continually fell into ecstasies, so much so that her sisters often had to carry her back to her cell from church. She was regarded as a saint. Barbe was asked to examine her and concluded that the ecstasies were merely the result of illusions. Each time, before she rendered one of her judgments, Barbe experienced that inner flash, that almost dizzying moment of conviction. Was she right in exposing these creatures? She was certain that she must do it in the service of God.

Having often observed Barbe during her own ecstasies, René Monnet was baffled by how she could tell that someone else's were mere self-deceptions.

"You were once so uncertain of your own trances," he said. "You wondered whether they were real and where they came from. Yet when you see others having the same sort of experience, you are quick to judge them. What makes you so sure?"

With a slight, superior smile, she replied, "In all humility I believe God has given me this insight. I simply *know.*"

It struck Monnet that Nicole had said the same in explaining her visions and predictions.

He could not help wondering whether sooner or later Nicole herself would come under Barbe's judgment.

•   •   •

Father Pacifique de Souzy seemed agitated when he arrived at the Acarie mansion and asked to see Nicole. As he waited for her to be fetched—pacing nervously—Barbe appeared.

"What brings you to us today, Father?" she asked.

"I am looking for Nicole," he replied.

He had expected Nicole and two companions at Mass that morning at his church, he explained, and had prepared three Hosts for communion. When it came time for the Eucharist, Nicole was nowhere to be seen and there were only two Hosts on the plate. What could have happened?

"I have no idea," said Barbe.

Nicole came in, pale but radiant. "I am sorry, Father," she said. "I was feeling poorly this morning and I was slow getting ready to come to church. Suddenly I saw a blinding light in front of me. It was an angel. Before I knew what was happening, a Host had been placed on my tongue and the light faded and the angel was gone."

"Are you saying that an angel brought you communion?" asked Father de Souzy, stammering in excitement, his pointed beard quivering.

"Yes, Father, that is what happened."

"How very extraordinary," said Barbe. "Are you sure that you did not merely imagine this?"

"I am sure, Madame, it was very real."

"And what did the angel look like?"

"My eyes were dazed by the light, but I believe that the angel looked very much like you."

Barbe gave a sharp laugh. "Scripture tells us that angels can take many human forms, but I doubt that an angel would have chosen to appear in my humble image."

"Why not, Madame?" said Father de Souzy. "I believe it would have been very appropriate."

Barbe thanked him for the compliment and asked no further questions, but she was plainly doubtful. She believed that Nicole had imagined the incident or invented it. As for the Hosts, perhaps the priest had simply made a mistake and put only two on the plate to begin with.

Father de Souzy had no such doubts, and within hours he told any number of people about Nicole's miraculous communion.

Nicole and Barbe were now the most famous women in Paris. Both were adored and admired. To René Monnet it began to look like a contest. One day he would hear Barbe propose a plan for reforming a convent. Within a day or two Nicole would create a stir performing some seemingly miraculous act. One day Barbe would publicly judge the validity of a mystic, and soon afterward Nicole would excite the city with some astounding prediction. Some Parisians regarded them as competing sibyls.

Once when Barbe was asked to attend Mass at the Capuchin church at Meudon, not far from Paris, Nicole accompanied her. During Mass, as happened so often, Barbe became completely absorbed in her devotions. Emerging from that state she realized that Nicole had disappeared. When she returned an hour later, Barbe asked her where she had been. Nicole replied that she had been at Tours.

"But Tours is five days' journey away," said Barbe. "You could not possibly have gone there and come back in one hour."

"I was transported there by an angel."

"Another angel!" exclaimed Barbe.

"Yes, Madame. I spoke to a very high personage and warned him about a dangerous plot against our Holy Church."

"What personage? What plot?" asked Barbe.

"I'm sorry, but I have been asked not to tell."

Barbe did not press Nicole any further, because she simply did not believe her story.

"I am convinced she invented this tale to make herself important," Barbe said to Andrée. "And even if she was really transported to Tours, it may not have been the work of an angel. I am beginning to believe that very possibly it was the work of the Devil."

Although Andrée had never trusted Nicole, this idea shocked her. The girl, after all, had won the approval of the archbishop, of Father Coton, of any number of other priests who considered her divinely inspired. Paris worshiped her. Even Barbe, with her reputation as a judge in these matters, would find it difficult to convince anyone that Nicole was a fake, let alone in the hands of the Devil.

"They won't believe you," said Andrée. "Unless you have some proof."

Nicole recognized the change in Barbe only gradually. One evening when she was about to join her for prayer as usual, Barbe said she preferred to make her devotions alone. Increasingly she attended church with Andrée, who had resumed her old place as Barbe's closest companion. Several times Barbe declined to walk with Nicole in the garden. She stopped talking when Nicole entered a room and was unusually silent at meals. Once Barbe walked into her husband's study and found Nicole seated on a low stool, looking up at Pierre raptly as he was telling her one of his stories from his time of exile.

Barbe said sharply, "I would like to be alone with my husband." Startled, Nicole rose and left the room.

"You seem to spend a great deal of time with her," said Barbe.

"Well, I like her. She has time for me and she's a good listener."

"I, for one, no longer trust her," said Barbe.

The next time Monnet was at the Acarie mansion, Nicole took him aside.

"Doctor," she said. "Madame suddenly treats me so coldly and distantly. I believe she suspects me of some serious fault. Everyone in the household looks at me strangely. Can you tell me what is happening?"

Monnet thought he knew. Barbe Acarie was increasingly suspicious of Nicole's predictions and wonders. He himself had always been skeptical about them. But he did not want to tell Nicole so because he had grown fond of her. He wondered what drew him to her. There was nothing of carnal seduction about Nicole, but he thought there was something like spiritual seduction. He felt its pull strongly. In some part of his mind he wanted to believe in her.

"Madame Acarie has always been good to you," he said. "But

perhaps it might be best if, for a while, you did not work any more wonders."

"I do not work wonders. God does," Nicole said. But then her mood changed and she looked contrite.

"I am sorry, Doctor. I know you mean well. I only do what I must do."

But Monnet did not hear the usual note of confidence in Nicole's voice.

On the next morning, as Barbe prepared to go out, she handed Nicole a letter. It was addressed to Father de Souzy.

"This is an important message for the good father," Barbe told Nicole. "It will be fetched by one of his servants while I am out of the house. Guard it carefully and remember that it is for Father de Souzy's eyes only."

After Barbe was gone, Nicole paced anxiously. Could this have something to do with the change in Barbe's attitude? Was the message about Nicole herself? As she weighed the letter in her hands, she realized that it was not sealed. Prompted by her fears, she decided to disobey Barbe's instructions and read it. Just then, a noise from the garden outside startled her. Suspecting that Barbe might have forgotten something, Nicole hurriedly scanned the note. It proved to be some innocuous suggestion to de Souzy, not even mentioning Nicole's name. Greatly relieved, she refolded the letter and put it on a table. The noise, as it turned out, was caused not by Barbe returning but by a servant doing a chore in the garden. Almost an hour passed and no one came for the letter.

"I see the messenger has not yet arrived," said Barbe when she returned. "Did you read it while I was gone?"

"Oh no!" said Nicole. "You told me it was for Father de Souzy's eyes only."

When Barbe was alone she unfolded the note, examining it carefully. Then she looked at the floor. There she found a sprinkling of tiny bits of paper, each no larger than the head of a pin and thus scarcely visible. She had placed these inside the letter, knowing that they would spill out if it was opened. Distracted by the noise, Nicole had not noticed the minute bits of paper as they drifted to the floor.

A few hours later, Barbe welcomed three visitors whom she had asked to see her on an urgent matter. They were Fathers Coton, de Souzy and Bérulle. They were joined by her husband, who, seeing the three priests, had wondered what was happening.

"I thank you, Fathers, for coming to me so promptly," she said after they settled into their chairs. "I would not have troubled you, but there is something serious that I feel I must tell you. It concerns Nicole Tavernier."

She went on to describe Nicole's disappearance from church and her claim that she had been transported to Tours by an angel.

"Father de Souzy will recall that some time ago she claimed to have had another experience involving an angel. I do not believe that either of these things happened or, if they did happen, I doubt that it was thanks to angelic intervention. I suspect quite the opposite."

The priests looked at her in alarm.

"The story is certainly unusual," said Father de Souzy. "But we know that such cases of bilocation have happened before. There is the instance of Saint—"

Barbe cut him off. "Nicole Tavernier is no saint."

Pierre Bérulle cleared his throat, like a lecturer about to go into action. "I have studied the idea of a body being in two places at the same time. Saint Thomas and many other Church fathers deny that possibility. On the other hand, Scotus, Bellarmine and others believe that the phenomenon is possible in some form."

Barbe had expected Pierre Bérulle to support her. Clearly this was a moment when, according to their pact, a warning was necessary. She said, "Forgive me. You are very learned but I cannot quite trust your judgment in these matters. You surely remember how mistaken you were about Mademoiselle Lasserre."

Bérulle lapsed into silence.

Pierre Acarie had been listening with growing anger. Now he burst out, facing Barbe, "What has put this into your head? What possible evidence do you have that she is a faker or, God forbid, possessed by the Devil? I suspect you are angry at her because she spends so much time with me and I like her company."

Barbe was stung: Was there some truth in what Pierre was saying? She quickly rejected the notion—surely she was above such petty feelings.

"I am only concerned with her soul, with her lies and deceit."

"But you have made some terrible accusations against her," Pierre said.

"These are indeed serious charges," said Father Coton. "So I must also ask you, do you have any proof?"

"I want to show you something," said Barbe, pointing to the floor. "Look carefully."

"I see nothing at all," said Coton.

"Take a closer look," said Barbe.

Coton shook his head but de Souzy, bending down awkwardly in his homespun robe, said, "I believe I see some tiny bits of paper. Is that what you are talking about, Madame?"

"Precisely," replied Barbe.

"But what does it mean?" asked de Souzy.

"It means that Nicole Tavernier is a liar," said Barbe, and explained about the letter and the telltale bits of paper.

"You played a trick on her!" exclaimed Pierre, indignantly.

"You may call it that," said Barbe. "I regard it as a test. She failed it."

Father de Souzy was not yet ready to give up on his protégée. "You certainly proved that the girl lied to you in this matter, but that does not mean that she lied about everything else, let alone that she was acting for the Devil."

"Exactly," said Pierre, still angry. "Obviously she gave in to her curiosity and then was ashamed to tell the truth about it. That was wrong of her but, as Father de Souzy says, it does not prove anything worse."

Coton said, "I think we had better talk to her."

Nicole was sent for.

"I must ask you some questions," said Father Coton quietly. "Don't be afraid to answer them truthfully. Madame Acarie gave you a letter this morning addressed to Father de Souzy. Did you open and read that letter?"

"No!" replied Nicole.

Coton sighed. Still gentle, but with a hard undertone, he said, "Nicole, we can understand that you may have been overcome by curiosity about what was in the letter and that you then were embarrassed to admit opening it. This may seem like a small thing to you, a small lie. But small lies can point to bigger faults. You are not in the confessional. But we are priests and we are concerned for your soul. We have proof that you lied about the letter."

Nicole was shocked by the mention of proof. She looked sharply at Father Coton and then by turns at the others in the room, who avoided her eyes. She plainly wanted to ask, "What proof?" but she did not dare.

First, there had been all the signs that Barbe had turned against her. Now came the accusation by a priest who had been entirely benevolent toward her. Nicole's defiance began to fade. Lowering her head she confessed, "Yes, Father, I did lie. It is as you said—I gave in to curiosity. I thought the letter might be about me. I should not have opened the letter and I should not have lied about it. I am heartily sorry and I ask you to forgive me," she said, turning to Barbe.

"It is not up to me to forgive you," said Barbe. "What you have done proves that you are full of deceit."

"If you cannot forgive her, I certainly can," Pierre Acarie interjected. "It is the first and only fault we have found with Nicole and that hardly proves that she is full of deceit."

Instinctively de Souzy and Bérulle looked at Father Coton.

At length he said, "I agree that this one fault is not enough to prove Nicole deceitful in all things. But, as I have said, even a small crack may indicate much larger flaws. We in this room cannot take the responsibility to judge her. She is no longer the obscure girl from the provinces we knew when she first came to Paris. The city has celebrated her, not to say worshiped her. Ordinary people as well as learned clerics and princes have looked to her for miracles and visions. If there is now doubt about her honesty, it is our duty to see to it that she is further examined. We must consult the archbishop."

"That will take time," said Father de Souzy, familiar with the pace at which business was done in the archbishop's diocese.

"In the meantime," de Souzy continued, "it might be best if Nicole did not remain in this house—considering how you now feel about her, Madame."

All this was said as if Nicole was not in the room. She stood silent, stricken; now she stirred and looked at the three priests one after another. "Fathers, you have agreed in the past that my powers came from God. Can this one sin, which I have now confessed, have changed your minds? But I am content to await the archbishop's judgment."

"So are we all," said Coton. "But I agree with Father de Souzy that it would be better if we tried to find another place for you. Perhaps a convent would take you in temporarily."

"In that case, I have a suggestion," said Barbe. "She could go to the Franciscan convent at Longchamp."

That was the convent where Barbe had spent some years as "a little boarder" and where she had met Andrée Levoix. She retained many connections there, and if Nicole was at Longchamp, her doings could easily be reported to Barbe.

"Madame," Nicole said. "I am sad to be leaving this house and sad that I have lost your trust. I pray that with God's help I will win it back."

Without a word, Barbe turned away.

The news that Nicole was in disgrace quickly spread throughout the household. Within hours she had packed her few belongings into a small bag. When she was about to leave, René Monnet arrived. He had ostensibly come to call on Barbe, but he really wanted to see Nicole. He had been concerned about her ever since she had told him of Barbe's growing coolness.

He was met by a very disturbed Pierre. "I do not know what has gotten into my wife's head," he said. "She suddenly accuses Nicole of being a liar, a fraud and worse."

As he finished explaining what had happened, Nicole appeared, ready to go. "Monsieur," she said to Pierre. "Thank you for your generosity. You will always be in my prayers."

"And I will remember you in mine," said Pierre.

René accompanied Nicole to the door. She took his arm and said, "What is to become of me, Doctor?"

This girl who had wandered across embattled France alone, had impressed priests and threatened an archbishop, had rich merchants kneel to her and the dying confess to her—this girl had never shown any fear. Yet now he realized that she was afraid.

"Nicole, I would like to help you," he said. "And there are others who feel the same way. But we do not know where to begin. You have told us nothing about yourself. You have said nothing about your early life, your family. That makes it difficult for people to trust you."

"I have no family," she said.

"But how did you come to take up what you call your mission?"

"I already told you. God led me to it."

Monnet tried to question her further, but Nicole pleaded with a mixture of fear and anger. "Please do not press me anymore. I will not say anything else. There is nothing else to say."

With that she joined Father de Souzy, who was waiting to take her to the convent.

CHAPTER 8

"They say she is a liar and a fraud."

"What, our Nicole? I don't believe it."

"Well, the good Acarie says she is a faker or worse."

"The good Acarie knows about such things."

"But what about the archbishop and all the other priests? They have been saying for years that Nicole is blessed."

"The king had good words for her too. The d'Entragues woman even brought her to the court."

"They could all be mistaken."

"No, I think it is all a plot to hurt the king."

"I am sure she is good. My little niece was sick a while ago and no doctor could help her. Nicole saved the girl."

"That could have been witchcraft. Some say she is really possessed by the Devil."

"God help us!"

Everywhere René Monnet went, people were talking about what had happened to Nicole Tavernier. He was amazed how quickly the rumors had spread, but hardly surprised by the way the event had been distorted. Some said that Barbe Acarie had struck Nicole, others that Nicole had struck Barbe. People gathered in front of the Acarie mansion demanding to know what had happened to Nicole, but they were dispersed by the servants. One man proclaimed with absolute certainty that Nicole had been put in jail. Partisans formed for and against her. A crowd in front of the archbishop's palace proclaimed that she was innocent, only to be shouted down by another crowd asserting the opposite. On one side it was said that she had been put up to her tricks by the Protestants, who wanted to embarrass the Church. On the other side it was said that Nicole was being slandered by ultra-Catholics, who still wanted to embarrass the king. From several pulpits, priests declared that Nicole Tavernier was in league with the Devil and should burn.

As always, Monnet was appalled by the way in which the Devil haunted the lives of the people. The Devil lurked in every corner and sat in every mind. He was thought to be behind every misfortune. If milk turned sour, if a two-headed calf was born, if a husband became impotent, if a precious jewel was lost, if the plague struck, if a crop was spoiled—all was blamed on the Devil and his many servants. Even some of Monnet's fellow physicians believed that, in cases of demonic possession, every body part had its own devil—Leviathan resided in the center of the forehead, Beherit in the stomach, Eazaz under the heart, Nephthali in the right arm and so on. The Devil assumed many guises—a man in black, a black cat, a dog, a horse rider blowing a horn, a shepherd. He was described as a hideous triple-headed monster devouring sinners with each of its three mouths. But the Devil was not always seen as repellent. He might assume a benign and handsome shape, even performing good works to ensnare the innocent. He was believed to be supported by a vast underground army of witches, mostly female, who had engaged themselves to his service.

When Monnet complained to Father Coton about the ubiquity of Satan, the priest said, "My friend, the Devil is part of the divine scheme. You might say that God needs the Devil. Surely you learned that in the seminary."

He also learned, thought Monnet, that the Devil and his minions needed God's consent to act, and he never understood how a loving deity was so divided against Himself. He knew the theological explanations for this, but they never convinced him. He was not going to argue the point with Father Coton, however. What concerned him at the moment was how Nicole would fare. Would the Church really find her diabolically inspired?

"I'm afraid that is entirely possible," Coton replied.

The prospect filled Monnet with anxiety. They talked further about what might happen to Nicole and at length Monnet pulled out his watch. "I must leave you now," he said. "I have been summoned by the king."

Coton was not surprised. He had guessed long ago that his friend was serving Henry. "What a coincidence," he said with a smile. "I have been summoned too."

Henry had started out the day in excellent spirits. The previous afternoon he had attended a play at the Hôtel de Bourgogne, a political farce lampooning lawyers and judges, tax collectors and royal officials. An overzealous police "adviser," or informant, found the play outrageous, an insult to the king. At the end of the performance, the actors were arrested. But Henry instantly pardoned them because he had found the piece hilarious. He was still chuckling about it the next morning, but his good mood did not last. He was disturbed by a report on the affair involving Nicole Tavernier— which apparently had Paris in an uproar. While he was still trying to sort out the facts Henriette appeared. She was in a stormy mood. Henriette was clever, witty, ruthlessly ambitious and she had alternating methods of getting what she wanted—feline seductiveness or violent anger. This time, the king realized, she was employing the second method. Ever since Nicole had accurately predicted her pregnancy, Henriette had championed the girl, even though the baby had been stillborn. Henriette had even contrived to have Nicole visit the court. Henry had been glad to see Nicole, because, somewhat superstitiously, he still thought she had brought him luck, and he had publicly praised her. Now Henriette was furious.

"Nicole is in trouble with the Church," she said. "I am afraid of what they will do to her. You must help her."

Henry did his best to calm his mistress, but he found that she was not alone in trying to get him involved in the case. One of his secretaries, looking anxious, placed a pamphlet on his desk. "Sire," said the man. "This has been circulating in the city. You may want to see it."

The pamphlet summarized the accusations against Nicole Tavernier. It noted that a certain person close to the king had been Nicole's patron and that the king himself had lauded her. It was legitimate to ask, the anonymous writer went on, whether Henry would now defend her or whether he would allow the Church to destroy her.

"It is atrociously written," grumbled Henry. "And poorly argued." But he realized that he was in danger of being dragged into the affair. He felt that he needed information and advice, which is why he had summoned Monnet and Coton.

He knew that many of his people at court were puzzled by his reliance on the Jesuit Coton. After all, a few years before he had found it necessary to expel the Jesuits from his kingdom when one of them had the foolish notion to try to assassinate him. But he had allowed Coton to stay. He liked the man for his shrewdness and his honesty. In fact, he was so honest that he had the audacity to admonish the king about his many mistresses. That did not matter because his judgment on everything else was sound. The king's good view of Coton was confirmed when he discovered that the priest had befriended René Monnet.

"I have asked you here," said the king as he faced them both, "because I am troubled by what I hear about Nicole Tavernier and her clash with Barbe Acarie. I always thought of the Acarie as a kind and good woman, as does everyone in Paris. But here she is suddenly turning against this remarkable girl. For years she sponsored her. What could have happened?"

"Barbe Acarie is indeed good and kind," replied Father Coton. "She is also a very shrewd judge in spiritual matters and I'm afraid she has caught Nicole in a lie."

"Be that as it may, many people obviously believe in Nicole. I do not want to become caught up in this conflict, which could get out of hand. I am thinking specifically about that wretched case of—what was her name again?—Marthe Brossier."

Coton and Monnet knew what the king was talking about. A young woman from Romorantin, a village in the province of Berry, developed symptoms of diabolic possession. She suffered violent fits and convulsions, writhing on the floor, rolling her eyes wildly, foaming at the mouth. In her calmer moments she seemed to understand Latin, Greek and English, although she had never been taught these languages. Assuming that she was in the grip of demons, her father, a weaver, took her on pilgrimages to various shrines around France to be exorcised. Everywhere crowds began to gather to get a glimpse of the exorcisms, which were regarded as something of a diverting spectacle. When the formula of exorcism was pronounced over her or when she heard words from scripture, she would writhe on the floor, gesticulate violently, shout and grimace, but the evil spirit never seemed to leave her. Finally she appeared in Paris for the ultimate in exorcism, presumably far superior to what was available in the provinces.

Marthe Brossier was examined by various doctors, both of theology and medicine. The usual tests were applied. Her body was pricked in many places and she showed no sign of pain, which was taken as evidence of possession. Witnesses reported that she mysteriously rose four or five feet into the air. She was addressed in Latin, Greek and English, and some of the examiners were sure that she understood the words, while others maintained that she did not respond correctly. Day after day the wise men could not agree on whether Marthe was truly possessed or whether she was a faker. One of her exorcists was Pierre Bérulle, who had developed a reputation in this liturgical specialty. He was convinced that Marthe Brossier was indeed possessed and eventually the church authorities agreed with him. But the matter did not end there.

Marthe Brossier had started to say publicly that her devil went daily to the Protestant stronghold of La Rochelle to capture the soul of a heretic. Such statements were eagerly seized on by the last adherents of the League, who remained unforgiving toward Henry. Large crowds gathered to hear Marthe, and preachers invoked her name in sermons against the king. Henry was furious and alarmed. He forbade further exorcisms and the assemblies in her support and ordered Marthe Brossier to be imprisoned. This brought about an angry conflict between the crown and the Church, which argued that Henry had no right to take action in a case that fell under clerical jurisdiction. Henry argued back that he believed Marthe Brossier to be a faker and that what was involved therefore was a secular case of fraud. The conflict between the crown and the Church continued to simmer.

"I do not want to go through this sort of thing again," he told Coton and Monnet. "I do not need another quarrel with the Church."

Always restless, Henry rose from behind his oak desk and began pacing about the council chamber with its grand tapestries of the four seasons.

Coton pointed out that in certain respects the cases were quite different: Marthe claimed to be possessed while Nicole claimed the opposite. She never behaved violently and did not demonize the Protestants or the king.

"That is true," said Henry. "But if I get involved at all, my enemies will find a way to use the affair against me. What do we know about Nicole Tavernier's past?"

"Sire, we know almost nothing," replied Monnet. "I have asked her about her family and upbringing and so have Barbe Acarie and Father de Souzy. She refuses to talk about these things."

The king sighed. "Then she probably has something to hide. We must try to find out more about her. Are there events in her past to show that she is dishonest? Has she been accused of being a faker before? Has she dabbled in witchcraft or that sort of thing?"

"We simply do not know," replied Monnet.

"I cannot accept that," said the king. "Monnet, you have rarely failed me before. You know the kind of information I need. You had better get to work."

Monnet said he would do his best, made his farewells and set about his task. He was eager to do it not only because it was the king's order but because he found himself increasingly concerned about Nicole. She had become a mystery that he wanted to solve and if she was in danger, he wanted to try to protect her. He sought out Father de Souzy and other priests who had dealt with her. He went to see the nuns at Sainte-Catherine's, where Nicole had lodged years before. None of them told him anything useful. But then he recalled a curious incident involving a new charity launched by Barbe. She had acquired a small house not far from the Acarie mansion, which she had turned into a hostel for former prostitutes who had been persuaded, or had persuaded themselves, to rehabilitate their lives.

The profession was widespread in Paris. Many young and not-so-young women were attached to brothels, whose keepers were ironically known as abbesses. Others walked designated streets but often strayed beyond. Scandalously, Notre Dame Cathedral had become a gathering place for prostitutes, despite frequent efforts to disperse them, and some even solicited customers inside the church. Many grew sick and came close to starvation when they lost their looks and their earning power. In her hostel, Barbe saw to it that the "Magdaleni"—as they were called, after their patron saint—received food, medical treatment and spiritual advice.

A few months before, Barbe had asked Monnet and Nicole to accompany her on a visit to the hostel. In the parlor the women had gathered to greet them. Some were touchingly grateful, some were just sullen and resigned. Suddenly one girl came forward and approached Nicole. She was about to speak but when she saw Nicole's blank look, she muttered something inaudible and retreated among the others.

On the way back home Barbe said, "The poor thing seemed to know you. Have you ever met before?"

"Not that I can remember," Nicole replied.

Monnet had thought it was an odd answer and he was sure that Barbe felt the same way. Now he made his way back to the hostel to look for the girl who had seemed to recognize Nicole. He described her as best he could and was told, "You must mean Pauline. She left some time ago and I have no idea where she went."

Monnet concluded that there was nothing else that he could learn about Nicole in Paris. To find out anything more, he would have to go to the place she came from. The next morning he was on his way to Reims.

CHAPTER 9

The trip should have taken three days, but it took him closer to five because the autumn rains had turned the road into a quagmire. At times, he had to leave it and ride through trackless country. The marks of the interminable religious wars were everywhere—half-tilled fields, overgrown gardens, cottages collapsed into muddy heaps.

He was curious about the city in which for centuries the kings of France had been crowned. From a distance he saw the sturdy ramparts and what looked like two scarecrows. As he drew closer, he realized that they were corpses, hanging from gallows. He wondered for what crime these men had been executed.

He rode into the city and through narrow, bustling streets, loud with the cries of hawkers and water-carriers and chimney sweeps, trying not to collide with rumbling carts full of merchandise. He kept an eye on the signboards swaying overhead: "At the Bear," "At the Four Puckering Cats," "At the Shield of Reims." He finally found what he was looking for: "At the Big Stag," marking the inn that had been recommended to him.

After he settled into his room, he asked the landlord whether he knew any people named Tavernier. He did not.

"I am not saying that I know everybody in town, but I have owned this place for more than twenty years and there are few families I have not at least heard of."

The next morning Monnet asked tradesmen and shopkeepers and fellow physicians. None of them had heard of the Taverniers.

Monnet reluctantly decided that he would have to consult the records in all the city's parishes—fourteen of them.

He found nothing at Saint-Rémy, nothing at Saint-Hilaire, nothing at Saint-Symphorien. Finally he came to Saint-Jacques. Here, too, the curé had never heard of the Tavernier family. But just as Monnet was about to leave, the priest remembered something. The name Tavernier did sound familiar. He slowly searched through the marriage records, mumbling to himself, "Tavernier, Tavernier," and finally there it was. On July 21, 1591, one François Tavernier, journeyman carpenter of Châlons, was married to Nicole Petit of Reims.

Monnet asked whether there was a Petit family. There was not, but then the priest noticed that the wedding had been witnessed by one Jean Lapin, a well-known and prosperous builder and property owner. The curé did not know what became of Nicole and her husband.

Monnet was amazed. There had never been any hint that Nicole was married. He found out that Monsieur Lapin was still alive and decided to call on him. He was a broad, stocky man, probably in his early seventies, with wispy gray hair and a self-assured voice.

"Monsieur Lapin," Monnet said. "I am a physician from Paris. I want to inquire about a young woman I know. She goes by the name of Nicole Tavernier."

Lapin stiffened, uneasily swept a hand over his thin hair and said, "Why are you interested in her?"

Monnet briefly told of Nicole's appearance in Paris and the role she had played there.

Lapin listened gravely with many sighs and frowns. "A procession, you say? Ordered by the archbishop? She preached? She healed people?" He shook his head in disbelief.

"Did she send you to me?" he asked, suspiciously.

"Not at all," replied Monnet. "She did not even give me your name. I had to work hard to find you, Monsieur. She adamantly refuses to say anything about her upbringing or family. She is in some difficulty now with the Church, but many people admire and revere her. You might say that I am here for their sake. If we knew more about her we might be able to help her. Is she related to you?"

"I see no reason to help her," replied Lapin gruffly. "And no, she is certainly not related to me. She lived in this house as a servant."

Monnet had the impression that he was about to be shown the door but after a few moments Lapin's attitude softened. He said, "Very well. I will tell you what I can."

With an expansive gesture that seemed to encompass his entire spacious house, he said that he was a very fortunate man and he always felt that he must repay God's favor by acts of charity.

"There is in Reims a place where a few devoted nuns receive and care for unwanted children. It is called Sainte-Claire's. Poor mothers who cannot afford to keep their children or have given birth out of wedlock can leave their babies there with the sisters. The hope is that the children will be reclaimed when the mothers have found a husband or some other means of support, but in most cases, the women never reappear. The church tries to find homes for these abandoned children, which is not easy. One of my closest friends is Father Joseph Lebrun, who has always made a special effort for these young unfortunates. Father Lebrun persuaded me to take in one of the little girls from Sainte-Claire's. That was Nicole. She was nine years old when she came into our house fifteen years ago, small for her age, but exceptionally bright. My late wife, may her soul rest in peace, was very kind to her. Nicole was useful enough, cleaning and running errands, but she was never happy going about her chores. She was moody and withdrawn. At the same time, she was pious—as we all were. We often found her kneeling in some corner, praying. For so young a girl she felt very strongly about the poor. On her way to church—

she was always eager to go—she would hand out bits of food she had saved from her own meals, to beggars. And when some needy person knocked on our door Nicole was always the first to fetch a piece of bread or a bowl of broth from the kitchen. I was struck by her evident intelligence. She had learned her letters from the nuns at Sainte-Claire's, and when I had the time I continued to teach her reading and writing. So it went for some years, and then François Tavernier came into our lives."

Tavernier was a young journeyman carpenter, originally from Châlons, who had moved from town to town practicing his trade. As Lapin told it, he took on Tavernier because he seemed to be a skilled worker and had a pleasant, winning personality—as it turned out, too winning. Like all journeymen, he lived in the master's house. After working hours he and Nicole would sit together, whispering; they walked out together on Sundays. Both Monsieur and Madame Lapin disapproved. He warned the young people that they were risking temptation and sin. As it turned out, said Lapin, he was proven right. One day Nicole confessed to her mistress that she was carrying Tavernier's child.

"When my wife told me about this I was furious. I had given Nicole a good home, I had given Tavernier good work, and this was how they repaid me."

He ordered the pair to leave his house at once, but when they asked for his help to get married he relented to the point of giving them a small sum of money and, at Father Lebrun's urging, he acted as witness to their wedding. A good Catholic, he wanted the child to be born in wedlock. Nicole and her new husband left Reims the next day, going to Châlons. That was the last he saw or heard of them.

The Sainte-Claire orphanage was a modest one-story house with a garden in back containing some vegetable patches and a few scraggly flower beds. There was a nursery, two small dormitories for boys and girls, and a large common room. The children, perhaps a score, ranged from infants to nine- or ten-year-olds. The girls were busy with needlework, the boys with various handicrafts. They were subdued and looked at the stranger curiously, expectantly.

The nun who had greeted Monnet asked, "Are you here to take away one of our charges?"

He was sorry to disappoint her and explained why he had come. "I wondered," he said, "whether anyone remembers a girl named Nicole who left Sainte-Claire's about fifteen years ago and joined the household of Monsieur Lapin."

The nun looked puzzled. "That was long ago and before my time. But perhaps Sister Marie-Margaret may remember something," she said, and returned a few minutes later with a frail, elderly nun who looked at him through kind, rheumy eyes.

"I do recall little Nicole," she said. "She came to us on Saint Nicholas's day, December sixth, and so we decided to have her baptized Nicole. We also needed to give her a surname, and because she was so small, I suggested Petit. She was an intelligent child, obedient, and kept very much to herself. She had one friend here, a girl who simply disappeared one day."

"Do you remember the girl's name?" he asked.

The old nun thought for a moment. "Paulette or Pauline—or something like that, I believe."

Monnet had half expected this. It was the name of the girl who seemed to have recognized Nicole at Barbe Acarie's hostel.

He thanked the sister and started to leave. On the way out he noticed an odd opening in the wall and asked Sister Marie-Margaret about it.

"This is where we receive our foundlings," she explained.

The device consisted of a box that fitted through the opening, part of it outside the wall and part of it inside. It turned on an axle. Women who wanted to give up an infant placed it in the outside part of the box and when the sisters heard the baby's crying, they turned the box inside, thus avoiding any contact with the mother.

"And this is how Nicole came to you?" he asked.

Sister Marie-Margaret nodded.

He left, followed by the wistful glances of the children waiting to be taken away by somebody, to places they could only imagine.

Monnet next called on Father Lebrun, the parish priest of Saint-Jacques, who had brought Nicole into the Lapin family. Erect and clear eyed at eighty, he remembered Nicole well.

"She was a very intelligent child. My assistant instructed one of the Lapin boys in Latin and he noticed that Nicole listened in on these lessons whenever she could. With my permission and Monsieur Lapin's, he offered to teach her some Latin as well—which was most unusual for a girl—let alone a servant girl. She was always eager to hear stories from Holy Scripture. Monsieur Lapin had bought some pamphlets retelling parts of the New Testament and Nicole read them avidly. She loved to go to church and she paid close attention to the sermons. Whenever traveling preachers came to town, and there were many, she persuaded Lapin to let her go and hear them. Occasionally we staged plays based on scripture or the lives of the saints. The performers were some of our more talented parishioners, and people flocked to see them. Nicole was often there in the audience. Once, in a play about Jesus and Mary Magdalene, she actually won a part as a beggar child. I remember her on the platform, her face shining, standing a little apart as if she were alone in the scene. And here is another memory. She came to me one day and asked, 'Father, how does one become a saint?' I asked her, 'Why, is that what you want to become?' She said yes and I reprimanded her. I told her that saints are created by God's grace and one could not deliberately try to be one. One could lead a good and pious life, practicing charity and the other virtues, but the rest was in the hands of the Lord. I'm not sure that she was satisfied with my answer. Eventually she began to change. She came to church less often. I cannot, of course, say what I heard from her in the confessional, but I can tell you that she was troubled. A few years later François Tavernier started to work for Monsieur Lapin, and I assume you have heard the rest of the unfortunate story from him."

"Do you know what happened to the couple?" Monnet asked.

"They told me that they were planning to move to Châlons, and that is all I know."

Monnet returned to his inn to jot down some notes about what he had heard and ordered a meal before setting out again. He knew he would have to follow the trail to Châlons, a few hours' ride away. He thought the quickest way to find out about Nicole and her husband would be to go to the carpenters' guild, where Tavernier must be known. The guild hall was marked by a statue of Saint Joseph, patron saint of the trade. The statue had been smashed by Protestant iconoclasts and had since been roughly repaired. A member of the guild received him with open curiosity. He was a young man with a bland face and a rather confused air that led Monnet to fear that he might not be able to give him much information. He was wrong. As soon as Monnet mentioned the name Tavernier his eyes came into focus.

"I knew him quite well," he said. "Why do you ask about him?"

"You say you *knew* him. Is he then no longer in Châlons?"

The fellow looked startled. "He is no longer in Châlons nor anywhere else on earth," he said. "You obviously don't know what happened to him. Tavernier came here with his new wife back in '91," he said. "He seemed to be a good journeyman carpenter, but he had no references from his last master in Reims and he could not find a regular place. He did odd jobs around town and his work was satisfactory. He and I became quite friendly and we spent many an evening together at the tavern. Unfortunately, he began to spend more time at the tavern than at work. I visited him and his young wife occasionally. They lived in very poor lodgings at the edge of town and I know that the neighbors worried about her. She was expecting a child and she had a hard time making ends meet. I suppose Tavernier would bring in money one day and then nothing for two weeks. I know they were fighting all the time. As the birth of the baby approached, Tavernier tried harder to get work but he also drank harder. One day, just before sundown, Tavernier was repairing the steeple of our Notre Dame. The priest warned him that the light was beginning to fade and perhaps he should stop until the next day. Tavernier insisted on continuing and from his slurred speech it was clear that he was more than a little drunk. You can probably guess the rest. As it grew darker, Tavernier lost his footing on the scaffold and fell to the ground. He broke his neck and died instantly."

It was a lot to take in, and Monnet was silent for a few moments. Then he asked, "What became of Nicole? And of the child she was carrying?"

"The child was born three days later, much too early," was the sad reply. "It died within a few hours."

On the way back to Paris, Monnet pondered what he had learned. In his mind he tried to find the little servant girl and the destitute young widow, scarcely seventeen years old, inside the Nicole he knew. He began to understand why Nicole had never wanted to talk about her past. He was sure she was ashamed that she was abandoned by a mother she never knew and then conceived a child out of wedlock herself. It was odd, he thought, that princes, dukes and kings, including Henry, not to mention any number of priests, were openly sprouting bastards, while among the good burghers and tradesmen illegitimacy was considered a disgrace. And she had another reason for not talking about where she came from or what had happened to her—the fact that she had been married. Everyone in Paris assumed she was a virgin and that gave her a special aura. She had never claimed to be a virgin, but she certainly did not deny it. She simply allowed people to see in her what they wanted.

He had found out much, but not what had turned her into the Nicole Tavernier whom Paris had worshiped.

"There are still too many missing pieces," he said when he met Father Coton back in Paris. He told the priest what he had discovered and concluded, "It is not enough. It will not satisfy the king. And it does not satisfy me. I somehow must persuade Nicole to tell me the rest."

Coton agreed. "Perhaps you should make it clear to her that she is in danger."

From his years as a lawyer, Coton retained the habit of lining up his arguments.

"When she is examined, it may be decided that she is indeed what she claims to be, blessed by a special grace; but, considering her prominent accuser, that is not likely. Or it may be decided that she is a faker and pretender, using clever tricks to impress the faithful. In that case, she will not be hurt but she will be disgraced. Or else it may be found that the Devil is acting through her. If so, an exorcist might be brought in to expel the evil spirit. If the evil spirit is seen to leave her, she will be left in peace. But if there is no sign that the Devil has been expelled, there is another possibility. It might then be concluded that she is not simply possessed against her will, but that she actively engaged herself to the Devil. In that case, she may well be accused of witchcraft. The result might be prison—or worse. After all, we burn witches in France."

CHAPTER 10

Monnet was alarmed by Coton's words. Fear of witches and demons seemed ever-present, like a pulse beating under the skin of society. Usually it was individuals who were accused, but sometimes scores went into the fire or to the gallows. It happened more often in small towns and villages, but it was not unknown in educated Paris.

When he was at the university one of his professors recommended that the students look into a book called *The Witches' Hammer,* which had been published a century before but remained in wide circulation. It attempted to treat the whole subject of demonology with academic precision. It included such topics as "Whether children can be generated by Incubi and Succubi," "Whether witches can sway the minds of men to love or hatred," "How witches deprive men of their virile member," and so forth. None of it seemed to Monnet to have any connection with Nicole. And yet he knew that some of the very acts that Nicole had claimed—her clairvoyance, her transportation to a distant town—were considered signs of witchcraft as much as signs of possession. The dividing line between the two struck him as vague, arbitrary—and dangerous.

Monnet made his way to the convent at Longchamp. It stood on the banks of the Seine, with a thick forest at its back, which made it seem remote. The mother superior had been instructed by the archbishop to keep Nicole at the convent until her formal examination, and Monnet had to do some negotiating before he was allowed to see her. He was led to the parlor.

Nicole was brought in. She was pale and plainly anxious. "Have you come to take me away, Doctor?" she said. "I am very badly treated here. I think they all believe the worst of me."

"I'm afraid I cannot take you away," said Monnet. "But we have much to talk about. I have seen Monsieur Lapin."

Her small chin came forward pugnaciously. "I did not want you to do that," she said. "How did you ever find him?"

"That does not matter. I also saw Father Lebrun. I spoke to Sister Marie-Margaret at Sainte-Claire's. I went to Châlons. I learned about Tavernier."

Nicole flinched with the mention of each name.

"I know about the death of your child. I am sorry, it must have been a terrible time for you."

She turned away. He thought that she might be weeping, but when she spoke again her voice was steady. "Now that you know all this," she said bitterly, "what good does it do you? What good does it do me?"

"You must believe that I am only trying to help you. But I will not be able to do this unless you tell me more about yourself. I have asked you this before. It is important. I must know about your healing, your miracles."

"These things are between God and me."

Monnet resisted an impulse to seize her and shake her.

"Nicole, you must realize that you are in great danger. Everything you have said and done will be examined. You will be tested in all sorts of ways. Your judges may very well decide that it is a devil who is acting through you."

A scream from Nicole: "That is not true."

"Worse, they may decide that you have given yourself to the

Devil of your own free will. You do know what will happen to you then."

She did. Some years before, during her wanderings, she had found herself in a small town in Provence. The place was in an uproar. A young widow, like herself, but rather free in her ways, was accused of casting a spell and poisoning her neighbor's husband. An angry crowd gathered in front of her house and threatened to deal with her on the spot. Someone proposed a frequently used test. Let the woman be thrown into the river; if she floated she was clearly a witch, but if she sank, and drowned, she would be considered innocent. The local magistrate, however, was a conscientious man and insisted on a formal trial. The woman was examined, witnesses were called and when she denied her guilt she was put to the torture, as was customary. Nicole did not know which methods were employed—whether the rack, the thumbscrew, hot irons or any of the other prescribed means. When the accused appeared in court, she confessed to the charges, although Nicole believed her to be innocent. She was condemned to death by fire—a slow fire, it was specified, to be achieved by the use of young wood. The various methods of execution were carefully detailed, including their costs (burning was relatively expensive compared to a mere hanging or beheading). Nicole did not watch the burning but saw it in her imagination many times, saw the flames gradually rising toward the woman's contorted face and heard her screams. Hearing Monnet's words, Nicole suddenly saw herself in that woman's place. In a blinding image she saw the archbishop—or was it Barbe Acarie?—presiding over the trial, saw the instruments of torture, saw herself on the pyre.

She jumped up and turned toward the door as if trying to escape, but then she sank back into her chair with a deep sigh that seemed to convulse her whole body. She began to speak. Her story came in fits and starts. She often sounded as if she were talking about somebody else, some other person called Nicole. Monnet had the impression that she was trying hard to reach inside her own mind, to explain to him—and perhaps to herself—what she had felt and how she had acted. Occasionally, when she was unwilling—or unable—to go on, he prompted her with questions.

Her recollections of Sainte-Claire's were mostly sad. She could not tell exactly how or when she learned that not all children lived in a flock, supervised by nuns, and that somewhere, beyond the gates, there were things like families and parents.

"I remember one of the nuns speaking of our mothers, and how some of them had committed a great sin of which we children were the result. I had no idea what they meant, only that it was bad and we must pray very hard to God to forgive them."

From time to time a woman would appear—one of those creatures called mothers—and take away her child. The other children looked on with envy, pretending to themselves and one another that they too would soon be claimed. It happened only rarely. The word "mother" had a certain magical quality among the children at Sainte-Claire's, always pronounced with a tremor of awe and mystery. When Nicole tried to imagine her own mother, she did not picture her as one of those poorly dressed and anxious women who sometimes appeared, but as a lady in a flowing blue dress, with a beautiful, serene face, holding a baby on her lap, like the image of the Virgin Mary hanging on the wall in the common room. She did not confide this idea to anyone except a tall, strongly built blond girl a year or two older than herself. Her name was Pauline and she had befriended Nicole.

"Real mothers don't look like that," said Pauline. "Anyway, you had better stop waiting for your mother—I stopped waiting for mine long ago."

Nevertheless Nicole continued to hope, if not for the appearance of her mother, then for some other wonderful event. A strange incident had given her the sense that she was destined for something special.

She had fallen ill one day, she recalled. "I was found cold and stiff and given up for dead. They moved me from my bed to a table and wrapped me in a shroud. They were about to sew it up when I suddenly sat up, fully recovered. I was so moved by this miracle that I decided that I must find a way to thank God for it. That is what I have tried to do ever since."

Sometimes Father Lebrun would appear at Sainte-Claire's with a stranger and would stroll about the common room, carefully looking at the children, stopping to talk to one or another. The visitor, Father Lebrun and one of the nuns would whisper together and then the stranger would leave alone, or else one of the children would go with him.

"The nuns explained that these gentlemen were performing a great work of charity and that we must all be grateful to them. Once we caught on to what was happening, whenever a stranger appeared with Father Lebrun, we children pretended to be indifferent, going on with our needlework or some other task. In fact we hung on every word and every move, desperately hoping to be chosen."

And so one day Father Lebrun came in with a man whom he introduced to the nun as "my friend Monsieur Lapin." While the priest watched, he spoke to several children and then approached Nicole. He asked her name, her age and if she was a good girl who liked to work hard. "Even then, at nine, I thought those questions were a little silly. What was I going to say? That I was a bad girl who didn't like to work hard? But then he asked an even odder question: 'Are you happy here?' I replied: 'I am happy enough but I would be even happier, Monsieur, if you took me home with you.' I don't know where I got the courage to say this—but he seemed delighted by my answer."

Lapin, Father Lebrun and two of the nuns spoke to one another for a few moments in low voices, while Nicole waited anxiously. Then the priest told her, "You are a very lucky girl, Nicole. Monsieur Lapin has agreed to take you into his house."

Nicole felt a pang of guilt when she saw the disappointment and longing of the other children, especially Pauline, who was the only one she would really miss. She left Sainte-Claire's with Monsieur Lapin's hand on her shoulder.

During her years there, she and the other children had only

rarely been outside and only for short distances. Now she saw the streets of Reims with amazement, both delighted and alarmed by the jostling of so many people, by the noise made by carts and animals, by the bright colors of the shop signs. She was struck by the many men without legs or arms—soldiers who had barely survived one of the countless battles between Catholics and Protestants— and by shabbily dressed women begging for alms who had fled with their families from these wars, which Nicole did not yet understand.

As they approached Monsieur Lapin's house she was awed. It had three stories, the top floors protruding over the lower ones, and they seemed to the child like a looming menace overhead. The interior was very different from the sparsely furnished rooms at Sainte-Claire's; every space was crammed with furniture, and very dark. Lapin led her into the parlor, where a tall, robust woman in a black dress and white lace cap stood waiting for them. Her face was round and soft and for a few moments Nicole thought of the mother image that she had formed in the likeness of Mary. But when the woman spoke, her mouth seemed contorted and there was nothing gentle in her voice.

"So this is the child you want to bring into our house thanks to the good Father Lebrun," she said coldly, addressing her husband.

"Yes, this is Nicole," said Lapin. "She is nine and I believe very bright."

Madame Lapin looked at Nicole long and hard, as she might inspect a cabbage in the market or a length of cloth in the shop.

"She is quite small and I hope she is stronger than she looks. I wonder what use she will be."

Then she spoke to Nicole. "Monsieur Lapin is doing a very charitable thing in bringing you here. But charity goes only so far and you will have to earn your place. If we are going to keep you, you will have to work hard like the other servants."

As Nicole continued to tell her story, Monnet realized that Lapin's account of her experience in his household was quite different from her own version. According to Nicole, Madame Lapin was hardly kind. She believed all servants to be lazy and deceitful and was especially hard on this foundling whom her husband had brought into the house against her better judgment. As for the children, only the oldest boy, Jacques, who was sixteen and preparing to be a priest, was kind to her. The others—a girl of fourteen and two boys of thirteen and ten—enjoyed tormenting her. She worked in the kitchen, scrubbed, cleaned, carried water up and down the steep stairs. She sewed and mended clothes and made her own clothes out of the ones cast off by the daughter. The Lapin children would make Nicole do things over again if they decided that they had not been done right the first time—a bed would have to be remade again and again, a table scrubbed endlessly to remove imaginary stains. These things Nicole minded much less than the taunts. "Nicole no-name," the daughter, Clarice, would call her. "Even your own mother didn't want you."

The middle boy would say, "I wonder who your father was. Some vagabond?"

In contrast, Nicole was warmed by the oldest boy's kindness and still sounded excited when she recalled how she had begun to listen to his Latin instruction and how Lapin had allowed her to take lessons. Despite everything that happened later, she remained grateful to him for that. Her teacher praised her quick and retentive mind and she picked up some passages from the gospel. She began to consider herself smarter than the rest of the household. But she was troubled. Whatever she had learned did not help her to understand her own soul.

"I did not know how I really felt about myself," she said. "And," she added earnestly, "about God."

Ever since her earliest childhood, when she imagined her mother in the image of the Virgin Mary, religion had been her cherished dream world, a realm of wonders and glories. She loved being in church, with its banks of flickering candles that seemed to make the saints' pictures move and come alive. She loved what sounded to her like the sweet thunder of the organ and was rapt by the ritual of the Mass, the chants, the tinkling of bells, the incense, the mysterious business with the wine and holy bread, even before she understood their meaning. She listened attentively to the sermons by the parish priest or visiting preachers.

"I thought it must be wonderful to stand up there on the pulpit talking to the whole congregation," she recalled. "I wanted to be up there myself, although I realized that this was not permitted to a woman. Back at Sainte-Claire's I often played at being a nun, and sometimes even a priest. I once climbed on a stool and started repeating some of the words that had stuck in my mind from the sermons in church. I think what I said was probably just a tangle of phrases that did not make much sense, and at first the other children just laughed at me. But after a while, some began to listen. That made me feel so good, so happy, so satisfied that I could never forget it."

And then there were the saints. They seemed to be everywhere, not only in the images she saw in church but in ordinary life. She took pride in memorizing the saints that were attached to each trade or event. She knew that the carpenters had Saint Joseph, the vintners, Saint Amand, and on and on. Even thieves, she discovered, had a patron—Saint Dismas. She learned that when people were about to go on a journey, they prayed to Saint Christopher, and when a child was about to be born they prayed to Saint Leonard or Saint Elmo. She found that when people were sick they prayed to different saints for each disease: Saint Vitus for epilepsy, Saint John of God for heart problems, Saint Bernadine of Siena for hoarseness.

Monnet knew this very well because he often heard his patients invoke those names and was sure that they relied on them more than on him. This did not trouble him. He had no exaggerated expectations about what his science could accomplish, but he was doing his best. Let the saints, if they existed, do theirs.

Mostly, the saints were taken for granted by people, part of the order of things, and few wondered about what was behind these blessed names and their powers. But Nicole wanted to know their stories. She kept asking the nuns at Sainte-Claire's and later Father

Lebrun to tell her about them. She could not believe that the Protestants wanted to do away with the saints. She lost herself in their lives and she found certain favorites. There was Saint Lucy, patron of the blind, a virtuous virgin in Roman times who had her eyes put out for being a secret Christian and later found them miraculously restored. There was Saint Dorothy, also martyred in Roman times, who joyfully proclaimed before her execution that she would soon be in a lovely garden; when a young lawyer made fun of her for saying this, an angel appeared with a basket of roses and apples, which so astonished him that he became a Christian himself.

"I wanted to be like them," recalled Nicole, "heroic in faith. I always remembered my pledge, after my miraculous recovery, to find a way of thanking God, and I thought that I could do that by being like the saints. With all my heart I wanted to share in their miracles and I wondered how I could make this happen.

"I once asked Father Lebrun how one became a saint and he scolded me. He told me that was not something I should wish for, but I did not believe him. I knew that saints were touched by God, that He spoke to them and they to Him. That is what I kept wishing for. I prayed and prayed and waited to hear God's voice and I heard nothing. I felt nothing. I became very miserable and thought that I must be wicked and sinful. Everybody saw me go to church eagerly and watch holy processions and plays, everybody saw me pray and called me pious—but they did not know that I felt nothing inside. I tried to tell Father Lebrun about this in the confessional, but he only told me that I must pray harder and open my heart to God. I tried as hard as I could but I still felt empty. How could I thank God for what He had done for me if I could not feel His presence?"

Then one day François Tavernier came to work for Monsieur Lapin. As Nicole described him he was as handsome as a statue, with dark curly hair and an angelic face. His voice was soft, his movements gentle, as if he wanted to make sure not to hurt anything or anyone around him. He was polite to the entire household, but almost at once he paid special attention to Nicole. The affair developed very much as Monsieur Lapin had told it. He had stated the facts, but now Nicole recalled not only the facts but her emotions. At first she felt merely warm and protected whenever she was with him, and her loneliness disappeared when he sat or walked with her, encouraged her to talk and listened to her every word. But then a stronger feeling overcame her, something she had never experienced before and could not name. When François began to make love to her she realized it was wrong, but eventually she could not resist. That force seemed to cure her feeling of emptiness, replacing the longing for the saints and God as her entire being became concentrated on François.

When she realized that she was pregnant she was ashamed, frightened, but also triumphant—because after all, it was *his* child.

"I wanted very much to be married to him," recalled Nicole, "to be with him forever. But I also wanted to be married because of the child. I was troubled when I found out how angry Monsieur Lapin was with us and I thought he was very harsh in turning us out of his house, but in the end I was relieved to get away from the Lapin family and looked forward with joy to my new life with François."

CHAPTER 11

Nicole's eyes stared into the distance—or into the past—as she tried to recapture the mood of hope that had long since vanished. She resumed her story. As she described it, soon after she and François arrived in Châlons, disillusion set in. Nicole gradually realized that behind his gentle manner there was weakness, that under his angelic features there was the face of a self-indulgent child. She could not understand why he worked so irregularly and brought home so little money. The small amount Monsieur Lapin had given them was soon gone. They quarreled about this. From the poisonous solicitude of the neighbors, she learned about all the time François was spending at the tavern. They quarreled more. They discovered that passion is a temporary fever that sooner or later cools.

When Tavernier fell to his death and the baby died afterward, Nicole was devastated. "I thought I was being punished for my sin with François and because I had forgotten my longing for God. Even though I had not heard Him or felt Him, I realized that what I felt for François could not be a substitute. If I could not feel God's love, I wanted to feel none."

"But eventually you did feel it," Monnet said. "How did that happen?"

Nicole was now near tears and took minutes to collect herself. Then she resumed. "I remembered how I felt when I preached to those children at Sainte-Claire's, the warmth and happiness in me. The same thing happened a few times later. After hearing some passage from the scriptures, I would try a little sermon on Jacques Lapin or on some of the servants. In Châlons, François and I sometimes visited neighbors, sitting about the chimney and telling stories. My stories always turned into sermons. Each time I felt that same joy. In those moments I believed that God touched me."

Tavernier's death had left her virtually destitute. She turned to the carpenters' guild in Châlons, but as Tavernier had been only a journeyman and not in good repute, Nicole received only a pittance. Reluctantly she decided to return to Reims and to ask Monsieur Lapin to take her back. One of her neighbors told her of a crockery merchant who was about to leave for Reims, and he agreed to let her ride in his cart. But when she came to the familiar door she found that she could not face the prospect of begging a favor of Lapin and especially his wife. Her hand, which had been about to knock, dropped to her side.

"For hours I wandered through the busy streets at a loss about what to do. At dusk, I saw a woman who looked somehow familiar. She was tall, fair, and her bright clothes with many ribbons and spangles made her stand out from the crowd. It took me a few moments to realize that it was Pauline, my friend from Sainte-Claire's."

The two young women embraced joyfully and walked along chattering until they settled down on a bench near the cathedral. They looked at each other.

"I recognized you right away," said Pauline. "Your face hasn't changed much at all."

Pauline's face had changed a great deal, thought Nicole, who was noticing hard lines and some touches of paint.

"We all envied you so when you left Sainte-Claire's with that gentleman," said Pauline. "How did it go with you? Are you still working there?"

Nicole shook her head and began to tell her story. As Pauline listened she clucked and drew in her breath sympathetically.

"My poor Nicole," she muttered. "I am so sorry. We should not have envied you."

"And what about you?" asked Nicole. "How did you leave Sainte-Claire's? Did someone take you away? Are you married?"

"I am certainly not married and no one took me away. I simply ran off one day because I could no longer bear life there. But I met a very kind woman who gave me work."

"What kind of work?" asked Nicole.

"You will see by and by, but right now we must take care of you. Do you have a place to stay?"

Again Nicole shook her head and Pauline said decisively, "You can stay with me for a while."

As darkness fell, they walked through many winding streets until they reached a building with closed shutters and peeling walls. Pauline led Nicole into a small, dark room. It contained a bed, a wash stand and a few other odd pieces of furniture.

"You must be exhausted," said Pauline. "Would you like some food?"

When Nicole replied that she was too tired to eat, Pauline gestured toward the bed. Within moments, Nicole was asleep.

She awoke the next morning to the sound of voices in the room.

"I suppose she is pretty enough," she heard a woman say, "but she does not look very strong."

"She has always been stronger than she looked." That was Pauline's voice.

"Well, do you think she would be willing?" said the other woman.

"I don't think she has much choice."

Nicole sat upright, opening her eyes. There was Pauline, and next to her an ample woman in black with a cluster of keys dangling from her belt who reminded her unpleasantly of Madame Lapin.

"Good morning, Nicole," said Pauline. "You have slept a long time. This is Madame Blois, our abbess."

"Abbess?" asked Nicole in wonderment—and then she understood. She was innocent, but not so innocent that she finally failed to realize where she was.

Madame Blois looked her over carefully and said, "I am ready to take you on. You can come here, on trial. You will have your own room, you will be well fed and you will have all the clothes and trinkets you want. Your clients will pay me and I will give you part of the money. But don't ever try to make special deals with the men. Believe me, I will find out about it."

Nicole was horrified. She jumped from the bed, startling both women.

"Never," she said. "I could never do this."

"Don't be hasty," said Madame Blois. "What I am offering you is much better than cleaning floors and washing dishes and being kicked about in some fat merchant's house, even if you could get that kind of work. It is certainly better than starving in the street, which is how you would probably end up. Think it over carefully."

"She is right, you know," said Pauline, after Madame Blois left. "When I first met her and she offered me a place here, I too wanted nothing to do with it. But I soon realized that there were worse things. She treats us well, the other girls are kind and the men—well, the men are often quite generous. It is certainly not the life I dreamed of back at Sainte-Claire's, but girls like us are not likely to have our dreams come true. You certainly would not find work as a servant here in Reims. Or," she added sarcastically, "do you expect to find a husband, without a dowry?"

"I expect nothing, but I know that I could not do this." She shuddered. "And you should not be doing it either. But you can still save your soul by getting away from this place."

"And where would I go?" scoffed Pauline. "And what would I do?"

"Mary Magdalene might have said the same, but she repented and followed our Lord," said Nicole.

The comparison came to her quite naturally, because she had always loved the story. Without realizing it she began a sermon, and again she experienced the exhilaration that she always felt at such times.

"Our Lord came to the house of a Pharisee, where He encountered a woman of the town who had led a sinful life. The host did not offer water to wash the Lord's feet or oil to anoint Him, but the woman knelt and washed His feet with her tears and dried them with her hair and anointed them with myrrh. 'Her great love proves that her many sins have been forgiven,' said the Lord. And then He told her, 'Your sins are forgiven . . . Your faith has saved you; go in peace.' You too can go in peace, Pauline. Leave this place and come away with me. We will kneel in church before the Lord and weep like Mary Magdalene and pray for forgiveness."

"I'm not Mary Magdalene and you're not Christ," said Pauline. "If God wanted me to lead a good and pious life, He could have provided for me. I cannot come away with you—we would both end up begging and starving, as Madame Blois said."

Nicole continued to argue but finally saw that it was useless. "God be with you," she said as she embraced Pauline in farewell.

She hurried out of the building and along the street as if pursued. She had no idea where she was going. All she knew was that she had to get away from Reims.

She walked about aimlessly for a long time and then she had an encounter that she firmly believed to be providential. Near Venice Bridge she came on a group of pilgrims led by a Capuchin friar. They had apparently stopped in Reims overnight and were now preparing to continue their journey. She asked the friar where they were headed and he named the shrine of Saint Restitue of Sora, who was known to heal migraines, among other things. It was located near Soissons, a three-day journey from Reims. Nicole said resolutely, "Brother, may I join you—at least part of the way?"

The Capuchin looked at her curiously from under his hood and in his turn asked her where she was going and why.

"I do not know where I am going but I believe that the good

Lord will guide me. I have just buried my husband and my child and I know that nothing good awaits me here."

The friar was moved. After briefly consulting the other pilgrims he gave his assent. "But," he said, "we have very little money and we beg for food along the way."

Nicole said, "I will be glad to do my share."

The friar continued, "As you can see, we have three mules with us and we take turns riding them."

Nicole left Reims with the pilgrims, who gave her one of the mules for the first part of the journey.

As they made their way along the pitted roads through the war-devastated landscape, Nicole saw with increasing pain the ruined farms, demolished houses and not a few burned churches. Every so often they encountered ragged groups of disbanded soldiers and poor peasants looking for food. That evening the pilgrims took shelter in an abandoned barn and, sitting around a small fire, they talked about the misery they were seeing. Why was it happening?

"Surely it is a punishment from God for our sins," said Nicole. She was probably unaware that she was echoing what she had heard so often from the pulpit.

"The terrible heresy against our Holy Church is a divine scourge and so are the wars that are ruining our country. They will not stop until the people repent and lead their lives according to God's law."

Again Nicole was preaching and again, as the pilgrims listened attentively, she felt blissful.

The next day they reached a village, and the friar urged the pilgrims to look for food and alms. This was a sad task because most of the village seemed poor and hungry. In her search Nicole strayed from the others and eventually found herself at a half-destroyed farmhouse a short distance outside the village. Like so many others, it had apparently been abandoned by a family escaping one battle or another.

"Something told me to walk inside," recalled Nicole. "The place was in disorder, chairs overturned, clothes on the floor—the people must have left in a big hurry. I walked into the kitchen to look for food. I found nothing. I opened a cupboard and all the shelves were empty. I was just about to turn away when I noticed some scratches and finger marks on the back of the cupboard. I looked more closely and touched the back. It felt slightly loose. I pushed and pulled and before I knew it the back slid aside and there I saw, incredibly, a cache of bread, loaf after loaf, stacked high. Clearly the people in the house had hoarded the bread and had been unable to take it along when they fled. I broke off a piece and tasted it. It was very stale but edible, especially if you were hungry. At that moment, two of the pilgrims who had followed me came into the kitchen. They were astounded by what they saw. What should be done with this treasure—should they take it back to the others? 'No,' I said, 'there is too much to carry. Bring them here. And bring some of the villagers with them.' "

Before long a crowd of hungry people had lined up in front of the farmhouse and Nicole was handing out bread to one after another. She continued as long as the bread lasted, which was quite a long time. Whenever one of the recipients thanked her, she would say, "Do not thank me, thank our Lord, who has provided this for you."

Word of what had happened quickly spread throughout the village and the surrounding countryside. People called it a miracle and blessed the mysterious lady who had brought it about.

The pilgrims felt much the same way and the friar said, "It must have been divine providence that guided you to that house."

"I believe it was," replied Nicole.

By the time they reached Soissons the story had spread even there, and it was told in a rather special version. A divine messenger had spoken to Nicole, people said, and given her a loaf that multiplied in her hand without diminishing, so that she was able to feed all who came.

Monnet broke into Nicole's narrative at this point and asked, "Did you correct people when they said that? Did you tell them about the hoarding and about the hiding place behind the cupboard?"

"I did not," said Nicole without embarrassment. "I believe it *was* a miracle. If it was not a visible messenger who let me find the bread and distribute it to the poor, it was an unseen force."

He was surprised by this argument. It struck him as an overly ingenious justification, but she seemed entirely sincere.

Nicole and the pilgrims had been in Soissons only a few hours, resting near the fountain at the marketplace, when people started gathering around them curiously. They had heard about Nicole and the bread. They stared at her.

"Is it her?" they asked. "Is that the one who can work miracles?"

An old woman came up to her. "Blessed one," she said, "my husband is very ill. I beg you to come to him."

Nicole readily agreed.

"What did you think you could do for this man?" Monnet asked.

"I did not know what I could do for him. All I knew was that someone had asked me for help and that if God wanted to use me he would show me what to do."

Nicole followed the old woman to her house. She knelt at the sick man's bedside and began to pray. She prayed for a long time. Eventually the man, who had been feverish and restless, went to sleep peacefully. His wife begged Nicole to spend the night. She knew that her traveling companions were eager to continue their journey, but Nicole felt she should stay. She went to explain this to the friar and the other pilgrims, thanked them for having allowed her to travel with them and returned to the sick man's house.

Monnet was sure he knew what was coming. "And next morning," he said, "the man was better?"

"Yes, he was," replied Nicole earnestly. "The news went around Soissons very quickly. Other people came to me and begged me to pray with the sick."

She agreed every time. Once she was brought to a woman, apparently close to death, who asked Nicole to hear her confession. She dutifully pointed out that only a priest could give absolution but nevertheless listened to the woman's account of her sins. Nicole urged her to repent and even chided her for some past misdeeds she had not mentioned. Thus she began the practice for which she was later celebrated in Paris, when she worked among the sick at the Hôtel Dieu and was summoned to private houses to attend people in extremis. Monnet thought all along that she had simply made safe guesses about minor misdeeds that could always be found in people's lives. But he did not put that to her now, not wanting to interrupt her again.

Sometimes she was asked to repeat the miracle of the bread, but she explained that this could only happen if and when God directed it. Nevertheless, she continued her care for the poor and begged for provisions to distribute to them. People obliged her, also offering lodgings and even money. Often, as she left a house where she had prayed or as she emerged from a church, she was surrounded by a crowd. Some people were merely curious, but most expected something from her without quite knowing what. At such moments she would begin to speak to them in her usual vein—about the tribulations that France was undergoing, about how this was God's punishment for the people's ungodly life, about how they must repent of their sins. She quoted passages from scripture and interpreted them, drawing on what she had heard from Jacques Lapin's teacher and in various sermons but also using her imagination.

After some months in Soissons she decided that she must move on to spread the word elsewhere. She went on foot, sometimes joining other travelers, sometimes going alone despite the marauders who often made the roads unsafe. She trusted in God to protect her. She went to Villers-Cotteret, and after some time there to Gondreville. Reports came constantly about more fighting around Paris between the Catholic forces and those of Henry of Navarre. She had always heard of Henry as a heretic and imagined him as the brutal enemy of all good Catholics and especially of her dear saints. As she arrived in Nanteuil she found a large crowd assembled in front of the town hall. Robed dignitaries, magistrates, representatives of the guilds, and burghers were listening to a speaker who was addressing them from a raised platform. Above the man's spotted and carelessly fitted tunic she saw wrinkled features and a graying beard. But the face was shining with passion and the voice was strong.

"There has been too much bloodshed in the name of God," she heard him say. "Those who unswervingly follow their conscience are of my religion and I am of the religion of all those who are brave and good."

Nicole was greatly excited by those words.

"Who is that?" she asked a man standing next to her.

"You don't know? That is Henry of Navarre."

Henry was on one of his frequent forays to various towns, trying to prepare the ground for reconciliation between the faiths. He had used the remark that so stirred Nicole often before. Nicole listened raptly as he continued to speak, and at the end she rushed forward on some impulse. But before she could get close to him, he had moved inside the town hall. What would she have said if she had reached him? She was not quite sure, but she probably would have told him what she told everyone else: to repent of his sins and to leave heresy behind. From that moment on she prayed every night for Henry of Navarre's conversion. When word came in May of 1593 that he had asked to take instruction in the Catholic faith, she felt triumphantly that her prayers had been answered. Henry, she was now sure, would save France, but she also knew that the struggle for Paris, the heart of France, was not over, and she was seized by the idea that she must go to Paris. She moved on to Dommartin and then to Le Bourget, near the capital. There she heard the great news that Henry had announced his conversion and that he would attend Mass at Saint-Denis. She instantly decided that she must see that event and made her way the two leagues to Saint-Denis Cathedral.

After witnessing the Mass, Nicole stayed on in Saint-Denis for another month or two, planning what she had come to think of as her conquest of Paris. She realized that she might not be accepted there as readily as she had been elsewhere. She asked the advice of a traveling preacher who had stopped in Saint-Denis, and he told her that she must find a spiritual director. She liked the sound of that and she tried to imagine what such a person might be like. She visualized him in the form of a statue she had once seen: thin, sharp features, pointed beard, intense yet serene even in stone. It was a statue of Saint Francis of Assisi. Early in 1594, she walked into Paris through the Saint-Denis gate.

Reims had once astonished and alarmed her with its tumult, but Paris was overwhelming. The streets were thronged with people rushing past her; peddlers were announcing their wares at the top of their voices. Gray- and brown-robed friars were haranguing the crowds at street corners. She walked past a large graveyard (the Cemetery of the Innocents) where people laughed and joked, heedless of their surroundings. Whenever she looked up she saw churches of all shapes towering over the houses. She reached a large square, the place de Grève, with its ancient, ominous pillory. Then, across the busy river, she saw the large bulk of Notre Dame and, turning her head, the thin, golden spire of the Sainte-Chapelle. It took her a while to get used to all this, but she was not frightened. "I felt that I belonged here," she said.

The traveling preacher in Saint-Denis had told her about a place named Sainte-Catherine's that took in women who were looking for work, and Nicole found her way there. The next day she began to visit churches. In each, she tried to get a close look at the pastor. She was searching for someone to fit the image in her mind. On the third day she found him, in the pulpit at the Capuchin Church on the rue Saint-Honoré. He had the thin face, the pointed beard and the intense eyes of the priest in her vision. The next day she presented herself to Father Pacifique de Souzy.

Nicole had been telling her story for more than two hours when the bell calling the nuns to vespers was heard throughout the convent. One of the sisters appeared at the door of the parlor and told Monnet firmly that the time for visitors was over.

CHAPTER 12

"I must ask you more about your visions and your prophecies," Monnet said when he again sat opposite Nicole in the parlor the next day. Her girlish face looked drawn and tired. He felt uneasy about playing the inquisitor, but he knew that he was approaching the part of the story that held the most danger for her.

"You told Father de Souzy that an angel had brought you communion."

"Yes I did."

"Some people believe that Father de Souzy was simply mistaken about how many Hosts he had prepared, and when you heard that he thought one Host was missing, you then simply invented the angel."

"That is not true. I was not well that morning and slept late. I felt guilty when I realized that I would be too late for Mass and I wished with all my heart that an angel would bring me communion. I had heard that this was a favor once granted to a saint. I must have slipped into a trance and in that state I saw an angel bringing me the Host. Later, when Father de Souzy told me about the missing wafer, I *knew* that this had actually happened to me."

Monnet let it go at that and turned to the recovery of the stolen relic of Saint Geneviève. How had she known where it had been buried? He expected her once again to insist that she had *seen* the place in her mind, but this time the explanation was quite different. She had attended Mass at Sainte-Geneviève and had become so deeply lost in her prayers that she remained behind long after everyone else had left. Where had he heard of such an incident before? It had happened to Barbe, years ago, he remembered.

Nicole was roused from her state by sudden footsteps and low voices. She peered through the gloom of the empty church and saw the shapes of three men at the altar. She heard the sounds of a container being pried open and observed one of the men lifting some object, wrapping it in a cloth. She was puzzled but moments later realized that the object must be a reliquary. The men turned to leave and in their haste failed to notice Nicole, who had pressed herself deep into the shadows. After a few moments she followed the men out into the church square and, still unnoticed, pursued them at a safe distance until they reached the Cemetery of the Innocents.

"Why did you do that?" interrupted Monnet. "You could have given the alert and the thieves would have been caught."

"Something told me not to. I believe it was Saint Geneviève herself who wanted me to keep quiet."

"Well," said Monnet, "the saint certainly gave you useful advice. It allowed you to take credit for yet another miracle and all of Paris admired you even more."

"That is true," she said. "I did want Paris to admire me and my works. I wanted this not for myself but to strengthen the faith and have my message accepted."

"Many people will not believe that, Nicole. They will especially doubt your story that an angel—another angel—transported you to Tours and back within an hour."

Nicole twisted in her chair. From the nearby river drifted the shouts of bargemen and the creaking of a sawmill, sudden reminders of the outside world. Finally she said, "I was afraid that I was no longer trusted by Madame Acarie. I felt I had to do something to restore her faith in me. I had heard that the king was in Tours and there were always rumors of this or that plot against the throne or the Church. And so, I thought, how glorious it would be if I could be taken to Tours and give the king some warning against—I was not sure just against what. I thought that if I told Madame Acarie of such a mission, she would be impressed and forget her doubts about me. But I was wrong. The opposite happened."

Here, then, was a flat admission of deceit. Monnet was not truly surprised, but he could not suppress a surge of anger.

"I think it was very foolish of you, Nicole, to make up such an elaborate story," he said sharply.

She stared at him.

"I was afraid that if Madame Acarie stopped believing in me, so would everyone else."

She gave him a look that he took to mean "I really told you all this before but let me explain it again."

She spoke quietly, intensely. "I pray with the sick and I see hope coming into their eyes. I listen to their sins and I hear comfort in their breath. People ask me about some future event and when I see the outcome in my mind and tell them about it, I sense their relief. I face a crowd and bring them the words that come to me, telling them to mend their lives, and I see them looking back at me with hope. At those times I feel close to God and know that He touches me. But that sensation does not last. I soon find my faith flickering out again like a fading lamp and I am left in the dark, a terrible dark, without God or His saints."

Monnet's anger began to abate.

"The only way I can get out of that dark," she continued, "is to find another chance to preach, to heal, to prophesy."

"Or to fake a miracle," he said.

Nicole did not answer but silently began to weep. He thought the tears were prompted by resentment rather than contrition.

"Why is it," she said, "that faith is given so easily to others, like Madame Acarie, and not to me? In faith, I am so poor and she is so rich. Why is that? Why has God made it so difficult for me to be close to Him?"

Monnet did not know how to answer that. His immediate concern was how she should act and what she should say during her impending examination.

"When you are questioned, just tell the truth as you have told it to me."

She suddenly looked horrified. "I have only told it to you because I trust you," she said. "I will never repeat these things to anyone else."

On his way back from Longchamp, he tried to collect his thoughts. Must he now dismiss Nicole simply as a fraud? He could not quite bring himself to do it. Obviously her aim was not money nor fame and importance in the usual sense. But could she really feel close to God by cheating?

He put the question to Father Coton.

"I agree with you that she is no ordinary fraud," said the priest. "Not like many I have known who were simply looking for attention and maybe a few livres. I think she is one of those people who, try as they might, have great difficulty in believing."

"Sometimes I feel like that myself," Monnet said.

"To make herself believe," Coton continued, "she needs the feeling that others believe in her. It strikes me as a kind of self-intoxication. Like most people who rely on intoxicants, she apparently needs more and more of it."

"I am sure you are right," he said. "But where does that leave Nicole? I told her that when she is examined, she ought to tell the truth. Being exposed as a fraud, as I understand it, would at least save her from the charge that she is bedeviled. But I think she would rather die than admit publicly that she is guilty of some fakery."

"Actually," said Coton, "having her exposed as a fraud would not be the best outcome. It would certainly not serve the king's interests."

"So as you have seen, Sire, the evidence can support different courses," said Monnet as he concluded his account. "Those who believe in her can make a case that she is indeed genuine, but we also now know that she is a faker, at least in some respects."

Henry snorted impatiently. "Is that the only conclusion you come to?"

Unperturbed, Monnet continued. "But there is also evidence that could be used to show that Nicole Tavernier was possessed."

The king's irritation was mounting. "We knew that much before you started your investigation. The question I had hoped you would help me with is what, if anything, I should do about this case."

"I do have some advice on that, Sire," said Coton. "I believe that there is a course of action that will serve you as well as keep her safe."

"Well, let me hear it," said the king.

Coton resumed. "Let us consider what would happen if Nicole were to be exposed as a fraud. She would be disgraced, but more important, from your point of view, Sire, you might be forced to intervene in a secular case of fraud, which is precisely what you want to avoid."

"Exactly," said the king. "Besides, it would not be a good thing for you and your religious colleagues either. From the archbishop down, all of you praised her and proclaimed her to be a near-saint. What would people think of you if she were suddenly declared to be a fraud?"

"I take your point, Sire. The best outcome, for all concerned, would be if it could be shown that she was, in fact, diabolically possessed, against her will. Then, if the Devil could be observed to leave her, if he were visibly expelled from her body, no blame would attach to anybody."

Henry looked doubtful. "Surely people would still say that the churchmen who earlier praised her—including yourself—had been fooled."

"It is one thing to be deceived by the ruses of a young woman," replied Coton, "and quite another to be deceived by the Devil himself."

"I agree with Father Coton," said Monnet. "I know the mood of Paris. To have the demon expelled from Nicole would be a very satisfying solution."

"You mean that she should be exorcised?" asked Henry. "I do not want a big public show, as with Brossier."

"I think the archbishop could be persuaded to appoint me to that task," replied Coton. "If so, I can promise that everything will happen fast and without a spectacle."

"But with all due respect," said the king, "how can you be sure that your exorcism will succeed?"

"I can only do my best," said Coton.

"I am sure you will succeed," said Monnet.

CHAPTER 13

At Father Coton's direction the exorcism was not to take place in the chapel at Longchamp but, for greater privacy, in the room of the mother superior. It was a spacious room with a tile floor and a large fireplace. On one wall there were two paintings: the convent's founder, Isabelle de France, pale and angelic-looking, and her brother the king, Saint Louis, white of beard, in the posture of a penitent washing the feet of the poor. A cloth-covered table bore two heavy candlesticks. It was a quite ordinary, not to say banal, setting, but it gave Monnet a chilled sense of foreboding. An exorcism required the presence of a physician, and Coton had chosen Monnet, who had arrived ahead of everyone else. A group had now formed around the table: Father Coton, Pierre Bérulle and two Capuchins in their brown robes. Off to one side stood Father de Souzy. Although his authority as Nicole's spiritual director had been obviously superseded by Father Coton, he had asked for permission to witness the proceedings. In a corner sat a scribe with paper and ink before him. And there was Barbe, seated in an armchair, her bad leg resting on a footstool. A nun brought in Nicole and placed her in another chair. She was pale and plainly frightened. She slowly glanced around the room, looking startled when she saw de Souzy and pleased when she saw Monnet. Her eyes rested longest on Barbe, whose face was impassive. Father Coton made the sign of the cross and in a brief prayer invoked the guidance of the Holy Spirit.

"We are here at the behest of His Eminence, the archbishop, to consider the case of Nicole Tavernier, who is suspected of performing certain acts inspired by the Devil. We are to determine whether this person should be exorcised so that, by God's mercy, for the salvation of her soul, any evil spirits might be driven out. Father Bérulle, whom His Eminence has appointed as my assistant in this matter, will conduct the examination."

Pierre Bérulle squared his shoulders as if to take up a heavy burden and stepped forward. Although he had originally attempted to defend Nicole, he had given that up, unwilling to defy Barbe Acarie's judgment. When the archbishop named him to assist Father Coton, he felt flattered and eagerly took to his task.

Slowly, glancing at a piece of paper from time to time, he led Nicole through the list of her miracles and visions. Did she, in fact, receive an inexhaustible supply of bread from a supernatural source? Did she receive communion from an angel? Did she heal people who were sick and did she have knowledge of future and distant events? Did she recover a stolen relic of Saint Geneviève? Was she transported from Meudon to Tours and back in less than an hour? Each time Nicole answered "yes."

Finally Father Coton spoke, turning to Barbe.

"Madame, is there anything you wish to add?"

Throughout Bérulle's examination, Barbe had been silent. Now she was more than ready to respond to Father Coton's question. With some difficulty she rose from her chair and began to speak.

"In all humility before you learned servants of Christ, I say: 'She is either a fraud or possessed by the Devil.' "

Nicole jumped up, extending her arms as if to ward off a blow. "Not the Devil, not the Devil," she said. "My powers come from God."

"Someone so favored by God would not have lied and tried to deceive me," said Barbe.

The two women faced each other as if they were about to engage in a duel, but Nicole said quietly, "Why are you doing this to me?"

Barbe did not answer and the nun took her by the arm and placed her back in the chair.

Returning to his task, Bérulle laboriously summarized Nicole's deeds and said with a glance at the scribe, "She not merely admits having performed these acts, she brazenly proclaims her role in them. Moreover they have been widely observed by many reputable persons. Normally, in such a proceeding, witnesses would be called to confirm her testimony, but that was considered superfluous in this case."

Bérulle was obviously speaking for the record being kept by the monk who was scribbling in his corner.

"Besides this evidence," Bérulle continued, "there are certain tests recommended by Holy Mother Church to determine a demonic presence."

He then read a Latin passage from scripture and asked Nicole whether she understood it. She nodded and translated it fluently. Monnet knew that a knowledge of Latin or other languages in a presumably uneducated person was considered evidence of diabolic possession. He was strongly tempted to interrupt and to explain how Nicole had come by her knowledge of Latin. But he realized that even if he succeeded in eliminating this one count against her, there would be enough other evidence to sustain the case. Besides, he knew that Coton—and the king—wanted exorcism as a way to end the affair of Nicole Tavernier.

Bérulle next read out a passage from scripture, this time in French, and asked Nicole what it meant to her. She obviously did not realize that this was another trap, but even if she did she was probably too proud of her knowledge to hide it. She gave a cogent interpretation in accurate and well-chosen words. This too would be taken as evidence against her. Monnet found it hard to accept that her insight, which only a few months ago was taken as proof of her holiness, was now seen as proof of the opposite.

"There is yet another test, the one involving sensitivity of the body, or its lack."

With that Bérulle turned to Monnet. He was about to ask him to examine Nicole to determine whether any part of her was impervious to pain. Monnet dreaded the idea of having to poke Nicole from head to foot with a sharp instrument, and fortunately Father Coton intervened.

"In my experience as an exorcist, I have never found this method very reliable. I think we can dispense with it."

Bérulle was about to protest but thought better of it.

At that point de Souzy decided to speak. "With the deepest respect, Father," he said to Coton, "should we not consider the fact that we have failed to see the usual signs of possession, such as bodily contortions and foul language?"

Coton was ready for this, and he too was now speaking for the record.

"It is well known that the Devil is apt to disguise himself and to avoid the more violent manifestations, even making it appear that the subject is not possessed at all. I believe we must proceed to exorcism. If she has been involuntarily possessed and has not deliberately engaged herself to the Devil, and it is God's will, the Evil One will leave her."

Coton ordered the room to be made ready for the impending rite and started to walk out with Bérulle.

Nicole had listened quietly to all this almost as if her mind were elsewhere. But now her old fierceness seemed to be rekindled. Her eyes assumed a wild look.

"I do not need to be exorcised!" she cried. "I have had nothing to do with the Devil or he with me!"

Coton looked at her, made the sign of the cross and left the room.

Nicole took several steps toward Barbe. "Madame," she began.

Monnet expected her to plead with Barbe and he believed Barbe expected this too. But Nicole said only, "Madame, I forgive you."

Jolted, Barbe sank back into her chair.

The nun who had brought in Nicole now returned and led her back to her cell, accompanied by Monnet. He had been instructed to examine her to make sure that she had no illness that might explain her case and that she was well enough to undergo the rigor of an exorcism. He had long since concluded that Nicole was physically healthy but went through the routine of examining her again.

He also wanted to prepare her for her coming ordeal. He had never witnessed an exorcism and he had asked Coton what to expect. The priest outlined the ritual and said, "If it is to be considered a success, there must be some sign that the Fiend has left the possessed, some physical sign. Sometimes this can be quite dramatic. Afterward the behavior of the subject is expected to change. For instance, if the person continues to display unusual knowledge—of scripture or Latin or some other foreign tongue— that is taken as a sign that the exorcism has not worked."

Monnet repeated this warning to Nicole while he examined her, but he was not sure that she would heed it.

"Nicole, do not be frightened and do not resist. The exorcism can only help you. It is meant to prove that you have been possessed against your will."

She shuddered, her eyes wide with fear. Before he could say anything more, a nun summoned them back to the mother superior's room.

Most movable objects, including the two heavy candlesticks and the pictures on the wall, had been taken away because of the expectation that unseen violent forces might make objects fly through the air and injure the participants. A bowl of holy water had been placed on the table along with a crucifix and two small votive lights. Two more nuns came in and placed Nicole in an armchair. They took up positions behind her in case it might be necessary to restrain her. Finally, Fathers Coton and Bérulle reappeared, white surplices over their black robes. A purple stole was draped around Coton's neck.

In the hushed room, invoking the Father, the Son and the Holy Spirit, Coton asked protection for himself and all present. He sprinkled holy water, knelt and began to pray. He recited the

Litany of the Saints and the Lord's Prayer. He then continued, alternating with Bérulle.

"Save this woman, Your servant. Because she hopes in You, my God. Be a tower of strength for her, O Lord. In the face of the Enemy. Let the Enemy have no victory over her. And let the Son of Iniquity not succeed in injuring her."

More prayer and yet more. Monnet lost all sense of time. Such is the power of the imagination that he could have sworn he smelled incense although none was used.

"Unclean Spirit! Whoever you are, and all your companions who possess this servant of God," intoned Coton, "tell me, with some sign, the day and hour of your damnation. Obey me in everything although I am an unworthy servant of God."

Coton's voice was alternately harsh and gentle, commanding and imploring. The drone of his words filled Monnet's brain.

Carefully, Coton touched Nicole's neck with the tip of his stole and placed his right hand on her head. Nicole's eyes were closed and she shivered at his touch. Pointing to the cross that was embroidered on the stole, he pronounced, "Behold the Cross of the Lord. Depart, Enemies! Jesus with ancient strength, with noble power, is conqueror."

The words flowed on. Monnet, leaning against the wall next to the fireplace, kept his eyes fixed on the priest bending over the recoiling figure. The rest of the room seemed to fall away. He was spellbound.

Coton's voice rose. "I exorcise you, Most Unclean Spirit! All Spirits! Every one of you! In the name of our Lord Jesus Christ. He who commands you is He who ordered you to be thrown down from the highest Heaven into the depths of Hell. Be uprooted and expelled from this Creature of God. Get out, Seducer! Full of guile and falseness! Enemy of Virtue! Persecutor of the innocents! Prince of cursed homicides! Author of incest! Head of all the sacrilegious! Master of the most evil actions! Teacher of heretics! Inventor of all obscenity! Go out therefore, Impious One! Go out, criminal!"

As Monnet was listening to this litany of invective, familiar satanic images crept into his mind: the horned head, the ghastly or sly grimace, the smoldering eyes, the fanged serpent.

What happened next was stunning. Flames appeared in the fireplace and ran across the room to the opposite wall amid an explosion and a ghastly stench.

Father Coton himself seemed startled by the eruption of flames, but he proclaimed that it signaled the expulsion of the Evil One. Exhausted but joyful, he offered a final prayer.

"We pray You, all-powerful God, that the Evil Spirit have no more power over this servant of Yours, Nicole, but that it flee and not come back."

As if to make absolutely sure, Bérulle addressed a few words in Latin to Nicole and asked her to interpret some lines from scripture. She stared at him in confusion. In a hoarse voice she uttered a few incoherent words and then fell silent. Monnet realized that his warning to her about not displaying her knowledge had probably been unnecessary. She was dazed and on the point of collapse. The nuns helped her from the room.

Monnet looked at Barbe, expecting her to radiate satisfaction. After all, she must feel that she had been vindicated. He imagined her facing her husband and saying in effect, "Do you see? I was right."

But her face was solemn and without any hint of triumph as she approached Father Coton. "You have done God's work, Father," she said.

Father de Souzy seemed almost as shaken as Nicole. He turned to Coton. "Please forgive my doubts. I did not believe that she was possessed, but after what we have just seen, who could question it?"

The Devil's flaming exit would soon be talked about all over Paris and eventually make its way into the history books. None of the eyewitnesses who described the scene over and over again connected the trail of gunpowder, the fire, the explosion, with the physician who had been standing near the fireplace. They would have been amazed to learn that, in his other role as a spy, he had become adept at many things beyond the medical profession, including the uses of chimneys and gunpowder.

Monnet was concerned about Nicole and made his way back to her cell. He found her stretched out on her cot and asked the nun who was watching over her to leave him alone with his patient.

Nicole stared at him, still frightened and confused. "All those terrible words about the Devil," she said, as if trying to remember. "That cold hand on my head and then the fire. Did it really happen?"

"Everybody saw it, Nicole."

"And they think they drove the Devil out of me?" she said, some of her strength returning. "I tell you there was no Devil. I do not believe that I was possessed."

"But the Church has said so and Paris will believe it. You had best accept that."

At that point Father Coton came into the cell. As he approached the cot, Nicole shrank from him.

"You need not be afraid," he said. "Not anymore. You are free and no one will hurt you—as long as you do not fall back into your old ways."

"What does that mean?"

"It means that you must no longer preach or try to heal people or foretell the future." He looked at her gravely. "It means that you must not speak of angels bringing you communion or claim other such miracles."

"But these things may simply happen to me, whether I will it or not."

"They must not happen," said Coton sternly. "Otherwise it will be assumed that the Devil is still in you after all."

Nicole looked desperate. "But you are taking everything from me, everything that is dear to me, everything that makes me feel close to God."

"God is always close if you have enough faith."

Nicole put her hands over her eyes to suppress her sobs. At a loss to say anything else, Coton again made the sign of the cross and left.

Monnet told Nicole to rest and promised to return early the following day so that they could talk about what she might do next. He thought that he could get her work in a hospital or as a housekeeper.

The next morning, when he reached Nicole's cell, he found it empty. He went to the mother superior, and she instituted a search throughout the convent. Nicole was nowhere to be found. She had obviously slipped away unobserved. Monnet assumed that she no longer wanted to have anything to do with any of them, and although he was hurt by the thought, he could not really blame her.

CHAPTER 14

They say Nicole is gone. The nuns looked for her everywhere, but she just disappeared."

"She couldn't just disappear. I bet the priests are hiding her somewhere because they are embarrassed. They were wrong about her. They kept praising her. They said she was saintly and doing God's work. And then it turns out she was possessed."

"I hear she drowned in the river."

"That is not what I hear. I believe the Devil took her away."

"Nonsense. Don't you know that she was exorcised and the Devil was driven out of her?"

"How do we know that?"

"They tell me that she let out a huge scream and while her mouth was open the Devil jumped out."

"Out of her mouth? I don't believe it. Someone who was there told me that the Devil burst out of her belly. At any rate there was a fire and a huge stink and he left."

"How can we be sure he really left?"

"That Jesuit said so and he knows his business."

"Devil or not, I am sorry she is gone. She did many good things for people."

"Well, I think she was just a faker. Good riddance, I say."

• • •

Rumors about Nicole started immediately after she disappeared from the convent and continued for weeks. The year 1599 came to an end, but only a few people pondered that the world was entering a new century. (Pedants, of course, insisted that this new century would not really begin until the following year.) On New Year's Day, as was customary, the king distributed presents to courtiers and officials, and so did the heads of many lesser households. Pierre Acarie was generous. Barbe received a holy medal showing the Trinity in shining gold. Dr. Monnet's gift was a fine, white linen shirt. On Twelfth Night, the Acarie family and several friends gathered for a large meal that ended with the appearance of a special cake. By tradition the cake contained a bean, and whoever found it in his portion would be crowned the bean king and wear a wreath for the rest of the evening. To his embarrassment, it was Monnet who found the bean and was thus crowned amid much merriment.

Yet despite the good cheer, he felt a vague sense of unease and realized that it was caused by the memory of what had just been done to Nicole. As the months wore on, he often woke in the morning with the feeling that something was wrong, that he was neglecting some task or duty. Again the cause was Nicole. For a long time she had been such a presence in his life, and he had been so preoccupied with trying to understand and help her, that her absence left a void.

He was not alone in this emotion.

Pierre for one often wondered out loud what might have become of Nicole. Even the king asked about her several times. Barbe never mentioned her.

One afternoon in the late spring, walking with Monnet in the Acarie garden, Andrée said, "You have seemed out of sorts lately, Doctor. I believe that you miss Nicole."

He thought he detected a note of jealousy in the remark.

"I do think of her often," he admitted. "I can't help being concerned about her."

"We were all taken in by her for a time, but I am surprised that you still are. No matter what they said, after she was exorcised, I believe she was simply a fraud."

Monnet was startled by Andrée's asperity. He said, "I do not blame you for believing that, but the matter is not so simple."

Andrée shrugged to show that she was dropping the subject. She stopped for a moment in front of a rosebush and inhaled with pleasure.

"Let me ask you another question: Why do you spend so much time with us? I am always glad to see you and so is everyone else, but it does strike me as strange how often you are here."

"I have cared about Barbe ever since the time when she first became my patient. You remember that, of course."

Andrée was not satisfied with that answer. "It seems to me that the Acaries really have become your second family."

"You may be right. I have no family of my own. I was the only child to survive infancy, and my parents died long ago."

Andrée said thoughtfully, "I think you are a lonely man."

"Well, I always feel less lonely when I am talking to you, Andrée. You are another reason why I spend so much time here."

Monnet stopped himself abruptly. He realized that what he considered a merely playful remark might be misconstrued by Andrée. He sensed that she would welcome a proposal. It had often occurred to him that Andrée would make a very good wife—if he wanted one, which he did not. He had always been content with the companionship of undemanding women—discreet wives or widows who were satisfied with good company and the pleasures of the bed.

He said nothing further to Andrée. They were friends, he told himself, and that was enough. As for Barbe, he wondered whether she had really found it so easy to put Nicole out of her mind.

Some weeks later, Andrée sat reading to Barbe. Barbe had found that small print strained her eyes these days and she enjoyed listen-

ing to Andrée's smooth, precise voice. The book from which Andrée was now reading troubled her.

Saint Teresa of Ávila had died almost two decades before. Her
writings had recently been translated into French from Spanish,
and some of Barbe's clerical friends had recommended them to
her. Teresa had led a remarkable life. In her early years she oscil-
lated between piety and frivolity. She accused herself of always
wanting to be well thought of and of being anxious for "splendor
and effect." In short, of vanity. She entered a Carmelite convent
and suffered many long, mysterious illnesses. She found that the
once austere and contemplative rule of the Carmelite order had
given way to scandalously lax and worldly ways.

She conceived the idea of starting a reformed version of the
Carmelite order, closer to its origins. The nuns would be bound to
poverty, would never leave the cloister, would not be distracted
from their prayers by visitors or music and would go without
shoes, wearing only thin, canvas slippers.

The Lord Himself, she said, had ordered her to do this, but all
earthly authorities furiously opposed her plan. She persisted with
guile and passion until in the end she succeeded, and her new
order, the Discalced, or shoeless, Carmelites, spread throughout
Spain.

By her account she had many conversations with God, referring
to Him sometimes as "His Majesty," on other occasions in the ardent terms evoking a loving father or spouse. He once told her:
"Now you are mine and I am yours."

She saw Jesus many times "with the eyes of my soul." Once He
thanked her for her devotion and placed a crown on her head.

Satan was no stranger to her either. She had a terrifying and
quite original vision of Hell.

"The entrance seemed to me like a very long, narrow passage or
a low dark and constricted furnace. The ground appeared to be
covered with a filthy, wet mud that smelt abominably and contained many wicked reptiles. At the end was a cavity scooped out
of the wall, like a cupboard, and I found myself closely confined
in it. . . . I felt a fire in my soul."

As Andrée went on reading day after day, Barbe listened attentively but with skepticism and even distaste. "So many visions," she remarked to Andrée. "I am amazed that the Holy Mother found time for anything else."

She had always distrusted visions and revelations. In Barbe's own ecstasies, she experienced an inner illumination without, however, seeing God, let alone conversing with Him. But gradually she was won over by Teresa's piety, her passionate devotion and her success in organizing a new religious order.

One day when Andrée sat down with Barbe to resume her reading, she found Barbe distraught.

"Not today," said Barbe. "I do not want to hear any more today."

Andrée asked what was troubling Barbe. She replied after some hesitation, "I have had a very unsettling experience. I am not sure how to tell you this."

"Surely there is nothing you cannot tell me," said Andrée.

After another pause, Barbe said, "I have had a vision. A vision of blessed Teresa. While I was at prayer last night I suddenly saw her."

Andrée was amazed. The woman who so distrusted visions now claimed to have had a vision herself.

"How do you know it was Saint Teresa?"

"I only saw her as if in a dim light, but I know it was the saint because she talked to me."

Andrée exclaimed. "*Talked* to you!"

"Yes, she talked to me. She told me that I must establish the Discalced Carmelites in France. 'Just as I enriched Spain with this Order, you must bring the same benefit to France,' she said. And she added some very kind words about my restoring piety in our country."

Andrée still had Teresa's book in her hands. "Are you sure that your vision did not come from this?" she said, holding out the volume. "We have been reading from Saint Teresa for days. Are you sure that your vision was not just a dream or merely your imagination?"

"I am sure," replied Barbe. Immediately she began to carry out

Teresa's command. It did not prove easy. The Spanish Carmelites were reluctant to have branches in other countries, especially in France, which was still considered rife with heresy. When negotiations stalled, Barbe turned to her cousin, Father Bérulle, for help. She knew that he had acquired a growing reputation as a thinker, an advocate of reforms in the priesthood and an occasional envoy on diplomatic missions for the court. Having constantly seen him for years, she had not noticed the gradual changes in him. Now she realized that his soft brown eyes had hardened; his forehead seemed higher and more imposing under a receding hairline. His attitude was assertive.

"I believe your emissaries in Madrid have been very inept," he declared. "I have no doubt that I could do better."

And so, eventually, he did.

But there was another problem. The king would have to endorse the new establishment in France. Barbe asked for an audience.

Henry, who had taken pains to stay on good terms with Barbe, welcomed her cordially.

"I trust, Madame, that you have received my latest contribution."

The king was referring to his habit of sending Barbe his winnings from the gaming table as a gift for her charities.

"I have indeed, Sire, and I cannot thank you enough for your generosity. However, I am here to presume on that generosity even further. I would beg Your Majesty's approval for a certain plan I have conceived."

"A plan? What do you have in mind?"

"Sire, I hope to establish a branch of the Teresian Order of the Discalced Carmelites in your kingdom and bring in nuns from Spain to do so."

Henry was surprised. He had expected to be asked to support some new hospital or shelter for the poor, or perhaps for some favor benefiting Pierre Acarie. He knew that Acarie was a man adrift now, and never one to bear grudges, the king would have been quite ready to do a good turn for the former Leaguer. But he had not expected that Barbe Acarie would ask him to back a new religious order—of all things.

"With due respect, Madame, we already have a great many religious orders in France. Too many, some would say. Do we really need another one?"

"Unfortunately, Your Majesty, many of the existing orders are in sad decline. They have long been too lax, too idle, too worldly. They are an affront to God."

She did not have to point out to Henry, the former Protestant, that this situation had been one of the causes of the Reformation.

Moral reform in French convents was not of urgent interest to a monarch who had been the lover of at least two nuns, whom he later rewarded with their own abbeys. As Barbe spoke, Henry could not help recalling a visit to a convent of the Augustinian Daughters of Saint Louis, whose prioress appeared, powdered and scented, in fashionable clothes with silk stockings and gilded garters. However, he politely asked Barbe, "How would this new order be different from the others?"

"The sisters would not be secular nuns, teaching or treating the sick. Such work is very important, but this order would be different. The nuns would be completely cloistered and would lead hard, silent and simple lives devoted only to contemplation and prayer. They would be praying for the redemption of the sins of the world."

"A formidable task," said the king. "And undoubtedly worthy. But do we really need nuns from abroad to do this? Especially from Spain? You know very well that Spain has been my enemy and the enemy of France for years. Must piety be imported? Can't you find holy enough nuns in this country?"

"Sire, these Spanish sisters will be here only for a time to train our own young women to follow the rules of Saint Teresa."

Mollified, Henry said, "I will think about it."

To reinforce her case Barbe enlisted several aristocratic ladies, who also pleaded with the king.

As usual, the decision required the most delicate political calcu-lations. If he approved Barbe Acarie's request, he would anger his Protestant followers, many of whom had never forgiven him for joining the Church of Rome. If he rejected her request, he would anger the Catholics, many of whom had never quite forgiven him for having been a Protestant in the first place. After carefully weigh-ing the issue he decided that the balance favored the Catholic side, and he sent word to Barbe that the Discalced Carmelites would be permitted in France.

"If they are to pray to redeem the sins of the world, Madame," he wrote to her, "I take comfort to think that this will include my own many sins as well."

Barbe Acarie plunged into the enterprise. She found wealthy patrons who contributed influence and money. Some did so for the sake of prestige, because backing religious houses was an ac-cepted and admired way of shining in society. Others acted out of sincere conviction that they were doing God's work, and, in the process, ensuring their own future entry into Heaven, which was even better than society. Most of them were driven by a mixture of both motives.

Barbe's project was favored by the spirit of the times. After decades of corruption and bloodletting, the Catholic Church in France was experiencing a powerful revival. Religious orders were gradually reformed; lax and illiterate priests were slowly replaced by men of better character and education. Along with reform came a strong wave of spirituality. Mystics and inspired preachers flourished, many of them part of Barbe Acarie's circle.

Barbe bought a property with the financial aid of noble ladies to house what she hoped would be the first of many convents, an abandoned Benedictine priory, Notre Dame des Champs, at the edge of the Faubourg Saint-Jacques. She supervised the necessary renovations and, despite her bad leg, she could often be seen on the scaffolding correcting and encouraging the workmen. At the same time she selected French girls who would eventually enter the new order. She was quick and firm in making her selections. She rejected some because she felt that they had no true vocation or that they were insincere. She ignored rank or money, sometimes choosing shopkeepers' daughters over noble women. Barbe housed these future postulants—a dozen or so—in the Acarie mansion until the convent was ready.

Throughout all this Pierre was a disgruntled bystander.

"No doubt it is a very worthy goal to bring the Teresian Order to France, but look what it does to this household," he would complain to anyone who would listen. "Not only do we have a constant stream of callers who want my wife's advice, and not only is she busy with her charities, but now she is also founding a convent and filling our house with future nuns!"

Barbe ignored these complaints. She felt that she had always done her duty toward her husband; now she had other duties as well.

Pierre's sense of having become a superfluous man was aggravated by another circumstance: because of Barbe's injury, he had not shared her bed for years. Dr. Monnet had advised him that Barbe's health would not allow another pregnancy without endangering her life. This was obviously not her fault, but in his mind Pierre could not help blaming her. Many men in his position would have taken a mistress, but he was too upright and perhaps too worried about his reputation to permit himself that relief. It was ironic, therefore, that Pierre was suddenly surrounded by a cluster of young girls, mostly attractive, living in his own house.

He made the most of it and spent a great deal of time with them. He teased them, joked with them, regaled them with stories of his past. They put up with him amiably enough, with the exception of one Anne de Viole, an earnest, high-strung young woman from an aristocratic family, whose pale, somewhat pinched face wore a look of permanent disapproval. She was not charmed by Pierre and she had a difficult time with Barbe's rigorous way of preparing her candidates for the religious life. Barbe insisted that the postulants do manual work, regardless of their standing in the world, and Mademoiselle de Viole was obliged to clean shoes, sweep floors and wash clothes.

This rigid regime was often interrupted by Pierre. Whether he realized it or not, it was his way of rebelling against Barbe, much as had been his championing of Nicole Tavernier.

"You are much too pretty to become nuns," he might say, or, "Won't you miss me when you are behind those cloistered walls?"

Barbe discovered him one day dancing with a particularly vivacious young woman, his face flushed and his beard in disarray. Within a few days she moved her future nuns to the Acarie estate at Ivry, outside Paris.

Soon the first house of the Discalced Carmelites was established in France. Others followed quickly. Flocks of young women, many of whom had been raised in luxury by their rich families, were caught up in the new spiritual ferment; turning their backs on comfort, they were drawn to the austere and harsh life of the Carmelites. The fact that it was not easy to be admitted—the convents were small and there were long waiting lists—made the order even more attractive.

Pierre Bérulle and two other priests were appointed by the pope to supervise the French Carmelite convents. But Barbe remained the guiding spirit of the order. She was regularly asked for advice and judgment. That is how she became involved in the case of a novice, Madeleine de Sully de la Rochepot.

Madeleine was a young woman of excellent family but very poor reputation. Despite her youth she was notorious for having many lovers, and so she stunned everyone in her circle when she announced that she wanted to join the Carmelites. Her own father resisted the idea, and the order was not eager to admit her. At that point Pierre Bérulle became interested in the situation. He met Madeleine and decided that she had a true calling. The superiors of the Carmelites as well as her family still insisted that Madeleine was not fit for the religious life, but Bérulle would not give up. He went to see his friend Father Coton and asked for his support. Coton gave him a quizzical look.

"This is a strange request," he said. "You seem to have an odd affinity for these difficult cases, these young women of dubious vocation. I remember your efforts for that Benedictine nun whom you tried to prevent from leaving the convent. And you have not forgotten how that turned out."

But Bérulle was not to be deterred, and Coton finally agreed to help. Madeleine was admitted as a novice. After a few weeks she developed violent fits, screaming and thrashing about. For reasons no one could understand, Bérulle saw these as spiritual symptoms and pronounced that she had an extraordinary vocation. The mother superior asked for Barbe's opinion. Without hesitation she declared that the girl was an hysteric and totally unfit for the convent. Madeleine eventually left without taking her vows.

"It seems to me we have been through this before with Charlotte Lasserre," said Barbe. But Bérulle was furious. Rather than admit he had been wrong again, he blamed Barbe for repeatedly interfering. For the first time his deference toward her fell away. His eyebrows contracted in an angry frown.

"I have always respected you, Madame, but you have become high-handed and arrogant. You make these judgments as if you were the pope himself."

Barbe flushed. "Again you have gone too far," she said. But she realized that their mutual nonaggression pact was probably at an end. Something had changed between them, or, she thought, perhaps their bond had never been as strong or real as it had seemed. It did not occur to her then that there might be an element of truth in Bérulle's criticism. Having escaped long ago from her mother's domination, having gradually gained respect and authority in her world, she no longer doubted herself. Above all, she had the approval and special favor of Saint Teresa. In yet another vision, the saint told her that she was very satisfied with Barbe's work and that, as a reward, she would eventually enter the French order of the Discalced Carmelites herself. When Barbe confided this to Andrée, her friend looked startled. Being married and having lived in the world, Barbe could only be a lay sister, and even that could not happen while her husband was alive. Andrée pointed this out to her.

"I know," said Barbe. "I believe that he will die soon."

•   •   •

Rﬞené Monnet continued to feel strangely unsettled. His medical practice had long since become routine and even his activities as a secret informant were less exciting than in the past. While political intrigues continued and always would, religious wars had abated. The king had less need of his services. Besides, René was fifty-three, an age at which it was no longer easy to be a libertine. His current mistress was a distant cousin of Barbe Acarie's, a pretty, plump, cheerful widow he visited regularly, ostensibly to check on her health, which, in fact, was excellent. Somehow these visits were not as pleasurable as they had been.

"My dear, you should get married," she told him one day. "I don't mean to me, I would be too demanding. You should find someone else. Have you thought about Andrée Levoix?"

René had, in fact, thought about her, and his resistance to the idea was weakening. Andrée meant a great deal to him. He appreciated her as a confidante, a good companion with a stable temper, common sense and shrewd insights. All this he would be able to depend on if they were married.

The next morning he called on her at the rue des Juifs.

She was as cheerful as usual, but there was about her face an air of determination.

"I am glad you are here, because it gives me a chance to say good-bye to you," she said.

"But where are you going?" he asked, alarmed.

"Can't you guess? I am joining Barbe's new convent. For some time now Barbe has been training me for this."

He certainly could not have guessed it. He had often seen Andrée with Barbe's postulants, but he had not realized that she was one of them. Andrée had always struck him as devout enough, in a conventional sort of way, but also very matter-of-fact whenever they discussed Barbe's trances or Nicole's wonders or anything else regarding faith. Nothing had suggested to him that, underneath, there might be a spiritual yearning, a desire for the life of a religious. It took him a few moments to collect himself.

"I can't believe it," he finally said. "I can't believe that you really want to be hidden away, separated from everyone who cares about you and whom you care about."

"Forgive me, dear friend," she replied, "but you don't really know whom or what I care about most deeply. Barbe wanted to be a nun since we were children in the convent together. It took me much longer before I felt the same urge. Besides, consider my situation. I am unmarried and past the age of childbearing. Barbe offered me a refuge from my father's misfortune. I was happy to stay with her all these years, and I never would have complained, although it was not easy to live in someone else's house."

There was a touch of bitterness in her voice.

"She does not really need me anymore. Her children are grown, her husband is safe again and she has learned to rely on herself."

Monnet understood that she could not accept the notion of living indefinitely in Barbe's household. Many women in Andrée's position, without money or family to support them, made the same decision and sought a religious refuge from a precarious existence in the world.

Would Andrée still want to take the veil if she had an alternative? He could provide one.

"You say how difficult it has been for you to live in someone else's house. Well, I can offer you your own house and with it my great affection, my loyalty, my support."

She looked at him with astonishment. "You are asking me to marry you?"

"I am. You would make me very happy by saying yes."

Andrée gave an ironic laugh. "You are very clever and quick as a physician, my friend, but as a suitor, you are slow. I am sure you know that I am very fond of you and if you had spoken a few years ago, perhaps my answer might have been different. But it is too late. I have made my decision and I am at peace with it."

At this point Barbe joined them. She must have noticed his crestfallen look, and said, "I see Andrée has told you her news. It is not easy to let her go, I know. I will miss her very much and so will you, Doctor. So will we all. But we must be happy for our Andrée. It is a joyous thing to be a Bride of Christ."

The familiar phrase struck Monnet as ironic: here was a rival he had not anticipated and apparently could not eliminate. In his mind, he berated himself as a fool. He had finally and belatedly decided to propose to Andrée only to lose her to the convent. He managed to pull together some inadequate words of farewell, thanked her for her friendship and wished her well in her new life.

The next day Barbe herself took Andrée to the convent, where she was received by the nuns from Spain. Andrée's hair was cut. The nuns removed her clothes and robed her in the brown habit and white veil of the order and escorted her to the chapel. The prioress intoned a prayer: "When we make our vows, we hold out all that we are or may become, to Him."

Before the altar, Andrée extended her arms as the prioress pronounced: "We stretch out our emptied hands to take hold of the Light of Christ."

The prioress then asked Andrée if she promised obedience, chastity and poverty, and whether she made this pledge of her own free will. Andrée answered, "I do." There were other questions and then she lay facedown on the floor and was covered by a white sheet. This shroud was meant to symbolize the nun's death to the world.

From now on Andrée Levoix would be Sister Andrée of All Saints, and René Monnet would not see her again.

CHAPTER 15

When Nicole slipped out of the convent at Longchamp, all she knew was that she wanted to get away from the place where she had been humiliated and away from Paris, where she had been idolized but would now be scorned. Instinctively, she thought of Reims. This was strange in a way, because she had been miserable there and had fled the town in despair. But she still considered it home and found that she longed for its familiar streets and churches with their ever-ringing bells. Almost blindly she began walking along the road in the direction of Reims. At the end of one weary day, she stopped at a farmhouse to ask for a drink of water, and before she could empty the cup, she collapsed. She was weak and obviously ill. The kindly farmer took her in and allowed her to bed down in his barn, where she spent many days—she did not know how many. Feverish, she drifted in and out of consciousness, gripped by nightmares in which she saw the exorcist looming over her as a huge, black, menacing figure, and a trail of fire coming ever closer. When Nicole recovered she continued her journey.

Mostly she walked, but occasionally some merchant's cart would take her part of the way. She slept in the fields or in abandoned houses. When she finally reached Reims she had no clear idea about where to turn. She knew that she could not go to the house of Monsieur Lapin. And then she thought of the orphanage at Sainte-Claire's.

The nun who opened the door for Nicole was puzzled by this weary, bedraggled and distraught woman.

"If you have a child that you want us to take, you need not come in like this. We have a special way of receiving our charges," she said, and pointed to the opening in the wall.

Nicole, who well remembered the turning box, said, "I know. I came here that way long ago myself. I do not have a child to leave but I want to ask you for a great mercy."

She explained that she had been through a very bad time, that she had no place to go and no money. Could she stay at Sainte-Claire's, at least for a while?

"All I need is a cot or a corner to sleep in and a few bites to eat. In return I will do anything you want me to do. I will clean and wash and care for the babies—anything."

"I am not sure we can do that," said the nun. "But I will be glad to ask my sisters for their advice."

At that point Sister Marie-Margaret appeared. She was the elderly nun who had told Monnet about Nicole.

"Sister," Nicole asked. "Do you remember me? I am Nicole. Nicole Petit, as I was called when I was a child here. It was you who gave me that name."

"I do remember you," said the old nun. "You were a good child."

"I have come back here because I have nowhere else to turn." She repeated her request, adding, "I was married to a carpenter and we lived near here in Châlons, but he was killed. I bore a child, a little boy, but he was born too soon and died after a few hours."

Nicole was not sure how much she should tell about her life since then and about the events in Paris, but Sister Marie-Margaret saved her from having to make that decision. Moved by Nicole's misfortune and her obvious distress, the nun said, "Of course we will take you in. We will do it not only out of charity but because your help will be very welcome. There are only three of us here now and there is a great deal of work to be done. I, for one, am getting quite old and can no longer do as much as I would like."

Nicole was installed in a tiny room, no bigger than a broom closet, and went about her chores. She worked hard and silently. She spoke no more than was necessary to the nuns and when they asked questions about her, she said as little as possible.

The orphanage was even poorer than she remembered and in disrepair. The townspeople were not generous but some merchants sent supplies from time to time—foodstuffs, candles, firewood. Life at Sainte-Claire's went on much as it always had. Occasionally, new infants arrived in the familiar way, and from time to time a benefactor appeared, accompanied by the parish priest, to choose one of the children as a servant. The priest was no longer Father Lebrun, who had guided Nicole to the Lapin household. He had died and been replaced by Father Duplessis, a rotund man with a manner that alternated between servility and arrogance, depending on whom he was dealing with. He had hoped for a better assignment than this poor parish in Reims and he made up for his disappointment by building up his authority in petty ways.

The first time Duplessis saw Nicole at the orphanage, he looked startled. "And who is this?" he asked. Sister Marie-Margaret explained that many years before, Nicole had been one of the children at the orphanage, that she had run into misfortune and that the sisters had given her shelter.

"This strikes me as quite irregular," said the priest. "I should have been consulted. What do you really know about this girl now?" he said, ignoring Nicole.

"I know that she works hard, cares for the children and does every other sort of chore. She is quiet and modest. She helps us more than I can say."

"Well, I hope you are not making a mistake," said Duplessis, clearly not satisfied by the nun's explanation.

Nicole listened to this in silent dismay, afraid that the priest might cause her expulsion from Sainte-Claire's.

For a long time she did not leave the orphanage, but at length she ventured out. Almost against her will she felt drawn toward the old familiar streets and the Lapin house. It appeared as solid and prosperous as ever. As she stood looking at the place where she had lived for years as a servant, a tradesman came out after having made some delivery. Hesitantly, Nicole approached the man.

"This house belonged to Monsieur Lapin," she said. "Is he still alive?"

"He died not long ago," replied the man. "It now belongs to a Monsieur Colbert, who married Lapin's daughter."

Nicole bitterly remembered the daughter, Clarice, who had always harassed her. She wondered what had become of Jacques Lapin, the only one of the children who had treated her well. She found out later that he had been ordained some years before and assigned to a parish in Normandy. If she had seen him again she might have talked to him about her experiences, and she regretted that he was gone. As it was, she continued to keep to herself, utterly alone.

She kept remembering Barbe Acarie, and again and again in her thoughts, Nicole kept asking, "Why did you do this to me?"

She was numb and lost all sense of time; years passed like months. When she had come back to Sainte-Claire's she was twenty-four; now she could scarcely remember how old she was. She avoided going to Mass whenever she could find an excuse, and when she did go her mind and heart were not engaged in the ceremony. She found that she could not pray. She felt none of the old impulse to preach or heal. God was remote, silent. This gave her a sense of permanent loss. She felt it the moment she awoke in the morning, felt it all day long whatever she was doing, felt it in the last moments before falling into restless sleep. But gradually the kindness of the sisters and their appreciation of the work she was doing gave her a sense of comfort, a feeling of being at home.

Then one day a visitor appeared at Sainte-Claire's. "My name is Daniel Carnot," he said to the sister who had opened the door for him. "I am employed by the Colbert family and I am bringing you some things that you might find useful."

Through the still-open door he pointed to a cart outside that contained bundles of cloth. They were remnants of larger bolts. The nuns were delighted, and Sister Marie-Margaret explained how they could now make new clothes for the children and cut new bed linen.

"There will be other things from time to time," said Carnot as one of the nuns and Nicole carried the material inside. Carnot smiled at Nicole.

"And who are you?" he asked. "You do not wear the habit."

Nicole was not accustomed to being spoken to by visitors, and, in some embarrassment, she gave her name, adding, "The good sisters are allowing me to live here."

"And very glad we are to have her," said Sister Marie-Margaret. "She is so much help to us."

"I can see that," Carnot said and went back to his now-empty cart.

Carnot's employers, the Colberts, were one of the richest families in Reims. It was a large clan whose members—uncles, brothers, cousins—lived in various residences. Several of them were responsible for different parts of the business, which they ran from the family headquarters. This was an imposing mansion on the rue Porte Chacre, through whose huge gates rumbled a succession of wagons, stopping in the paved courtyard to load or unload merchandise at a big warehouse. The Colberts carried on a lavish trade, mostly in textiles but also in anything else profitable—salt, grain, wine, herring. They were people of vision whose ambition reached well beyond Reims and its nearby towns. They traded with many distant places elsewhere in France, which involved considerable risk. Roads had often been cut by war and more recently were made unsafe by marauding bands of demobilized soldiers, landless peasants and thugs of every sort. To carry on commerce in such conditions, the Colberts had hired a contingent of armed guards to accompany their precious cargo, and this operation was the responsibility of Gaston, one of the Colbert nephews, who was married to Clarice Lapin. The latest of these guards was Daniel Carnot. He escorted many of the Colbert wagons to and from

their destinations, and he proved so adept at frightening off brig-
ands and finding the safest detours that he was soon supervising the
other guides.

Whenever Daniel returned from one of his trips he found time
to bring supplies to Sainte-Claire's—and to talk to Nicole. He
might help her in the garden as she was trying to bring along the
struggling vegetables or spruce up the feebly blooming plants.
He might lend a hand with her heavier chores or watch her taking
care of the infants. He especially liked to observe her with the
older children, playing with them or giving them simple lessons in
letters or numbers. She was serene at such moments and the children clearly adored her.

The nuns did not object to Daniel's presence. He was, after all,
the bearer of needed gifts, and they liked him because he was
friendly and polite. He was a man of medium height and middle
years, thickset and muscular, with an open face that seemed always
on the point of breaking into laughter. Nicole found it easy to
speak with him. She talked mostly about the children, the sisters,
the needs of the orphanage, her struggles with the garden. Eventually she told him about her childhood in this very orphanage
and how she had gone to work in the household of Monsieur
Lapin, whose son-in-law now employed Daniel. Finally she told
him about her marriage and the death of her child, but nothing
else about her past. Daniel, in turn, told her about his trips, his ad-
ventures on the road, news from the town. He, too, spoke little
about his earlier life. Although they both knew that they were
withholding much from each other, a bond developed between
them. Despite his jovial manner she sensed that, like herself, he was
very much alone, and they both drew comfort from their companionship.

Occasionally, in the midst of a conversation, Nicole would stop
speaking for minutes at a time, her eyes unfocused as if turned inward.

"Where are you?" Daniel might say after a while. "Are you in
another world?"

Nicole would shake her head and with a visible effort return to whatever she had been talking about. Once Daniel found her silently weeping. "What is it?" he asked gently. "Why are you crying? Are you still mourning your husband and your child?"

Nicole collected herself. "No," she replied. "My husband did not turn out to be the man I thought I was marrying and my poor little baby was scarcely alive long enough for me to know him. I am mourning someone else. But please do not ask me anymore."

One day, as they were working in the garden of the orphanage, Daniel started to sing in a low voice. Startled, Nicole strained to make out the words. "What is that you are singing?" she asked.

Daniel seemed embarrassed. "I did not realize I was doing it," he said, and added after a moment, "It was a psalm. A psalm of David. I made up the melody myself."

"Please go on," Nicole said. "I would like to hear it."

Hesitantly, Daniel started to sing again.

"For his anger endureth but a moment; in his favor is life. Weeping may endure for a night, but joy cometh in the morning."

Nicole was delighted. She had never met a layman before so familiar with the psalms, and whenever she saw Daniel she asked him to sing her more verses.

Daniel would continue to surprise her. Once he took her to a morality play that was mounted before Reims Cathedral. Since the time when, as a child, she had taken part in one of these performances, the staging of religious plays had become rare, but deeply devout Reims still occasionally presented them.

This one was about the prodigal son. In high excitement, most of the town came to watch. An elderly notary took the part of the father, a butcher's apprentice played the older son and a young potter was the prodigal. With relish, showing off their homemade costumes, these performers and a large cast of other townspeople enacted the story: the division of the father's fortune, the younger son's departure, his riotous living in a foreign land (that involved some very nearly scandalous scenes), the famine and the son's return. The audience alternately jeered and applauded as the father had the contrite son dressed in a beautiful robe. There were shouts of delight as the fatted calf was brought in amid singing and dancing, and gasps of suspense when the older son appeared and berated the father for treating the bad son so much better than he had ever treated him. Many wept when the father said, "Son, you are always with me and everything I have is yours. But it is right that we should celebrate because your brother was dead and is alive, was lost and is found."

Deeply moved, the crowd began to disperse. As Daniel walked Nicole back to Sainte-Claire's he began to recite some passages from the prodigal son's story, not in the simplified language of the play but in the actual words of Saint Luke as rendered in the French translation of the Bible.

Nicole was enchanted. She herself had acquired her knowledge of Holy Scripture in part by listening to Jacques Lapin's lessons so many years before, but mostly through hearing paraphrases and summaries. Catholic laymen, of course, were allowed to approach the Bible only through the filter provided by a priest. She knew that Protestants read the Bible itself, and relied on it entirely. But in her excitement she failed to connect that fact with Daniel.

CHAPTER 16

Daniel Carnot was born in Amiens, three years before the Saint Bartholomew's Day Massacre, in 1572, when, during three blood-drenched days of riot, thousands of Protestants were killed at the hands of the Catholics. Similar, if less horrible, persecutions occurred elsewhere, and Protestants in many parts of the country felt compelled to flee for their lives. They left in great waves, whole communities going to England, to Switzerland, to Germany or to Protestant enclaves in France, to be among their religious brethren. The Carnots chose Sedan, a small principality not far from the Spanish Netherlands. Its ruler, Prince Henri-Robert de La Marck, was friendly toward the Reformed Church and eventually joined it. Sedan, whose population was half German and half French, soon swelled with Huguenot refugees, among them the Carnots. Daniel's father, Isaac, had been a prosperous and highly skilled clock maker in Amiens and had left all his belongings behind. Like most of the refugees, he and his family dreamed about returning to their old home and recovering their property someday. For the present, Carnot carried on his trade, which was not easy. Despite the prince's benevolence, not all the people of Sedan welcomed the newcomers and many preferred to give their custom to the old, established tradesmen and artisans. Carnot did his best, spending long hours in his shop next to his house on Clock Maker's Street, working with the springs, wheels, weights of clockworks in all shapes and sizes. There were standing clocks styled to look like towers or castles, made of gilt, brass or wood, resting on lions' paws or balls or columns. Young Daniel was occasionally allowed to see the workshop. He was especially intrigued by an odd structure with several dials, moving rings and chimes. When he asked about it his father said, "It is not finished, but someday I will complete it and it will be a wonder."

Over the years old Carnot kept tinkering with this device. Daniel realized that his father was trying to imitate some of the famous clocks he had heard about: the astronomical clock at Hampton Court outside London, which showed not only the time but the phases of the moon and the position of the stars; the huge tower clock in Bern, which displayed the signs of the zodiac and the comparative movement of the sun and the moon as well as the eclipses. This project connected Carnot's trade with his passion for astronomy. Whenever the sky was clear he observed the stars, and when they were hidden he pored over charts of the heavens. He read many almanacs, with their welter of information and often sibyline predictions. He had never heard of the theories of Copernicus and Galileo, which were beginning to find some adherents, and he would have had a hard time accepting the notion that the earth moved around the sun rather than the other way. Even less could he have coped with the view of an itinerant Italian scholar named Giordano Bruno, who believed that there were an endless number of other suns throughout the universe. That would have seemed patently absurd and sacrilegious. To old Carnot, the universe was a huge, divine clockwork, a vast version of the mechanism he was trying to build, and, like it, functioned according to certain fixed principles. It was a reassuring idea that compensated for the violent disorder of the times. Like many others, he tried to read the future in the stars, and especially the day when he and his family might be able to return to Amiens. Somehow that day never came.

Young Daniel grew up amid endless stories about the good old days before the exile, the splendors of France, and the comforts of the Carnots' former lives. But whatever their material circumstances, spiritually the Carnots felt thoroughly at home. Sedan had earned the appellation of "Little Geneva" for its austere, Protestant ways. Taverns were subject to strict rules, blaspheming and swearing were fined, gambling was forbidden. Private charity was banned—whoever needed financial help had to work for it. Theatrical performances were forbidden, and anything was prohibited that might inspire carnal desires: dancing, revealing dresses, finery. Fornicators and adulterers were excommunicated; prostitutes were driven from the town.

From his earliest childhood Daniel became accustomed to the bright, bare Protestant places of worship. Each evening he and his younger brother and sister listened as their father read from scripture and, as they learned to read, the children too recited long passages from the Bible. When friends came to call they would join the Carnots in singing psalms. Like the Bible, these would always remain in Daniel's mind. The inequities of the Roman Church were a constant topic of conversation, the blasphemy of the Mass, the idolatry of worshiping saints.

Daniel accepted his religion without qualms and was devoted to the simplicity and directness of its forms. But he was by nature merry and spirited, and his existence began to seem narrow. He was apprenticed to his father's trade but did not take to it. The constant, repetitive rhythms of the clocks in the small workshop, insistent hour after hour and day after day, irritated him. They seemed to be ticking his life away. He did not share Isaac Carnot's preoccupation with the heavens and was more concerned with what the earth held for him. Sedan did not seem to hold much. He admired the great citadel that loomed over the town with its towers, fortifications, arches, winding stairs and balustrades. Sometimes the gray walls turned ocher in a setting sun, creating the impression of a vision in the clouds. But the town itself, huddling below the citadel and descending toward the sluggish Meuse River, was drab in contrast. As he walked the muddy streets, Daniel was restless. He wanted to see France, about which he had heard so much—wanted to see its towns, its castles, its farms.

One clear, cold, winter night Isaac Carnot had been stargazing and Daniel grew concerned when he did not come back into the house for hours. He went to look and found the old man collapsed on the ground, clutching a sheaf of notes. He had suffered a fatal stroke. Soon after the funeral Daniel decided that there was nothing to hold him in Sedan. His sister was on the point of making an advantageous marriage. True, his mother was now alone, but he knew that his brother would take care of her as he would the clock business.

"He will make a much better thing of it than I," he told his mother. "He has always been more interested in father's trade than I have been. I feel I must get to know France, the country you and Father lost."

"I understand," she said. "But I do not want to lose you. I will worry about you as long as you are away. You do not know the papists as your father and I did. They are cruel as well as crafty. I beg you: trust no one."

Daniel told his mother that things had changed in France since Henry had become king. "No one will hurt me, Mother," he said. "No one will seduce me."

He set out with a light heart and a purse that would keep him going for a few months if he was frugal. He decided first to go to Amiens, the place where he was born. Choosing not the most direct but the safest route, Daniel started his journey on a flat-bottomed boat that carried him and his heavily laden horse down the Meuse. He then joined a group of other travelers and a guide for the trip through the thick Argonne forest. They were enveloped by a weird silence as the horses' hooves were muffled by a deep layer of leaf mold, broken occasionally by the grunting of wild boars, until they emerged into the plains beyond. Thinking back on it, Daniel found that the journey from then on was marked in his memory by the churches he encountered, structures of a grand

sort he had never seen before. In village after village he was astonished by the steeples, the statues of saints (some of them decapi-
tated by his fellow Protestants), the stained-glass windows with
their images, a few of which he recognized from his Bible reading.
Most of all he was overwhelmed, when he reached Reims, by the
city's great cathedral. He took in the accumulation of towers,
gables and pinnacles, the large sweeping arches and the great rose
window, stared at the elaborate stonework representing human beings, animals, flowers and especially, in niches above the buttresses,
graceful angels spreading their wings. One of the angels, on the
left of the porch, stayed in his mind for a long time because of its
sweet, mysterious smile. But the stunning edifice did not inspire
a religious feeling in him; he saw it as a monument to human
achievement. Wandering about inside he saw the painted saints,
the relics, the gilded statues, the clouds of incense he had always
heard denounced. Daniel was intrigued but also affronted. The experience reinforced his attachment to the austere Protestant temples and the plain, French biblical text that had become a part of
him.

Daniel moved on, traveling through the Vesles and Somme val-
leys, toward Amiens. He had only the dimmest childhood recollections of it. Strolling about, he found the town to be a thriving,
prosperous community whose firm Catholic faith was proclaimed
by an impressive Gothic cathedral, impressive but not as over-
powering as the one in Reims. The town was divided by many
branches of the Somme River. On the banks of one of them
Daniel located his parents' house, a two-story, half-timbered structure, solid enough but not quite as splendid as it had been described to him. He stared for a while at the small, heavy door and
the latticed windows, wondering whether he should ask for permission to visit what had been his home as an infant, but decided
against it because he doubted that the Catholic family who now
lived here would welcome him. Everywhere, lawsuits were going
on for the recovery of property lost by one side or the other during the wars, and he might well be suspected of planning such a

suit. He had no thought of trying this because he lacked the patience for a long, complicated and uncertain legal battle.

He thought it was time to find work of some sort, but he was at a loss as to what he might do. He met a traveling peddler, a thin, elderly man with an equally elderly mule that helped him carry the merchandise: trinkets, ribbons, combs, scissors, needles and holy pictures. He offered to train Daniel in his trade and, considering him trustworthy, confided to him in a whisper that he also had some French-language Bibles in his inventory, dangerous though this was. Daniel liked the man but had no intention of becoming a peddler.

He next met two "projectors." One of them was selling tulips, a flower that had recently been brought from Turkey and was fetching huge prices. He wanted to expand his business. The other was betting on a new drink, apple cider, which he hoped to manufacture in large quantities. Daniel was not charmed by the looks of the tulips and he hated the taste of the cider. Besides, he saw quickly that both men were interested in whatever money he might be able to put into their enterprises. Once again Daniel moved on.

He made his way to the coast, traversing several fishing villages and reaching Dieppe, a busy little seaport on the channel. He found work with a maker of nautical instruments, a craft for which he was qualified thanks to his training in his father's workshop. Daniel stayed in Dieppe for a year, interrupting his wanderings. He found the place exciting, with its crowd of sea captains, shipowners and enterprising merchants. There was little religious conflict. He realized that in some parts of France, people of the two faiths lived side by side, more or less peaceably, and even intermarried, while in others, Catholic and Protestant communities were still separate and hostile, with mutual provocations and clashes commonplace.

It was ironic that fate eventually led him back to Reims, the last city to fall to Henry IV and still fiercely Catholic. Even after several years, Daniel realized how strange it was that he worked for a devout Catholic family and spent so much time in the Catholic atmosphere of Sainte-Claire's. (What would his mother have thought!) But he had become used to living among papists and he knew that if he wanted to keep working for the Colberts, he had to keep his religion to himself. The job gave him a kind of home and yet allowed his restless nature the freedom to wander.

CHAPTER 17

"So, she has finally had her coronation. And what a show it was."

"Well, she has been waiting for it long enough."

"How long has it been since he married Marie?"

"Ten years, I believe."

"Coronations cost money and he wanted to spend it on more important things. Roads and bridges; that's what we needed."

"We need a lot more. He promised us a chicken in every cooking pot on Sundays. I haven't seen a chicken since Christmas."

"You're always complaining. Things are so much better."

"Actually I think things are going too well. It makes me uneasy."

"That's just superstition."

"No it is not. I have heard that this astrologer—his name is La Brosse, I believe—predicted that today is a very dangerous day for the king. You can't argue with the stars."

"Henry can."

Henry was still irritated that he had finally given in to Marie and let her have her own coronation. It had been a wasteful spectacle, and besides, he felt that it would bring him bad luck. He suspected that once Marie wore the crown her partisans would feel free to get rid of him.

"Oh, this damned coronation," he had exclaimed. "It will be the cause of my death."

He had heard of La Brosse's prediction, and his retainers warned him not to leave the palace. On the other hand, he had business at the arsenal.

"Shall I go or shall I not?" he asked the queen with uncharacteristic vacillation. In the end he decided to ignore the warnings. Then he kissed her good-bye.

He could not help noticing again that she had put on more weight, and he found her full lips less appealing than ever. He had married Marie de' Medici after the Vatican had obligingly annulled his earlier marriage to Margaret of Valois. The match was strictly about money. Henry was deeply in debt to the enormously wealthy Ferdinand of Medici, grand duke of Tuscany, who acted as financier for half of the crowned heads of Europe. Not only was Henry unable to pay him back, but he wanted to borrow more. The grand duke was agreeable, providing Henry married his niece, Marie. Though unenthusiastic, Henry rose to the occasion and wrote her an ardent love letter even as he was dallying with Henriette, his mistress of long standing. She would never forgive him for breaking his earlier promise to marry her and turning instead to "the banker's fat daughter," as Henriette put it. But she nevertheless chose to remain the king's mistress.

He found Marie cold, stubborn and stupid. He was uncomfortable with the entourage she had brought with her from Florence, some of them very shady and, the king was sure, given to political intrigues against him. But Marie had borne him six children and brought him a great deal of badly needed money. If Paris had been worth a Mass, he thought, France was worth a wedding. He flattered himself that he had spent the Medici money well. He restored commerce and manufactures. The market stalls in the cities were bulging with produce, and shops were filled with silk and glassware and all sorts of goods now produced in France. And there was exotic merchandise from the New World.

Above all, the country was more or less at peace. How vexing, he thought, that he had not been able to make peace in his private domain.

When Marie arrived in Paris, he recalled ruefully, he had made Henriette kneel before her and told the new queen, "Mademoiselle has been my mistress; she will be your most obedient and submissive servant."

But things had not turned out that way at all. The women had been constantly at war with each other, mocking his reputation as a peacemaker and doing their best to render his life miserable. Fortunately, he had always found consolation elsewhere.

As he was about to get into his carriage the day after the coronation, May 14, 1610, accompanied by several courtiers, the captain of his guards asked permission to join him. The king declined. "For fifty years I have guarded myself," he said.

He looked forward to a talk with his favorite adviser, the Duke of Sully, who lived in the Arsenal. The building fronted the Seine and Henry often bathed there—in the nude, in full view of his subjects. This was a hot day for May, and a swim would be pleasant.

As the carriage, its leather curtains drawn back, turned from the rue Saint-Honoré into a narrow side street, it was blocked for a few moments by two carts. Suddenly a tall redheaded man jumped onto the vehicle and stabbed the king twice.

"It is nothing," said Henry, but he died instantly.

The next day his eight-year-old son became Louis XIII, while Louis's mother, Marie de' Medici, was proclaimed regent.

Paris erupted in grief over Henry's murder. Shops closed, people wept openly, women tore their hair. The churches were crowded and prayers rang out for Henry's soul and for the safety of France. Streets and squares, great houses and simple taverns echoed with rumors about who was responsible for the deed: it was the Protestants, it was the unreconciled followers of the Holy League, it was the Jesuits, it was Spain. As it turned out, the assassin was a Catholic fanatic, François Ravaillac, young, unemployed and deranged, who had become convinced that the king was planning war on the pope and moreover deserved to die because he had not brought the Protestants back to the true faith. Within weeks he was drawn and quartered before a huge crowd at the place de Grève.

Meanwhile the prolonged obsequies for Henry began. The exit of monarchs is never simple. Because of the unseasonable heat in Paris, it was decided that the king's viscera should be removed immediately. This procedure was done under the supervision of no fewer than fourteen physicians, including Dr. René Monnet. The sight of a corpse was nothing new to him, but it was somehow shocking to see this powerful man reduced to lifeless flesh, his muscles slack. The fatal stab wound, about two fingers wide, was visible between the fifth and sixth ribs. It was difficult to imagine this body alive, fighting countless battles and embracing countless women. The entrails were taken to Saint-Denis by an officer and six soldiers and buried without ceremony. But a great deal of ceremony would follow. Henry's embalmed remains were placed in a lead coffin covered with a gold brocade pall. For two weeks the coffin was on view between two altars in the hall of the Louvre. Elsewhere in the same hall, following ancient tradition, an effigy of the king was set up on a platform. The figure was in full regalia, including the royal mantle of crimson velvet decorated with gold fleurs-de-lis and trimmed in ermine. The Order of the Holy Ghost was around the figure's neck, the crown on its head. Its artificial eyes were wide open. At a nearby table, sumptuous meals were served twice a day, supposedly for the king. It was all meant to show that, in a sense, the king was still alive and the monarchy continued.

Monnet joined the crowd streaming past the effigy and found himself thinking of the extraordinary efforts people make to deny death.

Eventually both the coffin and the effigy were taken to Notre Dame. Through the night the coffin was on view in the cathedral with all of Paris—or so it seemed—trooping past.

Monnet had been the king's man, and, in a way, had loved him. He was deeply shaken by the murder. That evening he met Father Coton and they sat together and reminisced about Henry. Coton was holding a book, a copy of *Don Quixote,* which had appeared in France a few years before.

"It was his favorite," said Coton. "He laughed at that foolish old knight, but he really loved him, loved him for wanting the impossible."

"But Henry never tilted at windmills," said Monnet. "Only at real enemies—and he always forgave them."

The two men were silent for a few moments as images of past battles ran through their minds. Then Coton said, "I am glad that he made his confession to me on the day of his death." He smiled over a recollection. "When he first appointed me confessor, he refused to kneel; but eventually I made him do it."

Monnet looked at the death's-head watch Henry had given him and said, "Is it not typical that a man so tolerant and forgiving would be killed by a man who was neither?"

"The king is dead." The shout rang through the streets of Reims three days after the murder. The event provoked much the same commotion as it had in Paris. Houses were draped in black, people flocked to churches, groups argued in the streets about the meaning of the deed. Most of Catholic Reims had gradually come to accept Henry's conversion to the true Church and lamented his death. But there were also some adamant partisans who still saw him as a heretic. The identity of the assassin did not become known until later, and, in the meantime, rumors sprouted everywhere. Distraught mourners clashed with some demonstrators who actually rejoiced over the king's murder.

Nicole attended a Mass for Henry's soul and suddenly something very strange happened to her. It was as if a lock had broken open in her mind. The words of the Mass all at once had meaning for her again. She found the great, cold void inside her being filled

with a growing warmth. For the first time in years she was moved
to prayer. She remembered her earliest sight of Henry so long ago
in the town square of Nanteuil. She remembered seeing him after
the Mass at Saint-Denis, and later when he had called on Barbe
Acarie to tell her that Pierre was coming home from exile. Leaving the church, she was caught up in the crowd arguing heatedly
about the king.

"When all is said and done, he was still a heretic," shouted one
speaker.

A sudden impulse gripped Nicole and she said loudly, "He was
not. He repented and became a good and faithful Catholic. And
he brought us peace."

The crowd stared at her. She half knew that she should not go
on but the old familiar words rushed into her head and she could
not help herself. "We must all repent. We must all examine our
sins and confess them. We must all be united in serving our Lord."

Some in the crowd were both shocked and moved by this strange
figure with shining eyes and a commanding voice, but others muttered angrily at this woman who was trying to preach to them.
Suddenly Daniel Carnot emerged from the throng. He took in the
scene quickly.

"You had better stop this," he said, quietly but urgently.

As if waking from a spell, Nicole shuddered slightly and fell
silent. She allowed Daniel to lead her out of the square.

He said nothing for a while, but once they were back in the garden of the orphanage he asked her, "What made you do this?
When I saw you in that crowd I hardly knew you. How did you
get the notion of preaching in the streets? Have you done this before?"

Nicole shrank from the barrage of questions, but she knew that
Daniel's intentions were kind. After some hesitation she decided to
explain. She told him how she had discovered in herself the gift of
healing and of seeing distant places and the future. She described
how she had been taken up by the Holy League but how she had
come to admire Henry. She spoke in a low voice, painfully slow at

first, as if resisting the memories, but then faster and faster so that Daniel had a hard time following her: Barbe Acarie turning from patron to accuser, the exorcism, the warning that she must not continue what she considered her mission. She tried to describe how she had felt when she was preaching.

"Only then did I really feel alive," she said. "Only then did I feel close to God. For a long time I lost Him. That is what I meant when I told you I was mourning someone other than my husband and child. But just now, I began to feel His presence again."

Daniel had listened silently to Nicole's account. He had been raised not to believe in saints and miracles except those in Holy Scripture. He had certainly been assured of the existence of the Devil, but he did not believe that Nicole had ever been touched by Satan. As for her claims of extraordinary powers, he did not believe in them but understood how these things might become reality for a young girl growing up in the fervid Catholic world. He had no desire to argue with her about matters of faith, nor was he ready to tell her that he was a Protestant. His strongest impulse about Nicole was to protect her. He realized that he had come to love her even as he tried to tell himself that he was too old, at forty-one, to pursue such feelings.

He was startled from these thoughts when Nicole abruptly said, "There is something I must do. I hope you will help me."

He looked at her questioningly and was not prepared for what she said next.

"I want to be at the king's funeral. I saw him at Saint-Denis when he became a Catholic and I want to see him buried there."

Daniel tried to dissuade her. "The roads are dangerous," he said. "Do you really want to go back among the people who treated you so badly?"

"I will feel safe with you—that is, if you agree to take me. And no one will recognize me at Saint-Denis or pay any attention to me in the crowd."

He did not like the idea, but he already knew that there were few things he would refuse Nicole.

• • •

The funeral cortege moved past houses draped in black with burning torches in the doorways. A huge crowd welcomed Henry back on his last journey to Saint-Denis.

A grave had been opened in the middle of the chancel and the coffin was lowered into it. A herald descended into the grave and called out three times: "The king is dead! Pray God for his soul."

One by one princes and lords threw the royal insignia into the grave—scepter, wand of justice, mace, swords. Each landed on the coffin with a loud clang.

From her place in the packed, hushed crowd, Nicole Tavernier watched, her vision blurred by tears. The sounds made by the falling insignia struck her like blows, and she winced each time one of them hit the coffin.

Then the herald was heard again: "Long live the king! Long live Louis XIII, by God's grace king of France and Navarre."

The crowd cheered. Nicole looked about. She had spotted Pierre and Barbe Acarie and René Monnet among the dignitaries. Now as the throng made its way out of the cathedral amid drums, trumpets and fifes, they passed very close to her. But as she had predicted, they did not notice her in the crowd.

CHAPTER 18

On the way back from the funeral, as she sat next to Daniel in his rumbling wagon, she was still breathing hard with emotion and her cheeks were flushed. She thanked him for helping her to say good-bye to the king, her king.

"I was happy to do it," he said. "But we must talk about your situation in Reims."

By her own account, she had been warned not to go on with her sermonizing and her wonder-working.

"If you continue, you risk being discovered, and then who knows what will happen to you."

At first Nicole was unwilling to take his advice, but she understood his concern. In the following weeks, she resisted any impulse to resume her old role except with the children. She continued to tell them stories from the Bible and about the saints and she felt a glow of satisfaction when she saw their eager faces. It was preaching, of a sort.

One day Father Duplessis appeared at the orphanage in the company of a well-dressed matron in her early middle-age who looked familiar to Nicole. Even before the priest introduced her to the sisters, Nicole realized that it was Clarice, the daughter of the man who had taken her in and then banished her when she became pregnant. She looked remarkably like her mother—stouter, but with the same round, gentle face that Nicole remembered. As with Madame Lapin, there was nothing gentle in her manner.

"So this is the place we have helped support all these years," she said to Sister Marie-Margaret.

"You have never favored us with a visit before," said the nun. "We are happy to see you now and to tell you that we are very grateful for your help."

Clarice Colbert had come to the orphanage to take in a child as a servant, as her father had taken in Nicole so many years before. Suddenly she saw Nicole.

"I think I know that woman," said Clarice sharply. "Aren't you Nicole?"

Nicole only nodded.

Turning to Sister Marie-Margaret, Clarice said, "This person was a servant in our household many years ago. What is she doing here?"

When she heard the nun's explanation, Clarice grimaced. "She must be the reason why our man Daniel seems to spend so much time here. I have heard he visits very often."

Turning to Nicole she said, "So you have come back to where you came from. I hope you are behaving better here than you did in our house."

Clarice turned away and looked over the children who had assembled in the common room. She chose a young girl as a maid for her household. The child was ready to go with her at once, but Clarice shook her head.

"I will send for her presently, but right now there is a matter I need to discuss with Father Duplessis."

Outside she said, "Father, will you walk with me for a while?"

Duplessis bowed and fell in beside her.

"As I said, this Nicole was our servant. She was stubborn and thought she was better than anyone else. Then she took up with one of my father's workers and became pregnant. The pair left

Reims and I do not know what became of them afterward, but I do remember my father later telling me a very strange story. Nicole appeared in Paris. She started preaching in the streets and performing what people thought were miracles. She then got into some sort of trouble but I do not know what it was. I wonder whether such a person should be protected by those good, simple sisters and be inflicted on those innocent children. I think you had better get more information about this creature."

The priest eagerly agreed and promised to find out what he could.

That evening Clarice had a talk with her husband.

"A while ago I heard from the servants that your Carnot keeps visiting the orphanage at Sainte-Claire's. I did not pay much attention to it at the time, but now I have found out that he is visiting a woman who lives with the sisters. Her name is Nicole and she used to work for my parents as a servant girl."

Clarice went on to tell what she knew about Nicole and concluded, "Someone who is employed by our family should not associate with that kind of woman. You ought to put a stop to those visits."

"Carnot is one of the best people I have," he replied. "What he does with his own time is none of my business."

But, on reflection, he did summon Daniel. Colbert was several years younger than Daniel, but he spoke with an almost fatherly authority.

"Madame Colbert has just given me some facts about a woman you know. I believe her name is Nicole."

He briefly repeated what his wife had told him.

Daniel listened calmly. "Whatever happened in the past, she is a fine woman who works hard and takes very good care of the children. That is all that concerns me."

Colbert shrugged. "Very well. It is your affair."

When Daniel next saw Nicole, he mentioned the conversation with his master. Nicole said without hesitation, "When I told you about my marriage I did not tell you one thing. I was with child when we were married. That is why Monsieur Lapin turned me out of his house."

Given his upbringing in the strict, moralistic climate of Sedan, Daniel knew that he should be shocked. But he was not. His years of wandering had bred in him a large measure of tolerance, and, besides, he had grown too fond of Nicole to condemn her for something that had happened so long ago.

"It does not matter," he said. "We all have painful things in our past."

Life at Sainte-Claire's went on as usual. Daniel spent even more time with Nicole.

"I believe he is very devoted to you," said Sister Marie-Margaret one day. "You are a widow and he is single. Have you thought of marrying again?"

Nicole was startled. "Oh no, that is not for me anymore. I am devoted to my life here and to the children. Besides, I am thirty-five, I do not believe that Daniel has any such intentions."

But she discovered that she was wrong about that. One day Daniel took her on an outing to the countryside. He reminisced about his travels and especially about Dieppe. He described the scene: the white, windswept chalk cliffs beyond, which beckoned the channel and ultimately the great ocean. He told her about the reports of the New World that had excited the town, because from there, ships had sailed to Brazil, to Florida and the Carolinas, to New France. There were tales of bountiful lands, forests and lakes rich in game and fish; there were rumors of gold and pearls and, beyond all that, the fabulous wealth of China, wherever that was. He told her of hearing stories about strange, dark natives and how he had met some seamen who claimed to have actually seen two Indians brought back on an explorer's ship—although no one was sure that they were actually human beings.

Nicole detected a note of longing in his voice. "Were you yearning for that New World?" she asked. "Are you still?"

"On the contrary. The New World robbed me of something very precious. But I am not sure that you want to hear about it."

"I do. Please go on."

For a while Daniel seemed to pay attention only to the two horses that were pulling the wagon, and adjusted the reins. Finally he said, with a sigh, "Well, I fell in love with a girl in Dieppe. She was the daughter of a man I worked for. She was very sweet, very beautiful. I wanted to marry her. But her father had other plans. He was dissatisfied in Dieppe and intoxicated by the promise of adventure and riches on the other side of the ocean. He decided to join a group of craftsmen and merchants who were taking ship for New France. Naturally he wanted to bring his family along, including his daughter. I would have gladly married her and moved with her to that strange land, but her father forbade it. He knew that for some time I had moved from place to place without steady work and he considered me shiftless. And so she sailed away with her family and I have no idea what became of them."

"I am so sorry," said Nicole. "I can imagine what you must have felt."

"I stayed on in Dieppe for a while," Daniel continued, "but the place suddenly seemed gray and desolate. Just then I met an agent of the Colbert family. The port did a busy trade in cloth and all kinds of other merchandise, and this man had come with a wagonload of goods to sell. We became friendly and he offered me the work I have done for the Colberts ever since. I like what I do, but there are times when I feel very lonely. I had given no thought to a woman since that girl in Dieppe, but then I met you."

Nicole suddenly realized what Daniel was about to say and tried to stop him, but he went on.

"Perhaps I am a little old to speak of love but I do love you. I believe you are fond of me too. We could have a good life together."

Nicole was alarmed. "No, no. It is not possible," she said gently. "I am touched by your offer and I *am* fond of you. But marriage is no longer for me. My life is dedicated to other things. I serve God very imperfectly, but I must keep trying."

Daniel was not surprised by her reply and did not press her. He merely said, "Perhaps you will change your mind someday."

• • •

A few weeks later the routine at Sainte-Claire's was broken. It began on a bright morning when one of the nuns found a child, a ten-year-old boy names Jacques, sitting up in his cot and weeping quietly. "It is so dark," he said. "Why is it so dark?"

The sister first thought that the boy was shamming, because sunlight filled the room. But she soon convinced herself that he really had difficulty in seeing, and when she looked at him closely she found a pale film covering his eyes. Alarmed, she summoned the other sisters and Nicole.

Questioned, the boy said that his eyes had been hurting him for several days. Sister Marie-Margaret decided that his eyes should be bathed in a soothing lotion. Nicole did this carefully for two days, but Jacques's eyes grew worse. A doctor was called who declared that the boy had developed an inflammation of the cornea from causes he could not guess. He prescribed another lotion but warned that the child might well go blind. By evening, Jacques could not see at all. Later that night, while everyone else was asleep, Nicole slipped into the boys' dormitory and knelt beside Jacques's bed. As she had done so often before with the sick, she prayed for his recovery. Several times during the night she passed her hands over the boy's eyes. Once he stirred.

"Who is it?" he asked.

"Hush," she said. "It is only Nicole. I am here, I am praying for you."

She knelt again and pictured the shining eyes of Saint Lucy, patron saint of the blind, those eyes that had been marvelously restored to her after being put out.

In the morning Sister Marie-Margaret went to the boy's bedside. She shook him gently and he opened his eyes. They were clear.

"Thank the Lord," exclaimed the nun.

Jacques blinked and looked about the room, taking in everything.

"Nicole did it," he said. "She was here during the night. She touched my eyes and prayed for me."

When the doctor looked in later, he pronounced with great satisfaction that his lotion had worked. But Jacques insisted that he had been healed because of Nicole, and the nuns agreed with him.

Nicole was careful not to take any credit for what had happened. Back in her early days in Paris, she would have proudly proclaimed that she had been used by God as His instrument. Now she was silent. But she could not help feeling the glow of satisfaction, the inner radiance of faith that she had always experienced in her preaching and healing. Having been without that joy for years, she could not quite believe that her capacity to feel it had really come back. She knew that it would not last long beyond what had happened with Jacques, but she also knew that, despite all warnings and prohibitions, she would try to make it happen again.

In the meantime, Father Duplessis had received an answer to his inquiries about Nicole. He sent word to Clarice Colbert and to Sister Marie-Margaret that he had a matter of great urgency to discuss. He now faced the two women in his vestry. Swelling with self-importance he addressed Clarice. "Your suggestion, Madame, that I obtain information about the woman Nicole Tavernier was very wise indeed."

Sister Marie-Margaret looked startled.

"I don't understand," she said. "What is this about?"

"It is about the woman you have taken into your orphanage." He consulted some papers on the desk in front of him and again turned to Clarice.

"Several years after she left your father's household, she did indeed appear in Paris. Just as your father told you, she brazenly took on the role of preacher, sermonizing in public places, undertaking to heal the sick and even hearing confessions. She performed various acts that were thought to be miraculous by many. It must be said, unfortunately, that she even impressed some learned men of the Church. The Holy League made much of her. But then a very devout and wise lady named Barbe Acarie, who had generously taken her into her house, became suspicious. Nicole was caught in a lie and the Church authorities investigated all of her so-called graces. It was decided that she was diabolically possessed."

Hearing these words, both Sister Marie-Margaret and Clarice Colbert crossed themselves.

"Nicole Tavernier was exorcised. As a result the Fiend apparently left her."

The priest heavily stressed the word "apparently."

"The woman was warned not to resume preaching or healing or continuing the other acts she had performed. She then suddenly disappeared from Paris and evidently came here and found refuge at Sainte-Claire's."

Clarice Colbert heard this account with intense satisfaction. "I am not surprised," she said. "There was something strange and suspicious about her, even as a child."

Sister Marie-Margaret at first had been confused by what she heard, then turned indignant.

"I do not believe that Nicole was ever possessed. But if she was and if, as you say, Father, the Evil One left her after her exorcism, surely she is now in a state of grace."

"Not necessarily," said Duplessis. "We can never be absolutely sure that an exorcism has been effective. The Devil has infinite wiles and it is well known that he often only pretends to withdraw."

"With respect, Father, I do not believe that this is the case here. No, I do not believe it. I have been with Nicole every day for years now and I have never seen the slightest sign of evil in her. On the contrary, I believe she has spiritual gifts."

In her eagerness and innocence, the nun added, "Why, only the other night, Nicole prayed for a little boy who had lost his eyesight and laid her hands on his eyes while he was asleep. In the morning he could see again."

"Ah! You see!" the priest pounced. "That proves it. She was specifically forbidden to perform such acts because it was determined that they came from the Devil. If she is doing it again, there can be no doubt who is giving her the power. It is quite possible that she has voluntarily given herself to the Devil; in other words, that she is a witch."

The priest took another look at the paper before him. "Some of her actions are typical of witchcraft. The woman will have to be examined. It is my duty to bring the case to the archbishop's attention."

Clarice asked, almost eagerly, "Will she be exorcised again?"

"That is certainly possible. In the meantime, until I have consulted His Eminence, she will stay with you, Sister, but you will keep very close watch over her and you will see to it that she has nothing further to do with the children. I will send my curate to Sainte-Claire's to make sure that my orders are being followed."

Anxious and distraught, Sister Marie-Margaret returned to the orphanage. She found Nicole busy with the children and beckoned to her urgently. Nicole followed the nun into her small cell.

"My poor daughter," said Sister Marie-Margaret, putting her arms around her. "I have dreadful news for you. I do not know what we shall do."

She repeated Father Duplessis's report from Paris and his pronouncement.

"You are no longer to care for the children. I am to watch you and you are to stay here until Father Duplessis has consulted the archbishop."

Nicole suddenly saw herself back in the days when she was confined to the convent at Longchamp waiting for word from the archbishop of Paris about her fate. The nightmare seemed to be repeating itself in Reims.

"Was I wrong to pray for little Jacques and try to heal him? I suppose I should not have done it. But I felt that I had to."

"You were not wrong," said Sister Marie-Margaret, "but I fear that people are taking it the wrong way."

"What will they do to me?"

"I do not know. But Father did mention that you might be exorcised."

Hearing that word, Nicole barely suppressed a scream.

"Oh no! I could not bear that again. You do not know how horrible it is. And what if they decide that the exorcism does not work and that I am in league with the Devil? They will put me in jail, or worse."

"Surely not that," said Sister Marie-Margaret.

"Oh yes. It was all explained to me once before." She began to sob.

"Perhaps it will not happen," the nun said, but sounded less than reassuring. "We will pray for guidance."

She knelt and Nicole did the same, although she was much too alarmed and confused to form the right words. Sister Marie-Margaret prayed silently and intensely. Presently, she rose.

"I must look after the children," she said.

As she walked into the common room she saw Daniel Carnot at the door. She ushered him in eagerly. "You must be here in answer to my prayer," she said. "Nicole is in danger."

She explained the situation to Daniel in a confused rush, interrupting herself with exclamations of outrage and fear, but Daniel understood readily. "I believe she must get away from here as quickly as possible."

"I agree, even though I have been instructed to watch her and keep her here. I beg you to help her. Go into the garden. I will send Nicole to you."

The flowers seemed brighter and more fragrant than ever before and Daniel thought, ruefully, "Now that she has finally made something of this garden, she will have to leave."

Nicole joined him silently. "I have heard everything from Sister Marie-Margaret," he said, and he stretched out his arms toward her.

She stepped back, not letting him touch her, but she said warmly, "I am glad you are here."

"Nicole, you must leave," he said urgently. "No one can say what would happen to you if you stay. Surely you see that these people—the priests, Madame Colbert—wish you ill. Sister Marie-Margaret agrees that you should get away."

"This is the only home I have had for years." She sounded bitter as well as sad. "I felt safe here. Leaving would be very hard. Still, I understand that I must. But where will I go?"

"Listen to me, Nicole. We will go away together. I will take you to Sedan, where I grew up and where I still have family. You would be sheltered there—as my wife."

Nicole started to speak but he interrupted her. "Before you decide, there is something you should know. I have kept it from you so far because I did not believe that it mattered, but I must tell you now. I am a Protestant."

She was not as surprised as he had expected. "I should have guessed that. The way you sing the psalms and recite the Bible should have told me."

Daniel realized that what he said next would be very important and he spoke carefully, slowly.

"I know you are a devout Catholic. You look for God and try to love God only within the Roman Church. But think about how that Church has treated you. They raised you up and praised you and then threw you down and persecuted you. They saw the Devil in you when you were only trying to serve Jesus and to do good. They drove you from Paris and now they are driving you from Reims."

He paused to see if he had offended her. He could not read her face.

She was silent for a while and then said with a flash of anger that he had not seen in her before, "You are right. They did treat me badly. They forbade me to do the things I was meant to do. And now, after all this time, they attack me again."

Her reaction emboldened him to continue.

"I realize that when you were growing up you were told that Protestants were damnable heretics. But you have probably never known any Protestants until you met me. And you know that I am not evil."

"I know that."

"I remember very well what you told me not long ago," he resumed. "What you told me about reserving your love for God.

But you are not a nun and so surely you can love God while sharing your life with a man. Surely you do not have to choose one over the other."

Nicole felt dizzy with conflicting thoughts. She still believed that marriage was no longer for her. But she was crushed to realize that the Church she had tried to serve with all her heart had once again turned against her. Why was there no help from her beloved saints? She felt betrayed, abandoned.

"I need time to think," she said.

"There is no time," said Daniel. "We must leave before you become enmeshed in the net of the Church, before they have you in their grasp again."

She thought fearfully about leaving the shelter of Sainte-Claire's. Above all she could not imagine leaving her Church—and she knew that if she promised to marry Daniel, she would also have to promise to become a Protestant. But in the end all these doubts were outweighed by her growing desperation. In her mind she experienced again the fearful rite of exorcism, the horrific words, the evocation of the Fiend, the touch of the exorcist, which she remembered as deadly. Beyond that, might there be prison or the fire? She felt as if she were already in a dark prison from which Daniel offered the only escape. Finally she said in a near whisper, "Very well, I will go with you. I will marry you—if you still want me to be your wife after we are among your own people."

CHAPTER 19

Something is going on in the Acarie house. I hear the servants have all been paid off and the Acarie is finding other places for them."

"How do you know?"

"My niece has a friend who works there as a maid. She says the place has been full of visitors day after day. Friends and relatives are showing up who haven't been there for years."

"So what does that mean?"

"The odd thing is that they are all leaving with little gifts, souvenirs. It looks like the Acarie is giving away all her jewelry."

"I have heard that she is also giving away her clothes. She sent a whole load of them to Saint-Gervais for the poor."

"Is she moving away? Going on a journey?"

"You could say that. But it's a journey from which she won't come back."

When René Monnet called at the rue des Juifs, he found the house bustling with visitors. They were chatting and sipping hot spiced cider as if it were just another reception. But the atmosphere was different, subdued. They had all come to say good-bye to Barbe Acarie. She had been admitted to the Order of the Discalced Carmelites.

A few months before, Pierre Acarie had developed a high fever that would not abate despite Dr. Monnet's ministrations. When Pierre realized how serious his condition was he said calmly, "Bring on the priest."

He lost the power of speech, presumably from a stroke. He died a few days later, as Barbe had predicted. He was buried in the family chapel.

There were the usual flowery tributes to the deceased—his piety, his courage, his wisdom, his exemplary role as a husband and father. All these speeches, thought Monnet, were kindly exaggerations.

Pierre had indeed been pious, and downright fanatical in support of the League. He had also been reckless with his money and both self-pitying and self-righteous when he ran into trouble. But over the years he had mellowed and Monnet had sympathy for his fate, which had given him a wife more intelligent and able than he.

Almost immediately after Pierre's death, Barbe applied for admission to the Discalced Carmelites as a lay sister. This would involve much drudgery and manual labor that might be difficult for Barbe in her fragile state of health. But when Bérulle raised that concern, she brushed it aside.

"I do not want any special consideration," she said. "I want to do exactly what the others do."

Father Bérulle gave an exasperated sigh. "You should realize that excessive humility is also a form of pride," he said.

Barbe felt as if she had been struck. But she remained adamant, and in the end she was admitted.

She began to dispose of her property and to dissolve her household. Her daughters had preceded her in joining the order, and she saw to it that her sons were provided for.

As Monnet mingled with Barbe's farewell visitors, he looked about the familiar house for what was undoubtedly the last time.

"One more good-bye," he thought as he approached Barbe.

They both remembered the time so many years before when Dr. Monnet had first met the miserable young girl with chilblains, and remembered all that had happened since.

"I can never thank you enough for everything you have done for my family," she said. "And for taking such good care of my poor, weak body."

"I never thought of you as weak," he replied. "I believe you are very strong. But whenever your health requires it, please have someone send for me."

He realized that he had actually liked the uncertain, unhappy girl he first knew better than the high-handed and self-assured Barbe of later years. He could not forgive the harsh role she had played in banishing Nicole from both of their lives. And yet, he felt Barbe's retreat into the cloister was a loss for him. Nicole was gone, Andrée was gone and now Barbe.

"You are getting sentimental in your old age," he chided himself.

Still, he knew Barbe would leave a gap in his life.

Amiens, the place where Daniel Carnot was born, was still a prosperous and pleasant town. Barbe had only a glimpse of its winding canals and solid houses on her way to the Carmelite convent that had been chosen for her. The nuns were overjoyed, feeling honored that the foundress of their order would now be one of them. After two months as a postulant Barbe was ready to begin her novitiate. She moved through the ceremony as if in an ecstatic dream. During the Mass she was rigid, her face shining. She answered the usual questions: Was she prepared to vow poverty, chastity and obedience? Did she do so of her own free will? But when she was asked if she sought the holy habit out of pure love of God, she was silent and refused to answer. Given her obviously weakened state, no one insisted on a reply and the rite continued. After the robing she went to kiss the sisters according to custom.

At that moment she slid into one of her trances and had to be prevented from falling. The nuns carried her to a choir stall, where she remained for two hours. When Barbe awoke she went straight to the kitchen to go to work. During her novitiate, Barbe was constantly troubled by her injured leg and was often ill. When the time came for her to be professed, she was running a high fever and could not get up. Her bed was moved to the infirmary, which was connected to the church by a grilled opening in the wall. Through that grill, she took her final vows, and from that day in 1614 she was known as Sister Marie of the Incarnation.

The mother superior of the convent at Amiens had come to the end of her six-year term and a successor had to be chosen. By then Barbe was well enough to join the other nuns in the charter-house to welcome the new prioress, who had arrived from Paris. Sitting very straight in a chair on a raised platform, Sister Anne of the Blessed Sacrament addressed her new charges. At first Barbe did not recognize the severe features half hidden by her wimple. But when she spoke in a sharp, high-pitched voice, Barbe suddenly remembered one of the girls she had chosen nearly a decade before for her new order. It was not a pleasant memory. Sister Anne of the Blessed Sacrament was Anne de Viole. After the official welcome was over the new prioress asked Barbe to stay behind. The years had lined Anne de Viole's face and stiffened her manner.

"It may be difficult for you, Sister Marie, to be subject to someone who was once your postulant."

She did not mention it, but she obviously remembered the shoes she had shined and the laundry she had done under Barbe's roof. "But God has seen fit to reverse our roles. Even though you helped found our order, you will be treated here like all the other sisters and do the same work."

"Of course, Mother. I expect nothing else," replied Barbe, who could not help noticing how grudgingly Anne acknowledged the role she had played in bringing the Carmelites to France.

"Moreover, I know that our sisters here wanted you to be their new prioress. Our superiors prevented that. But I have been told that the nuns come to you constantly for advice and guidance. My predecessor encouraged this but I will not tolerate it. Your famous gift of spiritual discernment will count for nothing here."

The nuns at Amiens had indeed tried to elect Barbe as their mother superior, but they had been overruled because it was very rare for a lay sister to serve in such a position, and, besides, there were worries about her health.

"I never aspired to be prioress and I would have made a very bad one," said Barbe. "As for the advice I sometimes give to sisters who come to me with a problem, I will stop doing it. I will, of course, obey you in all things, Mother."

A year after Barbe was professed, René Monnet was surprised to receive a small packet from Andrée Levoix.

"I wanted you to see these," she wrote. "I am concerned about Barbe's situation, about the state of her health and her spirit. She would not want me to share these with anyone, not even with you, whom she trusts, but I am unable to help her from here. Perhaps you can do something."

The packet contained several letters from Barbe to Andrée.

"I remember very clearly the time when Mother Superior was one of my novices," wrote Barbe in one letter. "I found her somewhat proud and distant but I was certain of her vocation and was sure that she would make a good nun. And so she has. But I must say—and I would not confide this to anyone else but to you, dear sister—that she is very hard on me. But with all my faults, I deserve it."

And in another letter: "In the eyes of Mother I seem to be unable to do anything right. Day after day she reprimands me. I do not sweep the kitchen floor well enough. I do not know how to chop the vegetables properly. My laundry is not clean enough. And so it goes. I do not complain because I am sure she is right. I am very slow because my leg hurts me almost all the time but sometimes I do think that she goes further than necessary. She al-

ways dresses me down in front of the others to humiliate me. Of
course that is good for me, but it does hurt."

Reading these lines, Monnet remembered Barbe's mother and
how harshly she had treated her daughter. He found it ironic that
Barbe was reliving that experience under a new, religious mother.
He turned to another letter.

"I was forbidden by Mother to give any spiritual advice to the
other nuns, not that I want to do so. I have strictly obeyed. But the
other day one of the novices came to me in distress over some difficulty she had with her prayers and I said some words to reassure
her. Mother overheard this and berated me loudly. She accused me
of disobeying her order."

From yet another letter: "In my trances, which still occur often,
I have begun to hear strange and wonderful music, angelic music.
Of course I have told no one of this. But two nights ago Mother
saw me during one of those times. My face must have had an ecstatic look and she asked me what was happening. Taken by surprise, I forgot myself and blurted out something about the angelic
music I was hearing. 'How do you know it is angelic?' Mother
asked. 'It may very well have been the Devil's music.' If she really
believed that, surely she should have pitied me and I sensed no pity
in her. The incident made me remember Nicole Tavernier, that
poor, possessed girl. Looking back, I pity her, as I did not at the
time. I often wonder what became of her."

Monnet was startled by the sudden appearance of that name. He
thought of Nicole often, with a keen sense of regret that he had
not been able to help her more than he had, but he would not have
guessed that she was also in Barbe's mind.

Disturbed by Barbe's letters, he decided to consult Coton. They
met at the Golden Racket. Although their tennis games had become rarer through the years, they still frequented the place for an
occasional match and a companionable drink.

Coton was not surprised when Monnet described the situation.
He had heard about it already. Anne de Viole's persecution of
Barbe was not, he explained, merely a matter of personal malice.

It was part of a growing conflict with Bérulle, who was Anne's mentor, and suggested, if not dictated, her actions. For all his experience, Monnet found that he still had much to learn about theological divisions and the politics of faith.

Bérulle wanted to introduce a new vow of servitude to Our Lady as part of the nuns' regular devotions. Although Barbe was only a lay sister, she still had enormous prestige in the order, and Bérulle found it necessary to get her approval. She flatly refused, as did many of Bérulle's fellow priests.

Monnet was puzzled: How could anyone find fault with veneration of the Virgin?

"This proposed pledge is long and complicated," explained Coton. "It would take time away from the sisters' other prayers and from their various duties. Above all it would change the simple, austere spirit of the Teresian constitution. To some people this may seem like a trivial matter, but, believe me, it is not."

Coton assumed that Bérulle was using Anne de Viole as an instrument to curb Barbe's influence and to advance his own scheme. "My friend Bérulle is a very learned man and sincere in his beliefs," Coton went on. "But he is also very ambitious and eager to have his own way."

Coton thought that Barbe had best be removed from Amiens. He used his influence to have her transferred to the Carmelite convent at Pontoise, well beyond Anne de Viole's reach. But she was not beyond Bérulle's. Soon after her arrival at Pontoise, Pierre Bérulle came to see her and once again tried to promote the introduction of his new devotion. She kept resisting and the argument grew increasingly heated. It lasted for three hours, to the point where Mother Marie of Saint Joseph, the prioress, began to worry that an exhausted Barbe might not be able to withstand the strain.

"You are blind and stubborn," raged Bérulle. "You have a petty mind. You are simply wrong. Moreover, you have bungled everything you have ever undertaken."

It was clearly an unfair accusation, but Barbe said, "I am sure you are right. I am full of faults but I will not change my mind."

"You are arrogant even when you try to be humble," shouted Bérulle.

At that point Mother Superior came into the parlor to ask whether Sister needed to rest. Barbe shook her head, but Bérulle finally decided that he could not move her and left. It was the last time they saw each other.

After this wrenching scene Barbe grew weaker, and the mother superior sent urgent word to Dr. Monnet. He came immediately.

It was three years since he had last seen Barbe, and she had aged noticeably. The usual rosy glow of her features had faded. As he examined her, he touched one of her hands and saw her trembling, as if in pain. He asked her about this, and with some reluctance she told him that she often had sharp pains in her hands, her feet and her side; particularly on Fridays, Saturdays and during Lent, she added.

René was puzzled, but then he remembered the phenomenon known as invisible stigmata. He knew that some people experienced the pains of the cross without any bleeding wounds.

When Monnet suggested to her that this was the cause of her pains, she said anxiously, "We must not talk about such things. I do not want to draw any more attention to myself."

Monnet decided to stay on at Pontoise for a while to observe her. Two days later she had recovered some of her strength and he found her immersed in a book. She looked up as he came in, clearly troubled.

"I have been reading and rereading the life of Saint Teresa," she said. "I keep being struck by the way she accuses herself of pride and vanity. Listen."

Barbe turned the pages and read a passage: "I could not bear anything that seemed to make me look small. I delighted in being well thought of."

Next, Barbe read some sentences in which Teresa blamed herself for acting "with more vanity than spirituality, being anxious for splendor and effect."

She closed the book and said, "Do you understand why these words make me afraid? I am afraid that they apply to me. I never thought that I was looking for approval and renown, but did I really seek them? When I judged the spirituality of others and declared whether this or that person was truly inspired or not, was I being too rash, too ready to condemn?"

Monnet was at a loss, but he realized that Barbe was not really questioning him, but herself.

"A priest told me just the other day that I was arrogant even in my humility," she continued. "Perhaps he was right. I had been troubled by such thoughts before. When I took my first vows, I was asked, as our rules demand, whether I was acting out of pure love of God. I suddenly found that I did not dare answer that question. Can we ever be certain that we act out of pure love of God? We are so full of secret motives and self-seeking that often we think that we do only for God what is really for ourselves."

She paused and said hesitantly, "Do you remember Nicole Tavernier?"

"I certainly do."

"Lately I have been thinking more and more about her. Was I mean-spirited? Should I have been more compassionate?"

He was amazed and could not quite grasp at first Barbe's apparent transformation. Could it really be true that after nearly two decades, during which she had given no sign of even thinking about Nicole Tavernier, Barbe was now haunted by her? He had seen the first signs of her self-doubt in her letters to Andrée, and since then her qualms had evidently grown. How to explain this? Could it be her illness, her pain, her humiliation at the hands of Anne de Viole and Bérulle? Or were there more mysterious causes?

As if to answer the question in his mind, Barbe said, "I had a dream the other night in which I saw Saint Teresa kneeling and praying alongside Nicole, much as Nicole and I would pray together long ago. I feel that the saint is leading me back to Nicole and wants me to make amends."

He could only imagine how difficult it must be for Barbe to face that thought and he sensed the turmoil in her, but he was not prepared for what she said next.

"I feel that I must see her again. Do you know what has become of her and where she is?"

Monnet said that he did not. "After the exorcism, she disappeared without a trace."

"Do you think that you could find her?"

"It would be very difficult, perhaps impossible."

"But would you try?"

Monnet said that he would do his best.

With Henry's death, Monnet had assumed that his career as a spy was over. It was not.

Marie de' Medici proved to be a poor regent. She was greedy, luxury-loving, and she reversed many of Henry's policies, forming alliances with his old enemies, Spain and the Hapsburg empire. Her court was rife with intrigue. She was contemptuous of her son, Louis XIII, whom she considered feebleminded. He in turn hated her and would soon begin to plot against her. It was the perfect atmosphere for men of great ambition and small scruples.

Monnet was curious when he received an invitation to call on one of Marie's new advisers. Presently he found himself facing a surprisingly young man. He was short and slight of build, but one forgot those qualities looking into his face. His hooked nose and thin eyebrows gave him a domineering air. Armand de Richelieu, already a bishop despite his youth, had just begun his ascent, which would eventually lead to a cardinal's hat and the prime ministership.

"I've heard it said, Doctor," Richelieu began, "that you have been an extremely skillful agent for the late king. Well, I am in a situation where I need information, all the information I can get. I hope that you will be willing to help me."

Monnet had to admit to himself that he missed the excitement of his years as an informer, and, besides, Richelieu exuded an air of power that gripped him. Monnet quickly agreed. Richelieu soon developed the best intelligence network in Europe, employing merchants and sailors, monks and laymen by the hundreds. It was so carefully organized that identical coded messages were usually carried by two separate couriers in case one was intercepted. Before long Monnet played a leading part in that network and thus was able to use it in his search for Nicole.

He sent out word together with her description, although he realized that in the intervening years she undoubtedly had changed. The last time he had been on Nicole's trail, trying to track down her people, he had at least known where to look. This time his agents had to look everywhere. One might as well try to find a gold coin in the Ardennes forest, he thought, or a virgin at court. He did not have much hope for success.

CHAPTER 20

Nicole and Daniel arrived in Sedan in the early evening after nearly two days' journey. Daniel had managed to buy a cart and horse for the trip. Along most of the way Nicole was silent. Leaving Sainte-Claire's had not been easy. Late at night she said a stealthy and sad farewell to Sister Marie-Margaret, looked in on the sleeping children and hurried out of Sainte-Claire's to where Daniel was waiting for her. On the road, she was still in a daze. She was amazed by the decision she had made and kept wondering whether she was doing the right thing. Again and again she told herself that she really had no other safe choice. Daniel sensed her worries, and after a few attempts at reassuring her, he too kept his silence. He was wondering how he would explain his sudden return and especially Nicole's presence to his brother. There had been no time to send a message in advance, and so Daniel would simply have to arrive at his brother's doorstep with a strange woman who was also a Catholic.

They made their way into the town and across the cobbled marketplace. He remembered many landmarks, including the Inn of the Winged Wild Boar, whose shield had been reduced by time and weather to a mere faded outline of the mythical beast. The citadel towered above the slate roofs of the town, as imposing and seemingly impregnable as ever.

His father's house was much as Daniel remembered it, but it had a fresh coat of paint, suggesting that his brother had done well. Daniel halted the wagon and helped Nicole down.

Just then Jean Carnot emerged from the house. "I do not believe what I see!" he exclaimed. "Brother! Where have you come from? What are you doing here?"

"I have come home. Home to Sedan. I will explain everything later. And this is Nicole Tavernier, the woman who, I am happy to say, has promised to marry me."

Jean took a long, close look at Nicole: a slight figure in a plain, dark dress and a wool cap, dusty from travel, an anxious face attempting a friendly smile.

At that point Jean's wife came out of the house and took in the scene. She observed her husband's amazement and concern.

"Look, my dear, Daniel is home. What is more, he has brought a bride. Come and meet your future sister," Jean said uneasily.

Daniel had seen Sarah Carnot only once before, at her wedding. Now he was struck again by how much she resembled her husband. They could have been brother and sister, whereas the two brothers were not alike at all. Jean and Sarah were both short, delicately built, suggesting a pair of dolls. Their features were narrow and smooth, except for a struggling mustache on Jean's face. Like her husband, Sarah inspected the strange woman and seemed equally disturbed. She noticed that Nicole's dress was not made of good fabric and was very worn. The woman was obviously poor, at least forty, she concluded, and probably without a dowry.

Daniel said hastily, "I know all this is a surprise for you, but please make her welcome."

Sarah said, "You are certainly welcome." Then, noticing the fatigue in Nicole's eyes and bearing, she took her arm.

"There is so much we want to ask you, but that can wait. You must rest now."

With that she led Nicole into the house. Daniel and Jean followed and settled in the front room. The brothers were as dis-similar in temperament as in looks. Where Daniel was jovial, Jean was reserved, and where Daniel had always been restless, Jean was by nature content to stay in one place. True to Daniel's prediction, his brother had been very good at their father's trade. The ticking clocks in the workshop did not irritate him, as they had Daniel, but soothed him.

Daniel felt a little like a stranger facing his brother. They spoke perfunctorily for a while about family, health, business—their mar-ried sister had moved away, Jean and Sarah's children were growing up fast, everyone was well, the clock trade was good. Daniel told about the work he had been doing for the Colberts. At length he turned to the subject that he knew his brother wanted most to hear about: Nicole.

"I must tell you one thing about her right away—she is a Catholic."

"I guessed as much," said Jean. "After all, you have been living there among the papists all this time."

"Well, the papists have treated her very badly. She has suffered a great deal from their superstition and fanaticism. She is ready to turn away from Rome and join us."

"I am happy to hear it," said Jean. "But frankly, brother, I think you might have chosen a younger woman, one who could give you children."

"Things do not always happen the way one might wish," replied Daniel. "Children or no, I feel very fortunate to have found Nicole. When you come to know her I think you will recognize her goodness. But I must ask you for a favor. Her conversion to our faith will take some time. I hope you will allow her to stay here while she learns our ways of worship and living."

"It will not be easy for her," replied Jean. "Our friends and neighbors are bound to be suspicious, but we will try our best to make a place for her here." Then he added uneasily, "But what about you?"

"I will find lodging elsewhere," replied Daniel. "I know it

would not be proper for us to be under the same roof until we are married."

Jean nodded with evident relief. "You are right," he said. "But now, I think you need some rest as well. First I want to take you to the shop to show you what I have been working on."

The shop had not changed much since Daniel last saw it, with clocks of various sizes and designs everywhere. Jean pointed to one worktable with several small timepieces. "I have been able to shrink their size more and more," he said with satisfaction. "They are so popular that I can hardly keep up with the demand."

Daniel picked up one of them. It was exquisitely crafted and decorated. "Brother, you are just as good as Father, if not better," he said.

Jean thanked him for the compliment but sounded embarrassed when he continued. "Now that you are back, do you want to come into the business with me? It would have been yours, after all, if you had not left."

"Thank you, brother, but no. You are much better at this than I could ever be. I have learned a great deal about trading merchandise from the Colberts and I would like to set up such a business. I am willing to start modestly. Perhaps you would stake me to this."

Jean agreed eagerly, plainly pleased that he would retain his business for himself. Before they left the workshop Daniel saw his father's astronomical clock, still incomplete. "I tinker with it every so often," said Jean, "but I really don't have enough time for it. Besides, I'm not sure that anyone would want to buy it."

"Father did not build it to sell it," thought Daniel. "He built it for himself." But he left the thought unspoken.

Slowly Nicole became a part of the Carnot household. She offered to help with chores, but Sarah would not hear of it—there were two maids for that. She did spend much time with the children—a boy of five and a girl of nine—who were good-natured and well-behaved and readily took to their future aunt. This endeared Nicole to Sarah, who began to treat her warmly. On his long daily visits, Daniel was delighted and relieved to see that his family was accepting Nicole and she seemed to accept them. When Jean read aloud from the family Bible after the evening meal, she followed every word with delight but also with amazement; she had never before heard so much of scripture or seen it to be so much part of daily life. When neighbors came to visit she enjoyed listening to the psalms being sung by them and the family, just as she had enjoyed hearing them sung by Daniel, and she joined in, at first hesitantly and then enthusiastically.

But visitors were also a source of unease. "There is no need to tell them your story," said Daniel. "You will soon join our Church and be my wife. But in the meantime, my family's friends would be troubled to be with a Catholic."

After the singing, the neighbors would speak volubly about their families, their trade, the affairs of the town and especially about religion. Not knowing that Nicole was a Catholic, they said whatever they felt about the Roman Church, its superstitions and idol worship, its corruption, its persecution of Protestants. Nicole realized that, despite all public attempts at reconciliation, bitter hostility lingered. The talk of the neighbors pained her, but she remained silent, because she was imbued with the sense that her Church had betrayed and mistreated her. Besides, she felt protected and cared for in the Carnot family, as Daniel had promised. Nevertheless, she realized that she was now in a different world.

"I gave you a little time to get used to us," said Daniel one day, "but now it is time to begin your conversion."

He explained to Nicole that anyone wishing to join the Reformed Church had to undergo a careful process of study and examination. He took Nicole to the elder of their district, Gaston Roux, the proprietor of a woolen mill, who exuded prosperity and piety. It was his duty to question prospective converts, investigate them, and, if they proved acceptable, to follow their education in the new faith.

"Why do you want to join our Church?" the Elder asked.

Daniel answered for Nicole: "Her own Church has dealt with her abominably."

Roux was eager to hear just what the papists had done. Nicole gave a brief account. He was especially interested when she described how, in Paris, she had been taken up by the League but was later accused of being diabolically possessed.

"She was even subjected to the barbarous rite of exorcism," Daniel added.

He was uneasy mentioning this because he could not be sure what the elder would make of it. To his relief, Roux did not pursue the matter.

"These superstitious people see the Devil everywhere," said Roux. "We are not concerned about that. We use our own judgment in these things. What matters to us is that your future wife is truly prepared to abjure the Catholic faith and proves herself a good and virtuous woman."

The Protestant Devil was just as black as the Catholic one, and the Protestants feared him just as much. But as they believed that the whole Roman Church was diabolically inspired, they would never accept a Catholic's pronouncement on how and where Satan was at work.

Roux got up, leaning on a cane more for authority than support. "I will take up your case with the consistory," he said. "If they approve, you will then begin your road into our Church."

Nicole had only a vague idea about what the consistory was. Presently she learned from Daniel that it was a body composed of minsters and lay elders and that it was responsible for enforcing the spiritual and moral order of the entire Protestant community in Sedan.

A few days later Nicole was playing a game with the Carnot children and found that the usually cheerful youngsters were oddly subdued. Questioned, the girl explained that three of their friends had been observed outside a church eating cakes instead of being inside at the service. "They were reported right away," she said, "and the consistory ordered them to be punished. They were whipped. Maybe they deserved it but I am sorry for them."

Everyone was expected to inform the consistory of infractions, Nicole learned, and its representatives patrolled the streets of their district looking out for wrongdoers. They urged people to attend catechism, checked that shops were closed on prayer days or during offices, took note of who was spending his time and money at the tavern or even playing cards. Two by two they visited private houses, inquired why people remained at home instead of attending services, went on night watches at ten o'clock in the evening to check who was out-of-doors at that time. They reported to the consistory, which, every week, became a tribunal, meting out punishment.

Conditions were not as severe as they had been years before, in Calvin's Geneva, when those children might have fared far worse. In those days, a little girl was once beheaded for striking her parents. People were beheaded for atheism, sedition and repeated adultery. While no longer as ferocious, the Sedan consistory was still harsh. A man was banished from the city for three months because, when he heard an ass bray, he joked, "He brays a beautiful psalm." Three men who laughed during a sermon were imprisoned for three days. Adulterers, fornicators and prostitutes were excommunicated or expelled. Nicole heard about these things with alarm. She had come here with Daniel to escape what she saw as the harsh treatment by her Church. But were these Protestant people not just as harsh, if not more so? They imposed instant punishment for what seemed small offenses, and without the comfort of the confessional. Every time she heard people mention the word "consistory," she felt vaguely threatened. She could not have put it into words, but she sensed the paradox: religion could uplift and exalt the human spirit but could also suppress its natural feelings.

Eventually Gaston Roux summoned Nicole and Daniel to his house. With him was a minister whom he introduced as Albert Escagnas.

"I have told the consistory that I see no reason why your conversion should not proceed," said Roux. "Minister Escagnas will instruct you in our doctrine. But first you must make certain pledges."

Escagnas earnestly addressed Nicole. He asked her whether she would promise to follow the creed of the gospel she would be taught, accept the disciplines of the church, attend offices as well as the catechism sessions until she was judged able to take part in the Holy Communion.

"I promise," said Nicole.

The next day Daniel took her to her first Protestant service. As she entered the square, unadorned building that Daniel referred to as a temple, Nicole did not have the feeling that she was in a church. She knew enough about the Protestant religion to realize that there would be no elaborate altar, no stained-glass windows, no statues. Nevertheless, the bare, whitewashed walls shocked her. She vainly looked for images of saints or Mary or Jesus. There were no fonts of holy water. The very air seemed different: no scent of incense or of votive candles, which had always combined into the special aroma of every church she could remember. She enjoyed the psalms sung in pleasant unison by the congregation, and she listened attentively to the sermon delivered by Minister Escagnas. He was in austere black—no trace of the priestly robes she was used to seeing. He stood at a large, oak pulpit, an hourglass in front of him to keep him from running over his allotted time. He had a deep, resonant voice that occasionally approached passion. His theme was the duty to educate children in the ways of the Lord but also in human knowledge, and the sinfulness of failing in that duty. Many biblical quotations buttressed his points, and every time he mentioned the name "God," he lifted his cap. Nicole did not follow all the words because she was so preoccupied with the strangeness of her surroundings, but she responded to the preacher's earnestness and she felt the stirring of that old desire to be up there at the pulpit herself.

From then on she attended services regularly. Escagnas's sermons were surprisingly down-to-earth and varied. He talked about women and condemned their idle gossip. He talked about husbands and denounced them for drunkenness and for beating their wives. He spoke about liars. "Man makes bad use of language when he tells lies," he said. "Man is like those boxes of drugs bearing misleading labels: 'rhubarb' is written on the box but there is arsenic inside."

He also spoke of "people who rattle off prayers without understanding them" or "have pious thoughts that are useless and hypocritical—just like the Roman Catholics."

This censure of Catholics still disturbed Nicole. She was even more troubled by her lessons in doctrine. Every other day she found herself in a room with pupils ranging in age from six to fifteen, as Minister Escagnas drilled them in Calvin's catechism. She listened to all the tenets—the insistence on faith based on scripture alone, the condemnation of graven images, the rejection of the Mass.

There could be "no resemblance between Him who is eternal Spirit and incomprehensible, and corporal, dead, corruptible and visible matter."

The body of Christ could not be enclosed in the bread nor His blood in the chalice, for Jesus is not found in "these corruptible elements."

She dutifully repeated the words, but did she really believe them? On Sundays, at the regular services she attended with Daniel, Nicole observed the Protestant form of the Lord's Supper. It resembled the Catholic practice she was used to but it also differed from it, and the difference seemed greater than the likeness. What she saw was to the Mass as a partial sketch is to an oil painting. There was no tabernacle holding the Hosts, no incense, no tinkling bells. Bread and wine were laid out on a table as if for a meal. The communicants advanced and handed one of the assembled elders a metal disc signifying, as Nicole learned, that each was qualified to take communion. To her it almost seemed as if they were paying for a meal. The minister offered a piece of bread and a sip of wine. The familiar phrases—"This is the body of Christ . . . this is the blood of Christ"—echoed in Nicole's mind but were not spoken. Prayers followed and, like the entire liturgy, they were not in Latin but in French. She enjoyed this, just as she had enjoyed hearing the Bible in her own language, but there was also something strange about it: the mystery and the solemnity were gone.

Her education in Protestant doctrine took place outside the catechism lessons as well. An elderly neighbor of the Carnots had been ill for weeks and finally died. When the Carnot household heard the news Nicole began a prayer. But she was stopped firmly by Jean.

"We don't believe in prayers for the dead, and we don't hold with excessive mourning."

He explained that the dead woman would be placed in a coffin and the coffin buried quickly and quietly, after which everyone would go back to work. There would be no prayers, no hymns, no lamentation. In the strict Protestant view, praying for the dead was tantamount to asking for God's indulgence when He had already determined the destiny of each soul. To Nicole, the idea of burying someone without ceremony and without a prayer to help lead the departed soul into the afterlife seemed unnatural, if not cruel.

As if to silence her doubts, Nicole worked hard at her lessons and mastered the catechism quickly. She did so well that Escagnas reported her ready for conversion after only three months. The Carnot family was happy to learn this and Jean told his brother, "It is time for the two of you to be betrothed."

The traditional ceremony took place the very next day before the assembled household and several neighbors. Daniel and Nicole touched hands, sipped wine and exchanged the customary gifts—a linen shirt she had made for Daniel, a lace-trimmed dress for Nicole. They were now ready to become man and wife.

Soon afterward, René Monnet arrived in Sedan.

CHAPTER 21

"I see the banns have been posted."

"I am not surprised. We all knew he brought her here to marry her."

"Why does he have to marry a Catholic? Couldn't he have found a good Protestant girl right here in Sedan?"

"From what I hear she is not just a Catholic but the illegitimate daughter of some bishop."

"I believe she is a former nun who ran away from the convent."

"Daniel doesn't care. He is completely smitten. I must say she has acted very well since she came to live with his people, very quiet, very modest."

"But he could have found somebody younger."

"That's his affair. The important thing is, she has been studying our catechism and she will become a Protestant."

"Yes, but can you ever trust those converts? Once the papists have their grip on someone, they never really let go."

As soon as Monnet arrived in Sedan he started asking questions about Nicole Tavernier. He heard gossip and rumors about her everywhere.

He had been startled when, only two weeks after he had sent out his inquiry, one of his people reported that Nicole had been found in Sedan. She was engaged to a local citizen of good repute named Carnot, the report went on, and it was said that she was about to become a Protestant. Monnet could hardly believe that Nicole, who had been so fervent in her faith, could have gone over to the Reformed Church. But his informant was very reliable and Monnet could not doubt his account, however extraordinary. He decided to leave for Sedan immediately, not only because of his promise to Barbe but because he was anxious to see Nicole again. She had never been out of his mind for long.

Stopping to change horses on the way from Paris, Monnet met a traveler who was also going to Sedan. He suggested that they make the rest of the journey together and seemed eager to talk. His black garb made clear that he was a Protestant minister. He was intensely angry. Since King Henry's death many of the rights and privileges Henry had granted to the Protestants through the Edict of Nantes were being gradually chipped away. Protestants were having a hard time again in several regions. Minister Balladier had reluctantly decided to leave his parish at Meaux, not far from Paris, and head for Sedan, which was once again receiving a wave of Protestant refugees. He had been invited to preach there. He kept up his complaints about the situation almost without interruption until they reached the city. Before they parted, the minister urged Monnet to come to hear his sermon on Sunday.

Monnet found lodging at the Inn of the Winged Wild Boar and, having asked for directions, made his way to the Carnot house.

Told that a stranger wanted to see him, Jean Carnot came out of his workshop. He was polite but puzzled.

Monnet gave his name and said, "I am an old friend of Nicole Tavernier. I understand that she is engaged to a man named Carnot."

"That is right, she is engaged to my brother Daniel. I am Jean Carnot and she is staying with my family until the wedding."

"May I see her? I have a message of some importance."

Jean hesitated, but Monnet supposed that he looked respectable enough and his title of "Doctor" was reassuring.

"Very well, I will call her," Jean said. "But if you have important news, her future husband should be present as well."

A short time later Nicole appeared in the parlor, followed by Daniel Carnot. Even though Monnet had expected her to have changed, it was not easy to reconcile the woman before him with the image of the girl he remembered. Her small figure was still slim and lithe but her face had lost its freshness. There were lines around her mouth and eyes and the eyes themselves were duller, without their once-forceful gleam. But when she recognized Monnet, her features were transformed by a radiant smile.

"I could not believe it when I heard your name, Doctor," she said. "How did you ever find me?"

She turned to Daniel. "This is Dr. René Monnet, who has been a great friend to me in the past. He helped me through the bad times in Paris. He was always kinder to me than any brother and perhaps more understanding than any confessor."

The word "confessor" provoked a small frown from Daniel Carnot, as it might from any good Protestant, but he was courteous in greeting Monnet.

"I understand you have a message for my future wife," he said. "May we hear it?"

Monnet realized that he had a great deal to explain. "The message," he began, "is from Barbe Acarie."

Nicole's eyes widened. He guessed that she had not heard or spoken that name for a long time.

Monnet continued, "She is now known as Sister Marie of the Incarnation and she is a Carmelite nun."

Nicole seemed to have a difficult time taking this in. "If she has taken the veil, that must mean that her husband is dead," she said.

Monnet told her that Pierre indeed had died several years ago.

"I am sorry. May he rest in peace," she said. And he could tell that her days in the Acarie family still had an emotional hold on her, despite everything that had happened. She asked after Andrée Levoix and was surprised that she too had become a nun. He had the impression that Nicole really wanted to talk about old times, but Daniel interrupted.

"Doctor," he said, "just what is the message you have come so far to deliver?"

He faced Nicole and said, "The message is simply that she wants to see you."

Nicole looked not merely surprised but stricken. "But why? Why?" she stammered. "Why after all this time and after the way she treated me?"

"She has been thinking of you more and more lately," he said. "She has come to feel sorry about how she treated you. She has been through very trying times herself, and perhaps that accounts for her change of heart. She thinks she was too harsh toward you and unjust. She wants to tell you this herself and make amends."

"But why now?" asked Nicole.

"She is very ill, and she may not live much longer."

He could tell that Nicole was troubled by this, more so than he had expected. "I am sorry," she said again, her voice choking. But in spite of what he had just said, Nicole did not yet seem to realize what he was asking of her. "Barbe is in a convent at Pontoise," he said. "I would like you to go there with me to see her."

Before Nicole could say anything, Daniel jumped up from his chair, his face flushed. "That is impossible," he said. "We are to be married in little more than a week. You are making an absurd request, Doctor. You know very well what Barbe Acarie has done to Nicole. There is no reason in the world why she should leave here on the very eve of our wedding and go running to that woman."

He added more calmly, "I think of myself as a tolerant man, but I have seen enough not to trust your Church. Lord knows what might happen to Nicole once she is entangled again with those people."

"I am not acting for the Church but only for one woman who is in great anguish," Monnet replied. "Being face-to-face with

Nicole again would mean a great deal to her, and I think it would also mean a great deal to Nicole."

Nicole had been silent throughout this exchange, looking from Daniel to Monnet and back again.

"I certainly do not mean to speak for you, Nicole," Monnet said. "How do you feel about all this yourself?"

Nicole plainly struggled for an answer. At length she said, "Of course I must do what my future husband expects."

The answer seemed to satisfy Daniel. It also pleased Jean Carnot, who had kept himself in the background.

"Doctor," he said, "you must have had a tiring journey. Perhaps you will rest for a while now and then join us for supper. I think you may prefer our fare to what the Wild Boar inn can offer."

Supper proved to be a surprisingly pleasant affair. At one point Monnet looked at his watch, and Jean Carnot noticed the intricate little skull-shaped timepiece. He was fascinated by the workmanship and asked to examine it more carefully.

"It is very fine, very intricate," Jean said. "I too make watches."

"Perhaps you will show me some of them," Monnet said politely.

"Gladly," replied Jean. "But tell me, how did you come by this one?"

"It was made in Germany," said Monnet, preferring not to mention that it had been a gift from Henry IV. But he felt Nicole's eyes on him and noticed a slight smile. She obviously remembered the time long before when she had first seen that watch and divined its origin.

Daniel, evidently reassured that Nicole had properly refused Monnet's appeal, gave way to his usual good nature. He was friendly and volubly reminisced about his time in Reims and his courtship of Nicole. Monnet liked him and was disarmed by his obvious love for her and his happiness over their impending marriage.

At length he said, "I am only sorry that Nicole will have no family at the wedding. I think it would please her, and it would please me too, if you would stay for the ceremony."

Nicole exclaimed, "Yes, please do stay."

He readily accepted.

Monnet left the Carnot house amid more good feeling than he had thought possible, but he hated to think that he would have to disappoint Barbe Acarie.

He spent the next day exploring Sedan. He noticed the Protestant refugees who were crowding the town, looking for lodgings or lining up for public assistance at several houses of worship. In one rather dilapidated part of town he came upon a small structure that after a few moments he identified as a chapel. Monnet realized that he was in the midst of Sedan's tiny Catholic community.

An elderly priest came to the door to look over the visitor. "Are you Catholic?" he asked. When Monnet replied that he was, the priest became talkative.

"There are not many of us left here," he explained. "We are allowed to worship in our own way as long as we keep very quiet. We cannot have any processions, of course, or do anything else ostentatious. I would be very happy if you could come to Mass on Sunday."

As Monnet walked on he thought, "What a perfect contrast. Here the Catholics are crowded into a corner and lorded over by the Protestants. Back in France it is just the reverse. What are we to make of this? Is God wherever the bigger numbers are?"

Monnet weighed his two invitations for Sunday: Should he go to Mass, or should he hear Balladier's sermon? He chose Balladier not only because he was curious about what the minister would have to say but also because he had never been to a Protestant service before.

On Sunday morning the temple was crowded. Monnet saw the Carnot family and Nicole in the front row. Escagnas introduced Balladier as a distinguished preacher who had come to Sedan to share his experience and wisdom with the congregation. Then he stepped aside and turned over the pulpit to the visitor.

Balladier began quietly and slowly: life was getting bad again for

Protestants in France; promises of free worship and tolerance were being broken.

"It is time once again to speak out against Rome and to tell the truth about its abominations," he said.

His anger rising, he launched into an attack on the Catholic clergy. Curates were, for the most part, "not only the dregs of the clergy but the dregs of the people."

Bishops were ambitious and avaricious, living in high luxury with money that should go to the poor, maintaining "coaches with teams of horses, packs of hounds and, often, a swarm of whores."

He was no kinder to cardinals but reserved his most ferocious thunder for the pope. "He bears all the signs of the Antichrist. He sits in the temple of God as if he were God, he is clothed in scarlet as the whore in Revelation. He has his feet in Babylon, where all things are sold, even souls. He has sometimes been a sodomite, sometimes a sorcerer, sometimes a murderer, sometimes an adulterer. He has made a horrible traffic of sins, selling pardons for men who have lain with sister and mother and even beasts, for patricides and regicides. He himself has been seen killing, poisoning, robbing. . . ."

From where Monnet sat in the rear of the church he could not see Nicole's face, but he could only wonder how she might be affected by this aria of hate. Balladier went on to proclaim that the "corporal and real presence is a dream, transubstantiation a monster, purgatory a fantasy, the Mass a profanation of mysteries, the service of saints idolatry."

The preacher went on in this vein at length, well past his allotted time as indicated by the sand in the hourglass.

The service ended with hymns, a departing prayer and a benediction by Escagnas, but throughout all this the echo of Balladier's diatribe seemed to linger. Nicole left with the Carnots. She looked pale, stricken. She had heard Catholicism denounced since she came to Sedan, but Balladier's effusion of invective went beyond anything she had experienced.

Monnet decided to call on her the next day. He sat with her and

Sarah as they talked about the forthcoming wedding and about where Nicole and Daniel might live in the future. After a while a maid came and called Sarah away to deal with some household matter.

Nicole was silent for a long time. Then she said, "You were in church yesterday?" She shook her head as if in wonder. "You heard him say all those things. That Mary is not the Mother of God, that the Ascension is a fable and—and . . ."

She fell silent again and then reached into the pocket of her dress and pulled out a rosary.

"Madame Acarie gave this to me long ago. I will not be able to keep it anymore," she said, handing the beads to Monnet. "You take it. Take it back to Madame and tell her that I have kept it all these years."

"I wish you would bring it back to her yourself," he said.

At that moment Sarah returned. Soon afterward Monnet made his farewells.

He was at the inn several days later when he was told that a woman wanted to see him. She had not given her name. He went into the common room and found Nicole waiting. Almost apologetic, and very agitated, she said that she needed to talk to him.

"I am trying very hard to be a good and true convert to this new faith. I promised this to Daniel and I owe him so much. But it is very difficult for me to feel at home in his religion. Their heaven is different. Their God is so far away, we cannot really know Him. Even when I felt abandoned by Him, when I could not feel His presence, I took some comfort from looking at His image. Now that is forbidden."

She looked about furtively. "I understand that there is a Catholic church in Sedan. I want you to take me there. Soon I will be forbidden to pray in a Catholic church or even to set foot in one. But I want to do this one last time."

"I will take you, if that is what you want," Monnet said. But he knew enough about Sedan by now to add, "If we are seen, it will mean trouble for you."

She brushed this aside and they set out.

The elderly priest was pleased to see them and readily led them into the chapel. It was a dingy space, dimly lighted by a few flickering candles. Two oil paintings—one of the Holy Family and the other representing the Annunciation—were badly damaged by moisture.

Nicole slowly advanced to the altar, whose cloth covering was torn and mended. She knelt for what seemed to be a long time, looking up at the crucifix. Then she crossed herself, rose and rejoined the priest and Monnet at the entrance.

The old man said to Nicole, "I believe I know who you are. They tell me that you are about to renounce your faith and become a Protestant."

Nicole nodded.

The priest went on. "I understand you are doing this because you are planning to marry a Protestant. But you are risking eternal damnation."

Nicole stared at the priest and said only, "I have given my promise."

The priest shrugged. "Whatever you have pledged, your obligation to our Lord is greater. You must have some doubts, otherwise you would not be here. I will keep you in my prayers."

As they started on their way back to the Carnot house, Nicole said again, "I have given my promise. I owe him so much."

But Monnet realized that the old priest had been right: she was obviously torn by doubt.

The prayers and psalms rang out as usual, but Monnet sensed among some of the worshipers a special excitement. Before starting a sermon, Minister Escagnas addressed the congregation.

"My dear brethren, by God's grace, we are about to receive a new member into our flock."

At his nod, Nicole got up and stood facing him in front of the pulpit.

"Do you, Nicole Tavernier, promise to adhere to Jesus Christ, live in the fear of God and submit to the discipline of our churches?"

Almost inaudibly, Nicole said, "I do."

The minister continued. "Do you believe in Jesus Christ as the sole mediator between God and men? Do you detest the evil customs of the Roman Catholic faith? Will you give up all the superstitions and idolatrous rites of the Roman Church, especially the Mass? Do you pledge to turn your back on images and relics and never to pray to saints?"

There was a long silence. As it continued one could hear the uneasy shuffling of feet and the rustling of clothes as many in the congregation shifted to get a better look at Nicole. Suddenly her body seemed to sag.

"I cannot," she said softly, her voice tight with despair. Then, her head lifted and her voice now stronger and nearly defiant, she said again, "I cannot."

She turned abruptly and walked up the aisle amid the rising clamor. Looking stunned, the minister gestured helplessly, trying to calm his congregation. Daniel rushed after Nicole, his face red and contorted, catching up with her a few yards beyond the church door. Monnet followed at a distance.

Daniel seized her arm and she turned to face him.

"I could not do it," she said. "I am so sorry, but I could not do it."

Still holding Nicole's arm, Daniel said only, "Come away."

"When I heard the words I must agree to—the pledge of abjuration," Nicole told Monnet later, "I suddenly felt as if someone or something was throttling me. Everything turned dark, and then, through the gloom, I saw the face of Our Lady. My temples were throbbing and inside my head I heard a voice pleading: 'Do not betray me!' After a few moments the darkness lifted and the vision disappeared. I looked around the church and I knew that I did not belong there."

She remembered what the old priest had told her: that her

promise to a man was much less important than her obligation to God.

These thoughts only gradually became clear to her as she and Daniel made their way back to the Carnot house. Daniel was confused and angry.

"You have shamed me and my family," he said. "You have outraged my church. If you were not sure all along, why didn't you tell me before going so far?"

Nicole was distraught. "I am sorry, I am sorry," she kept repeating. "At first I truly thought that I could take your religion in good faith. When I began to have misgivings I tried to ignore them, because I had given you my promise and I owe you so much."

Daniel's anger gradually faded and he said gently, "It is not too late for you to reconsider. You would not have to make your abjuration in front of the congregation. You could do it quietly for the consistory."

Nicole shook her head. "I could do it only by pretending, which would be wrong. Daniel, don't you see: what your people call superstition is my faith. What your people call idols are my saints."

"How can you feel this way after everything your Church has done to you in the past?"

"It was not my Church that did these things, it was people. They cannot change what the Church means to me. I should have realized this all along, but I understand it now."

"I do not understand it."

At that point Jean and Sarah returned to the house. They were accompanied by Gaston Roux. The elder was in a fury.

"Nothing like this has ever happened here before."

He faced Nicole. "You asked to join our Church, you promised solemnly to accept its tenets and to submit to its rules. I believed you and recommended you to the consistory. But you deceived us."

"She deceived herself," said Daniel. "But please let us sort this out between the two of us."

"There is nothing to sort out unless you persuade her to change her mind. Otherwise, she obviously cannot stay here. I expect her to leave this house in two days. And no one in this family should have any connection with her."

With that Roux brought his cane down on the floor with a thud and was gone.

Jean was only slightly less angry.

"You were wonderfully kind to me and I did not mean to hurt you. I did not know that things would happen this way," said Nicole.

"You heard the elder," said Jean. "You cannot marry Daniel, and, even if we wanted to, we could not go on having you in our house or having anything to do with you. If we did, our family, our children, would be scorned by everyone."

When they were alone again, Daniel said, "My brother is right, you will have to leave here. But I will go with you."

He added with sudden resolution, "We can still get married. We can go to another town, or even another country, where Catholics and Protestants marry without much difficulty these days. I am even willing to be married in a Catholic church."

Nicole stepped toward him. "I cannot let you do this. I could not let you do something for me that I was unable to do for you. You would regret that decision and it would come between us. Neither of us would feel at peace."

Daniel continued to argue for a while, but she was adamant. Finally he said, near despair, "But if you leave here, where will you go? What would become of you?"

"What would become of me? I don't know, any more than I ever did. Any more than I knew when I left Reims, when I moved from town to town, when I came to Paris. I trust that God knows what he wants to do with me. But right now, I must go to Barbe."

Daniel tried once again to tell Nicole she owed nothing to this woman who had brought her so much misery, but he could not dissuade her.

Later that evening Daniel appeared at the Inn of the Winged Wild Boar. Following the events in church that morning, Monnet had decided to stay away from the Carnot house for the time being. But he was anxious to hear about what had happened afterward. Daniel in turn was eager to confide in him as a way to relieve his misery.

"I can't understand why she wants to do this," he said as he concluded his account.

"You may not realize what Barbe Acarie meant to Nicole. But I was there and I can tell you that Nicole was crushed when Barbe turned against her. It must be a great triumph for Nicole that Barbe has had a change of heart."

Daniel sounded resentful as he said, "If you had not come here with that message, none of this would have happened."

"It was bound to happen anyway," said Monnet. "I don't believe that Nicole would have been able to turn her back on what was so essential to her life."

Daniel now pleaded with Monnet. "Could you not simply leave, Doctor? Right now, without her?"

"I am sorry, I could not. At any rate, it would make no difference. I know Nicole. She would find a way to get to Barbe on her own."

Daniel finally gave up. "I am afraid for her. Please watch over her. If she ever needs me, you must let me know. I will be here."

Monnet said good-bye to him with true regret. He was a good man who suffered because he had been unable to give Nicole the peace he had promised her and instead had to watch as she, once again, left what had seemed like a safe haven for a world in which there was no safety.

The next morning Nicole and Monnet were on their way to Pontoise. In her pocket was the rosary Monnet had returned to her.

CHAPTER 22

Wen they approached Pontoise, Monnet considered it wiser not to bring Nicole immediately to the convent. He found lodging for them in a farmhouse and went on alone to the convent.

"I am glad you are here, Doctor," Mother Superior said as they met in the parlor. "Sister is very ill."

"I will see her at once," Monnet said.

Mother Superior led him into the small infirmary. Since he had last seen Barbe a little over a month ago, her health had deteriorated. The local doctor had diagnosed pneumonia followed by repeated, painful convulsions.

Barbe was stretched out on a narrow bed, her face pale, her eyes closed. She opened them when she heard him come in. She gave Monnet a tired smile. "It is good to see you, Doctor," she said.

Monnet found her alert and calm but extremely feeble. Her pulse was slow, her breathing uneven. He gave her a tonic without much hope that it would change her condition. He sat down on a stool beside her bed and said, "Do you remember asking me, weeks ago, to try to find Nicole Tavernier?"

She nodded.

"Well, I found her. I brought her here with me."

Barbe clasped her hands together in pleased surprise.

"I had given up hope that you would succeed."

He summarized as briefly as he could what he had learned from Nicole. "When a priest found out that she had once been accused of being possessed by the Devil, she was threatened with a second exorcism."

Barbe shuddered. "Where is she now?"

He replied that she was staying nearby.

"I must see her," said Barbe.

At that point her body was twisted by severe convulsions. The attack passed after a few minutes and Barbe spoke almost in a whisper.

"I know it will not be easy to bring her to me. I know the rules. But there are times when rules may be broken. I have learned that from Saint Teresa. The Holy Mother broke rules all the time. And if she had not, our order would not exist. You should come back at night. The sisters will be in their cells asleep and I trust you will find some way."

Barbe was obviously exhausted and Monnet quietly left the infirmary.

It was close to midnight when he returned with Nicole. There was a small enclosure next to the gate where a sister was supposed to keep watch at all times. Monnet went to reconnoiter and found that the woman had nodded off. He and Nicole slipped silently through the gate and moments later they were in the dim infirmary. A single night light glimmered in the corner. Barbe was asleep and Monnet touched her shoulder. She woke with a start and looked up in confusion.

"I am sorry to wake you," he said, keeping his voice low, "but Nicole is here."

Barbe tried to sit up but she was too weak and sank back against the pillows. Then she made out Nicole's form standing next to Monnet. "I need more light," she said, gesturing toward the taper in the corner. He brought it over and placed it on the bedside table. Barbe stared at Nicole in the flickering light.

"Nicole?" said Barbe. "I have dreamed of you so often lately. Is this real?"

"It is real," said Nicole.

"God bless you for coming. I would not have blamed you if you had refused. I treated you badly and made you suffer."

Nicole bent over the bed and kissed Barbe's hand. "Of course I came. I have never forgotten you, Madame."

Nicole held out the rosary and it glinted in the light of the taper. "You gave me this long ago. It has always been with me."

Barbe said, "Father Bérulle, who has known me most of my life, told me not long ago that I was full of faults, stubborn and narrow-minded. And that is true. I was also arrogant. I judged others, to determine their spiritual worth, to distinguish true vocations from false ones. I would not listen to anyone disagreeing with me. And so I judged you harshly, without pity, and I was too ready to see the Devil in you."

Barbe paused and touched her forehead, either in physical pain or else haunted by a memory.

"Of course we all saw how the Devil left his trail that time when you were exorcised. I have thought about this often. The Fiend was obviously there, but that does not mean that he was in you."

Hearing these words, Monnet felt a pang of guilt. He knew that the fiery trail had been his handiwork, but there was no way for him to say this now and there would have been no point to it.

"When I was young and began to fall into trances, I was afraid myself that the Devil might be behind them. I should have learned to be more careful about suspecting him in others."

Monnet was beginning to worry that Barbe was exhausting herself and also that someone might discover them, despite the late hour.

"Perhaps you should sleep now," he said. But Barbe shook her head.

"I have more on my mind. I must say these things and I know I do not have much time." With an effort, she again spoke to Nicole. "When it came to your cures and your wonders I was too suspicious. That is why I trapped you into lying. I did not want to believe you."

"You were not always wrong about me," said Nicole. "There were times when I claimed too much—or allowed people to claim too much for me."

"No matter. In the end only God can judge these things. I did not recognize it at the time but I see it now. I was jealous of you. When I saw how crowds adored you, how priests and kings deferred to you, how awed all Paris was by your prophecies, I believe I envied you."

"But I envied *you*," Nicole said. "I thought faith came so easily to you and it was so hard for me. You were so certain and I was in so much doubt. You were so close to God and I had to struggle to feel him near me. In these things you were so rich and I felt so poor."

Monnet remembered that Nicole had told him this in almost the same words long ago. He recalled how strong and bold she had been in the days when she had conquered Paris, and he was struck once again by the doubt and despair that must have been hidden underneath her confident exterior.

Barbe was again shaken by a convulsion and he thought it was time to end the encounter. He said so to Barbe and she weakly agreed. Seizing Nicole's hands she said, "Will you forgive me?"

"I have forgiven you long ago."

"Yes, I remember you said that to me on that terrible day. But I could hardly believe that you meant it."

"I meant it. Yes, there have been times since when I was angry with you. But that no longer matters."

"What will you do now? Where will you go?" asked Barbe.

"I will do what I was meant to do. I will go back out into the world and I will preach and try to bring people to God if He gives me the power to. I was wrong to let myself be frightened and give up what I always knew was my mission."

"God protect you on the way. But before you go, let us pray together as we used to do."

Nicole silently knelt beside the bed and folded her hands. Barbe also pressed her palms together and in unison they said the Pater Noster.

Barbe drifted off to sleep even before the prayer was finished.

As Monnet and Nicole made their way out of the convent, they saw that the sister at the gate had apparently not stirred. Monnet lit a lantern that he had left outside. By its light Nicole's face had a serene glow that seemed to transform her into the young woman he had first known.

When Monnet awoke the next morning in the farmhouse, he found Nicole pacing up and down in the yard.

"You talk about taking up your mission again," he said. "But you know that you were specifically forbidden to do that. Do you realize the danger you will be facing? What happened to you in Reims will happen to you again. You will find yourself driven from place to place and always in flight."

"I cannot think about that," she replied. "If God wants to keep me safe, He will. If He does not, so be it."

Monnet told her of Daniel's last words. "You can go to him, he is eager to have you back. It would be your best course. I feel strongly about this because, after all, it was I who took you away from Daniel and brought you here."

Nicole shook her head. "I could not have stayed in Sedan even if you had not come, even if Barbe had not called for me. I know what I must do, what I was always meant to do."

Monnet realized that she was determined and there was no further point in arguing. She had put together a small bundle of her belongings and he gave her some money, which she gratefully accepted.

"Be careful," he said. "Do not stay in any one place too long. Keep moving." He took her hand. "Nicole, I am not much for prayer, but I will keep you in my thoughts."

Later that day he returned to the convent and found Barbe much worse. Mother Superior was at her bedside.

"She should be anointed now," he whispered.

Presently the convent chaplain came into the infirmary carrying the holy oils. The other nuns of the community followed him and knelt around the bed. The priest began to recite the Hail Mary, and Barbe, who had appeared unconscious, moved her lips, which Monnet took as a sign that she knew what was happening.

The priest began to anoint her. Making the sign of the cross on her forehead he said, "Through this holy unction may the Lord pardon thee whatever fault thou hast committed."

Before he could go on to the other steps in the rite—the anointment of the eyes, nostrils, ears, lips and hands—Barbe gave a slight shudder. Monnet approached her bed and determined that she had died.

The chaplain began to pray, echoed by the nuns. "May her soul and the souls of all the faithful departed, through the mercy of God, rest in peace."

At the funeral two days later, Barbe's body was stretched out on a bier in the Pontoise church behind the grille separating the cloister from the outside world. The nuns filed past the body, touching it with their beads and asking for Barbe's intercession. Her eyes were closed, her hands folded, and people remarked that in death her face seemed serene and unlined. A great crowd pressed into the church to say farewell. She was buried in the cloister under a marker of hard limestone, bearing an engraved account of her life and deeds. Later, a mausoleum was built for her in adjoining chapels. On one side, in the chapel open to everyone, was a statue of Barbe. On the other side of the dividing wall, inside the convent, was a second, identical statue. This arrangement made it possible for both laypeople and those in the cloister to pay homage to her.

A few years after her death, one of Barbe's sons wrote to the proper authorities asking that they consider her for beatification, the first step on the road to sainthood. For many centuries saints grew up spontaneously, the martyrs, confessors and ascetics seeming to rise from their tombs or emerge from their cells in every corner of the Christian world by acclamation of the faithful. So many saints were venerated in so many places that Rome found it advisable to impose strict rules and procedures on this exuberance of veneration. Thus, by Barbe Acarie's time, a strict procedure was in place. It began with a petition on behalf of some person considered worthy of worship by the local community. It was up to the bishop to investigate such claims. If it was found that the person, in life, had indeed been holy, exhibiting heroic virtue, and after death had performed at least one miracle—in the judgment of Church experts—then the candidate might be beatified. With that went the appellation "Blessed." The next step, which might not happen for years or even centuries, required more examination, more arguments for or against the "cause," and at least one more miracle. With all conditions fulfilled, the pope might then canonize the candidate, meaning final recognition as a saint.

In Barbe's case, apostolic commissioners were appointed to take depositions from witnesses, to question her family and many others who had been close to her life and works.

As Barbe Acarie's doctor, Monnet was asked to testify about her illnesses and was allowed to witness many of the proceedings. Early on, the archbishop decided that the commissioners should visit Barbe's tomb at the Carmelite monastery at Pontoise. Monnet was with them as they viewed Barbe's mausoleum, an elaborate arrangement of a kneeling nun with an arch and sculpted curtains above her. The face was white, serene, with eyes closed and a faint smile on her lips—a beautiful face that was, but also was not, the living face Monnet had known for so many years.

The area around the chapel was covered with small ex-votos, looking as if silver flowers were sprouting all about. These were replicas of body parts—legs, arms, hands. They commemorated the miraculous healings purportedly brought about by Barbe Acarie since her death, in response to prayers of petition from those who believed in her.

Then the group moved inside the monastery, where a room had been set aside and the commissioners took testimony from people who were convinced that they had been cured by her. There was a long list of afflictions—lameness, tumors, broken limbs, hernia, bleeding, plague, continuous vomiting, genital inflammation—all supposedly healed.

Next came the evidence of Barbe's fellow Carmelites. One after another, sitting before the group in their brown robes and white veils, they told of her humility, obedience, charity toward her sisters and her uncanny ability to read what was in other people's hearts and minds. Nicole Tavernier was mentioned briefly by several nuns.

"This woman from Reims," related Sister Frances of Jesus, "feigned an extraordinary appearance of virtue and piety with the help of the Evil Spirit. She acquired the image of a saint even among people well-versed in spiritual matters who examined her repeatedly. Everyone in Paris knew about her. She did many utterly extraordinary things so that people for whom she prayed, or who merely talked to her, considered themselves blessed."

Sister Frances continued to describe many of Nicole's wonders, her procession in Paris, her preaching and the way she heard people's confessions.

"Despite all this, Sister Marie of the Incarnation, who was then Barbe Acarie, resisted the credence given to this Nicole and aggressively inquired whether all her works derived from the Evil Spirit."

The nun next related—sounding rather proud of Barbe's ingenuity—the story of the letter that trapped Nicole in a lie and went on to tell about the exorcism and the sudden burst of flames.

"In that instant the Evil Spirit who had assisted this woman departed from her and left her very obtuse, without her fine discourse or the knowledge she had displayed earlier. She grew so silent that there was no longer anything remarkable about her."

The nun ended by saying that Nicole had almost become a Protestant but had been rescued from that fate at the last moment.

Monnet listened to this version of Nicole's story with growing unease. Again and again he thought, "But this is not the full story, the real story."

But he knew that even if he found a way to tell the real story, with all its ambiguities and humanity, the people who were here to move Barbe Acarie along the way toward sainthood would not be interested. They needed to diminish Nicole, he thought, in order to further exalt Barbe. Nicole Tavernier, he realized, would be remembered, if at all, as an incident in the life of Barbe Acarie, known as Sister Marie of the Incarnation.

CHAPTER 23

Monnet and Father Coton had remained friends. The doctor was approaching eighty and was surprised by his longevity. His bristly red hair had turned white; his eyelid drooped even further. Coton was considerably younger than Monnet but in poor health. They had given up even their occasional tennis games and instead played cards. They talked about what was happening in the world, in France and at court. Richelieu, whom Monnet still served, was now prime minister and had finally succeeded after a long and bitter siege in taking La Rochelle, the last Protestant stronghold. The queen mother, Marie de' Medici, had turned against Richelieu, but young King Louis was his champion and the cardinal had more power than ever.

Monnet no longer treated many patients and was discouraged by how little progress physicians were making against the inroads of disease everywhere. He had taken on a younger colleague to help him, and keep him abreast of new ideas. The young doctor was especially enthusiastic about a plant brought back from the New World, tobacco, which he believed to be very effective against catarrh and other ailments. He also intrigued Monnet with the theories of a Scottish physician named Harvey, who insisted that blood is not stable but circulates throughout the body and that the heart acts like a pump. The medical faculty of Paris, however, dismissed Harvey's work as "paradoxical, useless, false, impossible, absurd and harmful."

"These men of science are producing new theories all the time," Father Coton said. "They undermine the faith. They threaten both Catholics and Protestants more than we ever threaten one another."

Often Monnet and Coton talked about Barbe Acarie and Nicole Tavernier and their intertwined lives.

"Barbe is safe," Monnet said during one of their reminiscences. "Safe in her grave, safe under her beautiful monument, safe in her saintly reputation. Nicole is out in the world somewhere, if she is still alive, and far from safe. Barbe built an institution that will perpetuate her memory. Nicole built nothing. She did inspire many people, but her memory will die with them."

Coton and Monnet knew nothing about what had become of Nicole, although they made some guesses. Richelieu insisted on hearing any evidence of religious unorthodoxy anywhere in the kingdom and so Monnet saw a great deal of intelligence. Occasionally he noticed reports of a woman appearing in some village, feeding the poor, in another place praying for the sick, in yet another place preaching in the town square. Descriptions were not precise enough to make clear whether this involved different women each time or whether it was the same one. If so, could it be Nicole? The name Nicole Tavernier never appeared, but that proved nothing. After everything that had happened to her, Nicole would be clever enough not to use her name.

Meanwhile, the process of Barbe's beatification was moving forward through the labyrinth of clerical procedure. The prioress of Pontoise reported that days and even years after Barbe's death, there was noticeable an extraordinarily sweet smell in the infirmary, in Barbe's cell, in the choir.

"The odor of sanctity," Coton said. "It will certainly further her cause."

And so here they were, an old skeptical doctor and an enlightened but devout priest, discussing the nature of faith and the meaning of sainthood. They contemplated the likelihood that Barbe Acarie would sooner or later be beatified and ultimately perhaps even canonized.

"In a way," said Monnet, "don't you think that Nicole is as much of a saint as Barbe—if not more so?"

Coton was startled. "How did you get that idea?"

"Nicole had to struggle so much harder to believe than Barbe," explained Monnet. "For Barbe, faith was a gift, while for Nicole it was a quest and a desperate goal."

Coton considered this, rubbing his temples as if to clear his mind.

"Well, I see your point," he said finally. "Perhaps people who have to try hard to believe are more blessed than people who accept their belief comfortably and without doubt."

Coton gave his old friend a long look that mixed irony and curiosity.

"I thought you were a confirmed doubter. Do you now believe that some of her wonders, her healings, were supernatural?"

"Well, she faked some things," said Monnet. "But she also did certain things that I cannot explain. In the end, perhaps what matters most is that she was willing to give up everything for faith. Her faith wavered, but that only made what she did all the more courageous."

Coton was beginning to warm to his friend's reasoning. Both as a Jesuit and as a former lawyer, Coton could not resist a good argument, even if it ran against his earlier position. Such an argument struck him now.

"In the rules the Church has laid down for beatification, evidence of at least one miracle is required, except"—Coton paused for emphasis—"except in the case of martyrdom. That signifies that martyrdom is as important as miracles. When Nicole left Daniel and the safety of Sedan, when she chose to go back out into the world to resume what she considered her mission, although it was forbidden to her by the Church, she knew that she was facing great danger. In a sense, she laid herself open to martyrdom."

"So you agree with me?"

Coton shrugged and sighed. "In the end, my friend, only God knows who His saints are."

Among the latest reports Monnet had seen, one was extremely alarming. Once again it involved a woman who appeared in a village, this time in Brittany, and prayed at the bedside of a very sick young girl. The next morning the girl was dead and someone in the village raised the cry of witchcraft.

"The witch has killed the girl!" people shouted. "The witch must die!"

The woman tried to escape but the mob chased her through the streets, caught up with her and pinned her against the wall of the churchyard. She was stoned to death. The account of this event once again gave no name. But both Monnet and Coton suspected that it might have been Nicole.

In our time, thought Monnet, faith and death are united in a terrible embrace, and he feared that it had finally crushed Nicole. He could not banish the picture of a hail of stones descending on that slim body, the fierce, small head bloodied, the dark eyes blank and lifeless.

He remembered what Coton had said: in weighing sainthood, martyrdom is as important as miracles; in effect, the ultimate miracle.

But then Coton had also said, "Only God knows who His saints are."

A CONFESSION (CONCLUDED)

The trip from Paris to Pontoise takes about twenty-five minutes. You drive westward from the Arc de Triomphe along the avenue de la Grande Armée, past the glass-encased monstrosities of La Défense and eventually to the motorway. For part of the distance, the route follows the Seine, but mostly what you see are factory buildings, warehouses, and prefabricated residences. You pass places with ancient names—Epinay, Cormeilles-en-Parisis, Patte d'Oie. These once were picturesque villages but they have been replaced by drab suburbs, only the quaint names remaining. Then you leave the motorway, follow a narrow street, take a sharp turn to the left and find yourself in a square at the center of the oldest part of Pontoise. At one end of the square you enter the rue Pierre-Butin and you soon reach the Carmelite convent. At one side of the gate there is an enclosure where a nun keeps watch and offers brochures and postcards for sale. You cross a cobbled courtyard with attractive flower beds and face the convent itself. As I look at the simple, unadorned façade, it strikes me as more ordinary than I had imagined, but, at the same time, I have an impression of order and peace.

My manuscript is finished. While I was engrossed in writing this book I had postponed what I knew all along I must do. I knew that I must see the place where Barbe Acarie died and was buried. That is why I have made this trip to Paris and to Pontoise.

Presently I stand inside the convent church. It is smaller than a parish church, with a high ceiling and half-timbered walls. Its austerity is softened by warm color—brown wooden floor, brown wooden benches and choir stalls. On one side of the church there is an arched opening leading to a small chapel with whitewashed walls and a round green-and-yellow latticed window. And there, on a large stone block, is the white marble statue of Sister Marie of the Incarnation, kneeling, hands clasped in prayer. Above the statue, halfway up the wall, there is a niche with a gilt, wood reliquary containing her remains.

I have learned about what has happened since Barbe was first proposed for beatification. Her cause lingered for more than two centuries, half forgotten, until finally in 1791, Pope Pius VI admitted her to the ranks of the blessed. The French Revolution was raging at the time and the Church apparently felt the need for more saints, much as it does today. But the Revolution ravaged Pontoise, as it did countless other religious establishments. Mobs looted the convent and the twin chapels, destroying Barbe's mausoleum. René Monnet had been wrong when he thought Barbe to be safe in her tomb. The coffin had been broken open and her remains scattered. A pious magistrate of Pontoise managed to collect some of these remains—the skull; bones, including her injured thigh bone. Eventually, when a new chapel was built, they were placed in the reliquary above her statue.

As these events pass through my mind, a short, middle-aged sister with wire-rimmed glasses and a winning smile approaches me and hands me a pamphlet published by the Association of the Friends of Madame Acarie. I look through it in the dim light. It gives a very brief account of Barbe's life and gently agitates for her advancement to the next and final level of holiness. It points out that it would require the confirmation of only one more miracle—in addition to the ones reported long ago during her beatification hearings—for her to be declared a saint.

Does she deserve it? I must leave that to other judges.

As I look at the beautiful marble statue, I see in my imagination next to it a slim, small figure with dark, glowing eyes. But there is no statue of Nicole. The time and place of her death are unknown, and her grave, wherever it might be, is surely unmarked. There is no Association of the Friends of Nicole Tavernier.

Well, Nicole, I have told your story. Many people who read it will still think of you as a fraud. Others will try to find some psychological term to label you. But I believe that some will think of you as a saint—more or less. As for me, I believe you should be the patron saint of all those who want to believe but cannot. There are many of us.

NOTES ON SOURCES: FACT AND FICTION

The life of Barbe Acarie is documented in her beatification proceedings, which are kept in the Vatican archives and at the Carmelite convent in Pontoise. An even more comprehensive source is a biography by Father André DuVal, a member of her circle, that first appeared in 1621, three years after her death (*La Vie admirable de soeur Marie de L'Incarnation*) and was later republished (V. Lecoffre, Paris, 1893). This biography forms the basis of all later accounts, including the section on Barbe Acarie in *A Literary History of Religious Thought in France* by Henri Bremond (Bloud et Gay, Paris, 1916, translated by K. L. Montgomery, Macmillan Company, New York, 1928) as well as *Barbe Acarie: Wife and Mystic* by Lancelot C. Sheppard (Burns Oates, London, 1953). The work that, as described in the opening section of this book, first led me to Barbe and Nicole is *Miracles* by Jean Hellé, a pen name for Morvan Lebesque (David McKay, New York, 1952), translated by Lancelot C. Sheppard from the French *Les Miracles* (Imp. de la Technique du livre, Paris, 1949).

My version of Barbe Acarie's life, her husband and her entourage is based on fact, with the major exception of Dr. René Monnet, who is entirely fictitious.

The situation of Nicole Tavernier is more complicated. She appears in all the foregoing sources about Barbe Acarie, which briefly note her activities in Paris, most of the miracles attributed to her, her adoration by Parisians and the fact of her procession. Also mentioned are her patronage by Barbe and Barbe's ultimate rejection, including the trick of the letter. The fiery trail caused by the Devil supposedly leaving Nicole is mentioned and I have used this incident to create the exorcism scene.

The record, however, says nothing about Nicole's origins or her later story, except that she was a young widow from Reims, that she returned to Reims after her disgrace, that she entered a second, unsuitable marriage and was rescued from turning Protestant, all of which is stated as bare fact without details. I have tried to accommodate these points (taking the liberty of changing her second marriage to a near-marriage), but all the rest of her story is fiction.

There is no evidence that Henry IV had any dealings with Nicole, but his involvement is made plausible by his well-documented actions concerning Marthe Brossier. In the description of Henry and his era, the following works were especially useful: *The Paris of Henry of Navarre as seen by Pierre de L'Estoile,* selections from his *Memoires-journaux* (originally published in Paris in 1574-1599 and translated and edited by Nancy Lyman Roelker, Harvard University Press, Cambridge, 1958) and *Henry of Navarre* by Hesketh Pearson (Harper & Row, New York, 1963), as well as *The Story of Civilization: The Reformation* by Will Durant (Simon & Schuster, New York, 1957) and *The Story of Civilization: The Age of Reason Begins* by Will and Ariel Durant (Simon & Schuster, New York, 1961), *La vie quotidienne au temps de la Renaissance* by Abel Lefranc (Hachette, Paris, 1938), *Henri IV, ou, La grande victoire* by Yves Cazaux (Albin Michel, Paris, 1977), *Magistrats et sourciers en France au XVII siècle, une analyse de psychologie historique* by Robert Mandrou (Seuil, Paris, 1980), and *Histoire de la vie privée. De la Renaissance aux Lumières* by Philippe Ariès and George Duby (T3, Paris, 1986).

HAG

ABOUT THE AUTHOR

HENRY GRUNWALD was editor-in-chief of all of Time Inc.'s publications from 1979 until 1987. Before that (1968–1977) he was managing editor of *Time* magazine. He subsequently served as United States ambassador to Austria from 1988 to 1990 and has since written the autobiography *One Man's America* and the memoir *Twilight: Losing Sight, Gaining Insight,* about his struggle with macular degeneration. Born in Vienna, Grunwald came to America at the age of seventeen and enrolled at New York University. He started with *Time* in 1944 as a copy boy, while he completed his education. He resides in Manhattan with his wife and their Australian Terrier, Harry.

ABOUT THE TYPE

This book was set in Bembo, a typeface based on an old-style Roman face that was used for Cardinal Bembo's tract *De Aetna* in 1495. Bembo was cut by Francisco Griffo in the early sixteenth century. The Lanston Monotype Company of Philadelphia brought the well-proportioned letterforms of Bembo to the United States in the 1930s.